Other Ross Duncan Titles

They Die Alone
Sleep Not, My Child
For A Sin Offering
To Catch Is Not To Hold
Unto The Daughters Of Men

SLEEP NOT, MY CHILD

A Ross Duncan Novel

Susan & Jon,

Again, thank you for your
friendship. I hope you'll get out
to visit us in Hawaii some day.
Warmly,

Christopher Bartley

Houston
Aug 6, 2013

PEACH PUBLISHING

ISBN 978-1-78036-186-4

Published by
Peach Publishing

Dedication

For my great-grandfather, Claude Brocklebank, who fought at the Battle of San Juan Hill at the age of 16 and later opened the first automobile service station in Michigan. He spent the rest of his long life as a devoted family man. Though he rarely talked about his war, he told me some of it when I was a child.

Author's Note

This novel is a work of fiction set within a specific historical context. Although the principle characters in this story are fictional, the broader historical context in which the story is set and the characters with whom they interact are based on real people and events from that time. For readers new to this period of Twentieth Century American History, John Dillinger was a famous bank robber. Also, Harry "Dutch" Sawyer was a real person. He was purportedly a liaison between independent criminals and the underworld of the Twin Cities, locally referred to as the "O'Connor System," after John J. O'Connor who had been Chief of Police in St. Paul until his retirement in 1920. Apart from its fictional elements, I have done my best to ensure that this novel is historically accurate to the period in which it is set. I apologize in advance for the inevitable mistakes and inaccuracies, which are my fault alone. Please feel free to let me know if you spot any or would like to discuss any element of the story.

My email address is rossduncan32@gmail.com.

It is June 1934 and America is in the fifth year of a Great Depression. Unemployment is running above 25%. Many people have lost their savings and their homes to bank foreclosures. Breadlines and soup kitchens are thriving. Bankers are the new villains of a populist society looking to place blame. The Federal Deposit Insurance Corporation, or FDIC, has been created as part of the Glass–Steagall Act, and signed into law by President Roosevelt on June 16th 1933 to prevent bank "runs." This federally mandated deposit insurance also has the unintended consequence of making depositors and banks essentially indifferent to robbery because the government will replace all stolen funds. The result is that mid-western states are now experiencing an unprecedented crime spree, with hundreds of bank robberies occurring every week, while the newspapers and a demoralized population cheer on the celebrity criminals.

Following the preaching of the Anti-Saloon League and Women's Christian Temperance Union there came the 1919 ratification of the 18th Amendment to the Constitution, followed by the Volstead Act – the prohibition of the production, transport or sale of alcohol – which was signed into law on January 17, 1920. By this time, the Volstead Act has destroyed the legal liquor industry, the seventh largest business in the U.S., along with tens of thousands of jobs. Although prohibition has recently been repealed on December 5th, 1933, it has provided a foundation for the now thriving illegal empires of organized crime outfits.

Now J. Edgar Hoover's Division of Investigation is building a reputation for law enforcement by glamorizing, demonizing, and hunting down the independent bank robbers who have emerged in the wake of the depression, while ignoring the far more powerful and insidious elements of organized crime. State and federal law enforcement officers have already begun to summarily execute the FBI's Public Enemies on the streets of America. Last month, Bonnie and Clyde were ambushed in Bienville Parish, Louisiana and went down in a hail of gunfire. John Dillinger, Pretty Boy Floyd, Homer Van Meter, and Baby Face Nelson remain at large, but not for long. Before the year is over, their deaths will result in national headlines and guarantee the continued existence and expanding budget of Hoover's fledgling FBI. The time of the celebrity bank robbers is almost over and the exploits of these

Public Enemies will recede into legend.

*

I use the name Ross Duncan. It is not the name my parents gave me, but one I have chosen for myself, an alias that serves to conceal my identity. I am one of the bank robbers and I foresee the end of our era. This past spring my childhood friend and partner, Colt Rollings, died violently – killed in a gun battle with law enforcement officers during a bank robbery. When we came out of the bank they were there, waiting to ambush us. The blame for his death, like so many others, is mine. As he was dying I promised to look after his younger sister, Elinore, a woman I have loved since our childhood on Hennepin Avenue, in our hometown of Minneapolis. Now she is dead too, murdered by an Irish florist – a gangster who presides over a criminal empire run from an ornate office above his Chicago nightclub, The Nightingale. I blame myself for that death also.

    Mine is a fast-paced world of Tommy guns, cold gin martinis, piles of cold hard cash, deadly betrayals, very expensive fun, and sudden violence. They say I resemble John Dillinger, though I have none of his zest for publicity and glamour. All I want now is to get out of this life. I feel weary with the weight of my sins, my failures, and my grief. I carry a Bible with me and I read it slowly, working my way through the Old Testament grasping for redemption as I maneuver my way through the atmospheric glow of slow motion sparkle and despair, and I find myself praying as I lie in wait for the soft, cool respite of a far-off dawn.

    Competing mobsters – Irish and Italian – vie for power and wealth, and Hoover works ambitiously to expand his Federal empire over the bodies of brave law enforcement officers and front page Public Enemies. They continue to die and they die alone, they always do – and sometimes I am the one who pulls the trigger.

Prologue

August 1933

As children we ran together.

Jimmy was three or four years younger than the rest of us on Hennepin Avenue, and he was the kind of kid who never could leave the older boys alone. He put up with the teasing and the bullying so that he could be part of the group. Every neighborhood had a kid like him. Colt Rollings was the surrogate brother who stuck up for him. Since everyone looked up to Colt, Jimmy was accepted and allowed in on the fun, which eventually included taking other people's automobiles for joy rides and reformatory stints for me and Colt.

The days inside were harsh, filled with early mornings and strenuous farm labor. Even the smallest infractions of the rules were met with beatings and the withholding of food. Each week seemed like a month and there was no comfort to be found, not a kind word anywhere. When we finally got out, Jimmy was waiting with enough cash to buy us hamburgers and sweets for a week. He figured we hadn't eaten too well in the reformatory, and he was right.

It wasn't long before armed robbery and stints in real prisons became part of the life that Colt and I chose. Jimmy managed to hang back from the trouble, but he was always waiting and helpful when we came out.

The last time we got out of prison, Colt and I swore together it would be just that: the last time. We weren't going back, no matter the cost, and to keep it that way we got serious about our chosen profession. That meant more careful planning, more firepower, faster automobiles, and hardened partners who knew what they were doing.

It was very good money, but eventually, like all the rest of them, we made a mistake that cost us more than we could afford: we allowed Jimmy to join our gang.

In the beginning it seemed to work. The first two jobs he was in on went off well enough. He helped with the planning and the getaway afterwards, though he didn't participate directly in the robberies. He didn't carry a gun. The support role fitted him, and the rest of the gang

1

appreciated his contribution. Then one of our crew got himself arrested and Jimmy agreed to be the replacement. That meant Jimmy carrying a loaded gun into a bank.

That meant trouble for all of us.

*

It was early August of 1933, two months after what they were calling the Kansas City Massacre, and Kansas City was a good week into one of the worst heat waves anyone could remember.

The bank we chose was at the edge of town, non-descript, not too close to a police station and near enough to an open road west to be an appealing target. There were seven of us and we were confident of our choice. Still, the job went wrong, all wrong, right from the very beginning. We didn't even have our bullet proof vests on at the rally spot when Jimmy informed us he would go, might even carry a gun, but he would not carry a loaded gun. He didn't want to have to shoot anybody.

Then, right into it, someone tripped an alarm that brought the city down upon us.

*

When the alarm went off, we quickly herded the bank tellers and customers together in front of the counter. Altogether there were nine of them, including three women and two small children.

"Kill 'em if they move," Colt shouted to no one in particular.

Jimmy pushed behind the counter to retrieve the cash. I drifted away from the group and stood with my back against a sidewall so that I could see everything and nothing could happen behind me.

The first shots were fired from outside the bank, from the front steps. A police officer simply walked up and shot Billy Cameron, our man outside on the top landing, at point-blank range with a double-barrel shotgun. Since Jimmy had refused to go in armed, we had only Billy outside the bank and now he'd been taken out by surprise. I looked over in time to see him fall back against the glass window. It flamed suddenly with the red of his blood smeared against it as it cracked apart.

The uniformed officer's silhouette rose up beside it to appear framed in the glass of the main lobby door. He fired the second barrel right through the glass at Martin Walsh, one of our crew who was standing in the lobby, catching him in the back of the head with a hail of buckshot and glass shards. Martin pitched forward to land on his chest, dead before he hit the marble. The Browning Automatic Rifle that he'd held muzzle down fell forward with him and clattered onto the floor.

I snapped aimed my .45 and pulled the trigger twice. Both shots hit the policeman square in the chest and knocked him backwards, down the bank steps and out of my line of sight.

A second officer appeared next to where the first one had been. He discharged a shotgun that knocked out the chandelier hanging over the center of the lobby. Glass rain sparkled. As the officer was racking the next cartridge into the chamber, I shot him in the chest and he too fell backward, out of sight.

The bank alarm continued to pierce the air, though for a moment all was still. Then shots started up from the street and more glass shattered around us inside the bank. It happened so quickly there was little chance to react or adjust. Several of the civilians in the bank went down in bloody heaps. One man screamed hysterically and clutched at his neck. Blood pumped into the air. Jimmy was behind the counter, in a small alcove, sweeping up piles of cash into a green duffel bag. The rest of us dropped to the floor where we stood. The barrage continued and was sustained. Another civilian was hit and cried out.

I listened carefully, straining to identify the weapons that were being fired at us. Most were single shot rifles and pistols. I rolled onto my back for positioning. From the floor, I returned fire in a wide arc, aiming through the broken windows out towards the street. From my position on the floor I knew my angle meant my shots would be high. I didn't expect to hit anyone, but it would give attackers outside something to think about. When my eight shots were used up, I ejected the magazine and inserted another one, quickly releasing the slide catch with my right thumb.

I started firing again, aiming more specifically now at large windows across the street. Shattering them would startle any shooters taking cover nearby and let them know we were returning fire.

Movement on the second-story rooftops across the street caught my eye. I paused and waited a moment to see if a target would present itself. It did. I aimed and squeezed the trigger three times. A man with a rifle fell back out of view.

After a moment, another face appeared. I fired twice and it too disappeared from view. My gun was empty now. I replaced the magazine and waited for another target. None appeared. After a ten-count I holstered the .45 and rolled onto my stomach so that I could crawl toward the Browning Automatic Rifle that Martin Walsh had dropped when he died.

The firing from the street continued. When I reached the BAR I pulled it to me and checked the action. It was already set on full automatic mode. It was an M1918 model, a heavy automatic rifle, almost sixteen pounds not including the ammunition, designed for advancing infantrymen to fight the trench warfare of the Western Front. It had a gas-operated tilting breech lock and could fire at a rate of 500 rounds per minute. A 20-round magazine of .30 caliber bullets was in and ready to go.

From where I lay, I stretched out to reach the kit, a shoulder bag, which carried additional magazines. It was still looped to Martin's shoulder, but I was able to pull it loose and toward me. There were seven or eight magazines inside. I lined these up together and placed all but two of them back in the kit so they would be ready when I needed them. I pulled the kit over my shoulder. Then, still lying on the floor, I fired a full magazine out the window, sweeping it all along the rooftop. Some of the shots cleared the roof ledge; others hit it, sending chips of brick and stone flying through the air. My mouth filled with the heavy taste of cordite and I found myself chewing on the tiny bits of grit that filled the air.

When the magazine was empty, I replaced it quickly and rose up a bit to repeat the process, sweeping at street level this time. I sprayed a line of slugs along the windows of shops and the automobiles that were parked along the street. Then I scanned the roofline again. Nothing moved there.

Something kicked hard at my leg. At first I thought it was a ricochet, but when I glanced back I saw a small boy, maybe seven or eight years old, in a brown cap scrambling over me. He was headed toward the bank door and the street beyond. At the periphery of my vision was a woman, a mother, hysterically trying to reach the boy, though unable to stand up to chase him effectively. Leaving the BAR on the marble floor I came up into a crouch and lunged once in his direction, but I was too late.

The shot that hit him tore a hole in his chest and pushed him back

4

towards me. I caught him as he fell. Panting hard with his hand on my wrist, a large glass marble fell out of his pocket and rolled across the floor away from us. I laid him flat on the cold, hard surface and with bullets still flying above us I tried to see if there was anything I could do for him – there wasn't. I pulled his shirt apart at the buttons and placed my hand over the spurting wound. Blood gushed through my fingers.

The small hand gripping my wrist tightened, as if holding me to him for dear life. I could feel his eyes watching me as he struggled to breathe. I looked at his face. It was oddly calm and he blinked unhurriedly as he gazed intently into my eyes. Then, very slowly, his mouth parted and I felt his last breath as he released it. His hand relaxed against my arm and his eyes rolled back in his head.

He had died just like that, as people do, without fanfare. His marble was still rolling away.

The boy's mother was on the floor beside me now grabbing at my shoulder. I pulled away from her to look about the room. My eyes found Colt's and we communicated silently across the distance between us. I pointed with a forefinger, and then jerked upwards with my thumb to be sure he knew about the men on the roofline. We both knew what we would have to do. It was a situation we had discussed and prepared for in the past.

I looked back towards the teller's cage and spotted Jimmy hunkered down there. He was covered from the fire, but kneeling in a place that he could move from when it was time. Next to him was the green duffel. With a movement of his chin and a hand-motion I knew he was with us. I looked back over at Colt and saw that he had seen Jimmy too. My eyes found Isaac's and he nodded smartly at me.

When the lull came we were prepared for it. Isaac and Colt each rose up on one knee, pouring suppressing fire out through the windows with their Thompson guns. They weren't aiming at anything in particular. We all knew that our only hope of escape was to lay down so much fire that the police officers and citizens waiting for us outside the bank were forced to take cover.

George Tucker, a former professional boxer who'd been with us for the past three months, crawled flat over to the front window nearest the wall. From there he proceeded to toss out four hand grenades, working as fast as he could to pull the pins.

As the sound of the explosions subsided, I stood up with the BAR. First, I swept the roofline again and then I began to fire out towards the street as I walked quickly toward the main entrance. When I reached it, I paused and rolled back behind the cover of a stone pillar to insert a fresh magazine.

Colt was up beside me now, firing through the door with his Thompson. He glanced over at me and I nodded.

"Watch the roof," I shouted at him.

He went through the door first and I was right behind him with the BAR pouring out fire.

From the top of the steps leading down to the street we could survey the entire area in front of the bank – it was a scene of carnage. The two policemen I had shot lay at the bottom of the steps together. They were both dead. One lay with his head on top of the other's back and an arm over his shoulder, as if he'd try to reach out to him in his last moment. I knew it was possible that he had. People did small things to comfort themselves and others as they were dying.

A pool of blood collected beneath them and flowed out toward the curb. Across the street, two more bodies were evident and all of the automobiles lined there were badly damaged from the grenade explosions and machine gun fire.

As I looked about, swinging the BAR in front of me, a man in civilian clothing rose up from behind one of the damaged vehicles. He sighted my way with a bird rifle, but quickly dropped down again when I released a short burst from the BAR towards him. I sprayed all along the length of the street for good measure until my magazine was out. Colt fired several shots from his Thompson while I replaced my spent magazine. We alternated like that as we moved.

Behind me Isaac was shouting, rallying the others. Jimmy came up beside me and nudged me gently to let me know he was there. Then we moved quickly in orderly fashion, all five of us as a unit now, towards the spot a half block away where we'd left our two automobiles.

Four of us took turns to fight a rearguard action as we retreated, at least one of us standing still always to fire while the others moved onward. We did not rush. It was standard small unit combat-tactics and we were better at it then the police officers and civilians who were shooting at us. I couldn't tell how many of them we killed, but their fire had all but dropped off.

A man in uniform holding a shotgun stepped out from behind a police truck that was parked at an angle in the middle of the street. He opened fire.

6

I cut him down with the BAR.

Shots continued to ring out. One caught me on the forearm; a moment later another grazed my thigh. We kept moving, moving and shooting, taking cover as best we could. Behind us the bank alarm was still ringing.

Since he wasn't pausing to return covering fire, Jimmy was the first to reach the automobiles. He had the Buick started and pulled halfway out of the spot by the time the rest of us caught up to him. Our second automobile, a Ford, was useless now: one of the tires had been shot out and it listed badly to one side.

When we were in, Jimmy accelerated. We hauled furiously down the street while I laid down fire with the BAR out the back window, blasting the glass out of my way.

After a few blocks, a single police cruiser appeared and chased after us with sirens blaring. Slugs from the BAR pierced holes across their hood and blew out their windshield. The cruiser swerved off the road, up onto a sidewalk, and ran into a telephone pole. Suddenly we were in the clear, though we wouldn't get far in the Buick. The windows and side panels were full of bullet holes, and from the feel of it, I assumed the radiator was leaking badly. Colt pitched an open 25-pound keg of roofing nails out onto the street behind us to slow any other pursuers on our trail.

Behind us we left a slew of dead: at least three officers that I knew of, probably six or seven in total; Martin and Billy, both cut apart with double-aught buckshot; several adult civilians in the bank; and the small child who hadn't done anything to deserve what he got that morning.

*

We barricaded in the one-room apartment that Jimmy had arranged while casing the job. The apartment house had only four units and was less than a mile from the bank and there was an open-air garage in the rear where we stashed the Buick. It couldn't be seen from the street, but it wouldn't be well hidden if anyone came sniffing around the back.

It would be very late before we could try moving again. The five of us huddled together in the small room that now reeked of our sweat, our anguish, and our quiet, unspoken fear as we cleaned and reloaded our guns and magazines and watched as the hands on a wall clock moved slowly, very slowly, around the big face.

It was still only late morning, but the day seemed to have gone on forever. The heat was sweltering already, and we had at least twelve hours ahead of us before it would be safe to move again.

"What a bloody mess," Colt said in disgust from his position by the window. "I hope the county morgue has a good stack of toe-tags handy."

In the distance we could hear the bank alarm still ringing. It continued to ring for another twenty minutes. We sat silently, waiting for something to happen, fingering our weapons and thinking thoughts that we didn't want to share with one another. The streets a few blocks over were filled with racing sirens and the commotion of heavy, fast moving automobiles.

My hands felt like they were still vibrating from the heavy pulsing of the BAR.

*

Colt was confident he could patch up the radiator well enough to take us the sixty miles west to where two fresh automobiles were stashed and waiting for us. The police had the city shut down for now, but by midnight they would assume we were long gone and would give up on the cordons they had erected throughout the city. If they didn't find us by the early hours of the morning, we had a chance to escape – at least those of us there were still alive or not too badly wounded to move.

Only Colt and Jimmy had managed to come out of the gun battle unscathed. I hadn't been so lucky and blood was seeping from my left forearm and my right thigh, and a two-inch shard of broken glass had gashed my shoulder. I'd bled heavily and the wounds were now wrapped in cloth bandages.

Isaac had it worse than I did. He'd taken a slug just above the knee and another that had shattered his collarbone. He couldn't walk. There was a very real risk that he might bleed to death within a day or so if we didn't get him medical attention. George Tucker was in the worst shape of all: a shotgun blast had caught him in the side. The buckshot had mangled his arm and some of it had creased the seam of his bulletproof vest, tearing into his abdomen. I didn't think he would live to see sundown.

Jimmy had bandaged us each up as best he could with his well-stocked first aid. Tucker and Isaac had some of the morphine in them now and were wrapped in blankets, though Tucker's blankets and most of the bed were now almost entirely soaked through with blood. It was too late for him, but if Isaac and I survived, we would owe Jimmy our lives.

Colt stood at the window with the curtains pulled back an inch so that he could watch the street. I staggered slightly when I rose to my feet. I was a bit dizzy from the blood loss. I stepped across the length of the window and stood very close to my old friend, close enough so that I could look out and see the same view he saw. He put a hand on my shoulder to steady me.

There was no motion in the street. Shuttered houses faced us, a long, angry row of neglected homes that held out only the disappointment and broken promises of the lives they contained. Dry and brown lawns stretched out in parallel. The sky was overcast now and moving quickly. Oblong gray clouds streamed across the city toward the open plains, flowing quickly, a rain-swollen river rushing to the sea.

"Hey, we can't move Tucker," Jimmy whispered, moving across the room to sit on the floor, staring up at me.

As an adult now he was still a bantam-sized young man with clear features and always short, awkwardly clipped hair that he probably cut himself. It would've been easy to think he was barely out of his teenage years unless you looked closely and noticed the lines that were developing around his eyes and mouth. They betrayed not only the years, but the hardship of those years. Yet still, there was a tranquil quality about his soft brown eyes that comforted people and made them want to live up to their best around him.

"I know," I replied.

"He'll die if we don't get him medical attention soon. Isaac could die too."

"Yes," I said. "I know. We'll do what we can for them. They're quiet now?"

"Tucker is out, completely out. Isaac is sedated, probably sleeping, but not too deeply. He's going to be in a lot of pain soon when the morphine wears off. We can move him if we need to, but ..." Jimmy's voice trailed off and he left the words unsaid.

"I know, it's bad," I told him. "But we're partners, we won't leave either of them to fend. We do what we can to take care of our own. We always do."

"It's my fault," Jimmy said, speaking louder now, with his thick Irish accent. "It's all my fault. We needed two men out there on the street. It was my post that cost us everything."

"Forget it," Colt told him. His voice was stern.

"No, I can't. It's my entire fault. A lot of people are dead and others are dying now because of me—"

Colt interrupted him. "A lot of them would have died anyway even if you had been out there. You might have been one of them."

"That makes it worse. It should have been me … All those people dead … Oh, God, a child too."

"That's not on us. If the police are going to open fire through a window like that, then civilians are going to be killed. They should know better – they do know better. Somebody out there panicked – or worse."

"We're to blame. Any reasonable mind would see that."

"We have to move on with it – forward only," Colt said. "These guys need you. Without you, they'd be dead men."

Jimmy hung his head and fell silent. My stomach churned and I was light-headed. I returned to my chair and sat down with my head between my knees before I fainted.

Chapter One

June 1934

There was cool speed under my wheels.

I was almost an hour past Davenport and the sky above held no texture. It was a flat, gray screen of indeterminate height, impossible to approximate, set above fields of waist-high corn and the hard, straightaway road I traveled. A rare slow tune from Fletcher Henderson's orchestra floated through my mind – lush strands of pure grace and sorrow.

Ahead, perhaps a quarter of a mile, I saw the automobile by the side of the highway. It was a long, low, dark blue Packard, one of the Sport Phaeton models from last year. It had a double cowl and red trim. There was no sun evident to make it shine.

I could see there was a man standing half in the road with his legs apart, jacket off. His hat was pushed back, and he stared unknowingly into some mystery inside the engine compartment. Even from a considerable distance, I could see his lips moving. When he heard me slowing down, he tilted his hat forward and watched me approach hopefully. I slowed to a stop. There was a Bible on the seat beside me, which I pushed down between my seat and the door.

The short man with a paunch over his belt and tight beads of sweat developing across a high forehead came around to my window and bent forward slightly, gentrified rows of teeth belied dark shadows that circled his eyes.

"I think it must be the radiator," he informed me.

"Do you need water? I should have a can in the boot."

"I fear it's worse then that. Can you give me a lift over to the next town, shouldn't be more than twenty miles or so? I'd be grateful."

"Sure, hop in."

He stood there for a moment without responding.

"It's no trouble," I told him.

"Wait," he said, nodding absently. "Let me collect my things."

His things included an expensive hand-sewn leather briefcase, a matching suitcase of moderate size that did not appear heavy, and a

11

small boy with reddish-blonde hair and quiet freckles. By the looks of it he had been sleeping on the seat of the Packard.

"What's your name?" I asked the kid after they were both loaded in.

The child straddled the back seat and leaned forward with his hands out before him. They trembled slightly. "Wilson," he said in response.

"How old are you, Wilson?"

He held up nine fingers. His eyes were droopy and there were indentation lines on his cheek from where it had rested against some textured surface while he slept. He was still in the process of waking up, not fully oriented to the change that had occurred.

The man beside me shifted impatiently. "Wilson will be ten years old next month. He's small for his age. I'm Kenneth Hamilton. We're coming home from Detroit, cutting a trip there short. I'm taking him back to his mother in St. Paul," the man explained. "She's been ill with a fever for several days."

I looked at him, unsure of exactly what he was intending to explain. "You okay back there, Wilson?" I asked the child.

Over my shoulder I could see he had settled in behind the passenger seat with his head in the center. His feet were tucked in under him and he already had his eyes closed.

"The boy's tired," the Hamilton said. "We've been driving much of last night, had hoped to at least make Mason City by this evening."

"It's a long drive for a child," I replied. "I'm headed toward Mason City, I can take you all the way there."

"Thanks, that would be great." Hamilton lowered his voice a bit for what he was about to say next. "The boy's had a tough go of it lately and he needs to see his mother. He's not my son, you understand. I married his mother almost three years ago. She was widowed early. I try to do for him as though he were my own. I try the best I can."

"That's good of you."

He nodded. "But it's not always easy."

"I hope she's not too ill."

"It's a fever. Worrisome, but it should pass."

"I hope so. What was in Detroit?" I asked, mostly to be polite and keep the conversation going.

"Investment opportunities … my work, future dreams."

"What line of work?"

"Finance. Investment broker. Creating money out thin air."

12

"It's a neat trick," I suggested after a five-minute lapse in the conversation. "The thin air part."

"Yeah." I could feel Hamilton smirking deliberately on the seat next to me. His smile was like a thousand broken mirrors, reflecting everything and nothing. "I like to think so. Especially these days with things so tight just about everywhere. It's nice to be one of the few coming out ahead."

"I'm sure it is. Where does the thin air come from?"

Hamilton chuckled, indulging me. "It's all around us. You just have to know how to see it. I work at a large bank – originally with Lee Higginson out of Boston, but we split off. We have investments and do make money, and I am good at spotting the opportunities and understanding the timing needed, even in these times. I'd be embarrassed to say how much I brought in last year. Almost obscene when I think about it, given the hardship of others."

"I can tell it's difficult for you."

"I said 'almost'. Sure, there have been rough spots this cycle. We were heavily into International Match, which is Krueger and Toll, a few years back. But we got out near the top, a few months before it all came apart. You know, at one point that Ivar Kreuger had a balance sheet bigger than all of Sweden's. He was loaning money to the governments of Germany and Italy, nearly made a deal with China – loans for monopoly."

"Heard it didn't turn out too well for him."

Hamilton clucked, started to laugh, and then caught himself short. He finished by shaking his head. "Shot himself through the heart in his Paris apartment last year. Couldn't face the bankers."

"And all over matches."

"Safety matches – a damn near world monopoly of them. But it was more than that—the Swede had businesses in construction, timber, mining, you name it. He almost made it work. Even the auditors didn't see it coming. Now, look what we got: a National Securities Act forcing groundless disclosure requirements on all the companies selling stocks."

"I suppose," I told him, "that somebody's got to stay on top of things."

"You believe that?"

"No."

"Aw, heck, I don't either. The banks aren't the bad guys. They're just businesses, helping move the money and the goods and the services around. I know it's fashionable, but they don't deserve the bad rap the politicos give them."

"Maybe you got a point there."

I smiled a bit to myself as I thought about it.

*

On we cruised, gliding down the ribbon at eighty miles an hour. I was driving one of my regular favorites: a black Ford sedan with a special V8 engine. It was nondescript to look at, which suited me fine, but it was solid, fast, and near bulletproof if you didn't worry about the windows. You could cross the country in it in a hurry if you needed to. I was driving very fast, as I always did, but carefully so. Sitting behind the wheel of a machine like it was one of the few times I felt in control of anything in this life.

"Coming up on Waterloo soon, right? Up ahead?" he asked.

I nodded. I caught Hamilton out of the corner of my eye scrunching his face as if deep thought caused him pain. I sucked a breath and kept my mouth shut while I waited.

"Saw they got another one of them bank robbers right there, just last week," he said.

There wasn't much to say to that, so I merely shrugged at it and studied the road before us.

"Don't remember his name, one of Dillinger's gang, though."

"Tommy Carroll," I heard myself say. I couldn't help it. I'd met Carroll a few times. He was a tough ex-fighter who'd had his nose broken at least once, maybe twice. He drank too much and he could be loud, but he was a stand-up guy when it came down to it. According to what I'd read, the police and Hoover's special agents of the Division of Investigation, who came down from St. Paul just before he died, got nothing out of him. The paper said his last words had been protective of his girlfriend. The exact words came back to me from the article: As he lay shot down in an alley he had said: "I got seven hundred dollars on me. Be sure the little girl gets it. She doesn't know what it's all about."

"Yeah, him," Hamilton declared, drawing me back to the present. "Tommy Carroll. A couple of alert cops got him as he was passing through town with his little girlfriend. A case of what turned out to be fatal auto-trouble. He was spotted at a service station; someone saw the

14

rifles and fake license plates in the back. They're going down, one by one, those bank robbers. Bonnie and Clyde three weeks ago. Dillinger's gang may be finished now, and perhaps the rest of the gangs too. The newspapers and the public love them, but they can die like dogs as far as I'm concerned. I wonder what will happen to the girlfriend, though."

"Year and a day," I said. "It's what they get for harboring."

I didn't know anything about the girl, though I'd met her sisters and by accounts she was stand-up too. I'd heard the agents questioned her all night, and got nothing out of her – squat.

Hamilton sighed and then he was quiet. After a quarter mile or so he spoke again: "To tell the truth, I don't know what to make of it. They can't survive. Not any more than Mr. Kreuger could. They've had a good run for a short while now. Shot up the cities and the countryside, taken the money from the banks while regular people cheered them, lived the high life on the lam. But they're finished soon; their time's about to be over. Hoover and his agents – the federal boys – are starting to get serious about taking them down. Soon enough they'll all be dead or in prison, every last mother's son of them."

I kept the large sedan steady on the road and did not reply.

*

Not too far from Waterloo, I turned off the main highway and hooked south for about thirty minutes on a smaller road. It narrowed considerably and had less shoulder on either side. If he noticed, Hamilton didn't give any sign of it. After a while, I connected with another larger highway and we were going northwest again. At that point we traveled in silence. Conversation had petered out and neither one of us seemed inclined to change that. From behind me, I could hear the child sighing occasionally as he shifted around in his sleep. The road was the pure geometric straightness of a flood plain, with silver maples and draped lakes gliding easily past us as if we were not moving at all.

Over the next hour, we made several more road changes before coming to the marker that had been set out for me. Without comment, I slowed to a near halt and turned the Ford carefully off onto a single dirt lane that ran first through early June corn fields, then a young bottomland forest, and finally came out from the trees to approach a large open area near a pond.

15

A simple white farmhouse waited for us against the dimming sky. There was a barn nearby, with a grain silo and a short dock out over the pond. Tall weeds collected around a rusting grain harvester that was parked beside the silo. It didn't appear to have been used in at least a season or two.

We crunched over sparse gravel as the Ford pulled up in front of the house. Sitting on the front porch of the house was a shapeless middle-aged woman in her brown stockings. She was scraping the skins off potatoes over a low, wide metal pail.

When I shut the automobile off I was struck by how quiet it was out there in the middle of nowhere. My ears filled with the little sounds that become noticeable when everything else falls away.

I looked at Hamilton and he looked back at me and yawned. "Of course I already know who you are," he said after he finished his yawn.

I turned in my seat to look at him. "Nuts."

"What? It never occurred to you I might take a hand in my own kidnapping?"

I stared at him quietly, sensing the blood pulse in my ears. The shoulder rig chafed as I sat twisted.

"Jimminy Crickett, this whole kidnap scheme was my idea in the first place," he exclaimed with a blinking, callous grin that evaporated as quickly as it formed. "I presented it to Harry Sawyer and the St. Paul outfit already wrapped in a bow. They brought you and the others in for the ride. You think you've taken me against my will? No sir, I'm your new partner in crime. My ransom should bring a pretty penny – from my rich wife and my rich bank – and I'll take a fair share of it. Like I said: creating money out of thin air."

My fingers tips worried at the leather edges of the Bible that I had slid down beside my seat out of view. The plan had seemed simple a few minutes before: pick up a stranded motorist and drive him to a farm, but suddenly I knew it was about to get complicated – which never led to good things. From behind us I heard the child stirring on the seat.

"Are we there?" he asked in a soft voice that quavered bow-like.

Chapter Two

As we went up to the porch the woman set her knife down and picked up a cigarette that she had going on the bench next to her. Her draw pinched her weathered face into a dried raisin, as lines around her cheeks and lips converged on a central point inside her mouth.

"Dinner's ready in an hour or so," she recited without energy after she exhaled. "Best head in and wash up. Take the first and second bedrooms at the top of the stairs."

"This here's Hamilton and Wilson," I replied, gesturing at my companions. "And they call me Duncan. We've been driving most of the day."

She just nodded and stared past us with squinting eyes as she took another drag. We went into the old house. It had fallen into poor repair, and the wood floors were unfinished and splintering in areas of high traffic. The small living room had three chairs, a low round table, and a cracked leather trunk with a framed photograph set on top of it. At the eastern face of the house, the room received little direct natural light in the evening. A kerosene lamp glowed from the table already.

"Who's that lady?" Wilson asked his father, pulling away from him to explore the room. "She's old."

"Now, Wilson. She's our host. We'll be guests here for a while until the old jalopy can be fixed up again."

"How long?"

Hamilton looked at me over the boy's head. His lips pulled back in a grimace. "Not too long, Wilson. Only a few days, as I told you: until the Packard is fixed and ready for us to drive again." His lies to the child rolled off easily.

"What about mother?"

"Don't worry about anything. Your mother will be okay. I'll call her tonight and let her know we're here."

Wilson crossed the room to look at the photograph that was on the leather trunk. He picked it up and studied it without comment for a long while, holding it so that it tilted to catch the available light. Over his shoulder, I could see the black and white outlines of a slender, pretty young woman posing stiffly in a white dress that was laced to the throat. She stared out from the last century with large eyes that peered anxiously from beneath a wide brimmed hat framed with piled ribbon.

"This house is creepy, there's old people about, and it smells," Wilson said after he had carefully replaced the photograph. The floor squeaked as we moved about.

*

At the landing before the stairs, Hamilton paused.

"Wilson, you can go on up. Take the first bedroom. Lie down for a little while. I'll be up shortly."

We watched the child take the stairs slowly.

"He's been lethargic like that for as long as I've known him—almost three years," Hamilton told me.

"Is he sick?"

"No. I don't think so. But he's not spirited. His mother spoils him. Be good for him to spend a few days in the country. Maybe fresh air will give him a bit of pep, especially if he moves around a little in the sunshine tomorrow."

"What does he like?"

"I don't know. What do any kids like?"

I stared at Hamilton, still trying to get a read on his angle. "If they're young boys, they usually like baseball and crackerjack, sometimes marbles."

"Never knew him to care about crackerjack."

"Maybe he hasn't tried it yet."

"His mother doesn't like him to have sweets. She's protective about his disposition." Hamilton paused and thought about it for a moment, as if wondering for the first time about his stepson. A narrow line formed between his eyes as he squeezed them for effect. "Well, he does like the Cubs. Took him to Chicago to see a home game last year. They lost, and then he was disappointed when they finished the season in third place."

"They could be good this year if Chuck Klein can hit like he did in Philly last year."

Hamilton shook his head, pursed his lips. The line between his eyes didn't go away. "I don't follow the game, don't see the appeal. To me they're all owned by the gamblers, can't trust any of them since the Black Sox. But Wilson seems to enjoy it, so I leave it to him."

18

"He was never part of the plan."

Hamilton took a step back. The line disappeared, finally. It was replaced by an expression that was no expression at all. With that blankness cultivated, he cleared his throat before responding: "Couldn't help it. His mother took ill. The boy had to take the trip with me."

"We make plans for a reason."

"Sure we do."

"You made your own plan."

"I don't want you to think we'll be any problem. This is just for a few days, till we get the ransom money, and then we all move on as though nothing ever happened."

"Sure," I answered. "It'll all be as easy as sweet potato pie. Let's put up our things."

*

The day had been long and dry and I was thirsty. After I set my grip in the room I'd been assigned, I came down through the kitchen to the back porch and drew myself a glass of water from the well pump. It was cool, with a slight metallic taste.

"Want a little whiskey to go with that?" said a young woman's voice that held an air of challenge.

I turned too quickly, spilling a bit of the water on myself in the process.

"Easy, I won't bite, at least not until we've been properly introduced."

She stood sideways, with an ankle out towards me, twisted a bit at the waist, holding a bottle up by her shoulder – deliberately provocative. Her hair was jet black and matted a bit with sweat. It stuck to her forehead and the back of her neck, and a few strands clung to her cheek. Even in the watery light I could see that her skin was smooth and sun-bronzed, like coffee with lots of milk and sugar stirred in.

"What are you doing here?" I asked, taken off guard and not liking the fact that she seemed so cocksure of herself.

"I'm Murph's girl; he brought me along for the thrill."

"He wasn't supposed to do that."

"Yes, well … can you really blame him? If you were him, would *you* leave me alone back in Des Moines all by myself?"

I didn't like the way she so confidently put the emphasis on the word "you" when she referred to what I might do. I took a sip of water and was aware that the distance between us had somehow closed without my having moved any.

"My name's Delilah, the name my daddy picked out for me before he went off to die in France a couple years after I was born."

"He was a doughboy?"

"One of Pershing's best, but then weren't they all?"

For a moment I was quiet while I did the math in my head. "That makes you about 17 or 18."

Delilah smiled, not about to answer my unspoken question, and offered me the bottle. I took it out of self-defense because I was trying not to notice some of the other little things about her that men tend to notice, even when they don't want to.

I poured a good slug of the whiskey into my glass, swirling it to mix with the water, and then I took a long swallow before handing the bottle back to her. The mixture managed to burn and soothe at the same time.

"Have as much as you like," she told me. "We brought a lot of this hooch, and some beer too. Though its warm and they ain't got any ice at the house."

"Where is Murphy," I asked. "Shouldn't he have appeared by now?"

I found a Chesterfield and got it going. With the help of the soothing tobacco, I was regaining my sense of rhythm now.

"He and that other guy, the swarthy fellow – what's his name?"

I released the smoke through my nostrils. "Isaac."

"Yeah, Isaac. Murph and Isaac went on a supply run, that little store a town up the road."

"I thought we'd already have plenty of supplies by now."

"Yeah, well. You know, they thought we needed some other things, especially with the kid along."

So the child had been part of somebody's plan all along. That didn't shock me too much.

"Like what for instance?" I asked. "What would we need?"

"Ice, for one. It's hot. Who wants to drink beer without ice?"

"What's that got to do with the kid?"

She waved at that. "They wanted ice, so sue them. Maybe they'll bring some ice cream back for the kid."

"Maybe they will. It's only for a few days. We could have stood it okay without the ice."

20

"Who wants to? And anyway maybe they got restless. You know how boys get."

"How come you didn't go with them?"

"Oh, do I seem like the restless sort too?" Her grin was too smart and too knowing and I didn't like it. "Maybe I am at times. Wanted to be here when you arrived, see you for myself. I've heard things about you that made me curious."

I took a long swallow of water and whiskey from my glass, and then another one. Even diluted as it was, two long swallows so close together burned my throat. At least the whiskey helped the metallic taste of the water.

Without making a specific effort to, I finished off the glass and then set the burning cigarette on my lower lip. I looked at her without speaking still. Her eyes were clear and sure, a pure color that you didn't often see in nature. Not even the lascivious shape of her mouth with its veneer of red lipstick could spoil her freshness.

"Hmmm …" Delilah intoned after a while, not backing down from the unspoken challenge of my stare. "They say you're a dangerous man." She moved up close enough to me that I could smell the heady scent of sweat mixed with lilac talcum on her skin.

She studied me with eyes that saw and had seen too much. Then she reached towards me to remove the cigarette from my mouth and put it slowly to her own lips. It glowed orange for a moment as she pulled at it.

"Yes," she said, after exhaling. "You look kind of like that other fellow in the newspapers – you both have that look in your eyes that makes you seem older than you actually are I suppose. Only I think you're better looking than he is by a good long yard or so."

"I don't know who you're talking about," I said, though I knew exactly who she was talking about.

She ignored my obvious lie. "What are you doing on a kidnap job?"

"I'm a criminal, aren't I? We commit crimes."

"I thought you were a bank robber – this doesn't seem your style."

"We'll see."

She squinted a little, as if she were puzzled and was now taking a closer look.

By way of response, I said, "Nuts. I didn't know about the kid, or you being along for the ride. I hope there aren't any other surprises in store."

Dusk was settling. Out over the pond, fireflies were starting to gather.

21

From the other side of the house I heard a vehicle moving over gravel.

"All right, Delilah," I said, ignoring the openings she had left me. "Let's go on inside and find out who else has joined this swell party."

She turned in front of me without another word and headed in, sashaying with my Chesterfield between her fingers, held out away from her hips in a well-practiced motion.

*

Dinner was an awkward affair, conducted under the light of four kerosene lamps. Apart from Hamilton, Wilson, Delilah, and myself, there were four other adults at the house.

I learned that the middle-aged woman from the front porch was named Mary. She was somewhere in her late fifties and well on the heavy side with sagging, fat arms, and washed-out gray hair that was piled in a tangled bun over her forehead. Tight vertical striations cut deep above and below her lips even when she wasn't smoking, which wasn't very often. Her eyes held a tired disappointment that suggested a lifetime of unmet expectations. Maybe she had been pretty at one time, but you couldn't tell it now. I thought about the photograph in the living room and wondered if it might be of her. Youth had slipped away a long time ago and her left eye sagged as if to emphasize that fact in case there was any doubt. I had never met her before, but I knew she was the wife of Hector Schulz who owned the house and, at some point in the past, had owned and farmed some of the land around us. He was a sallow man with large, drooped ears and over-sized lips. I'd never met him before either, but he was tied in to the other two men who I did know – they were yeggs operating out of St. Paul.

Isaac Runyon was heavy set, with dark features and a prominent mole above his lip that moved in a distracting fashion whenever he talked. He would never be confused for a ladies' man. In his early fifties, he had been doing this a long time. He had come out to the Midwest from the East, where he'd done a couple of stints in Sing Sing prison for racketeering and burglary. He was no criminal genius, but I'd worked a few bank jobs with him in the past and as far as I knew he had never crossed anyone. The last job had gone sour, though he'd proven himself a stand up guy and when he invited me in on the Hamilton kidnapping, I had accepted his explanation for the cause because I remembered where he had been and whom he was indebted to.

The other fellow, Murphy Pendleton, was slender and handsome, in his late twenties, with a penciled mustache that he must have worked hard at to keep in perfect style. I had never worked with him before, but I knew him by reputation – volatile, egotistical, mean. He was wanted in a couple of states for a variety of armed robberies and recently had been doing enforcer work in the Twin Cities. A rumor persisted that he wore an expensive cross-draw shoulder holster and fancied himself a trick shooter. From across the table I couldn't see it, but then maybe he didn't wear it to the dinner table. I didn't like him, or the fact that he had brought his teenage girlfriend along, as she had said, "for the thrill".

Murphy was already a bit drunk and sullen by the time we sat down and he continued to drink steadily from a tall glass of straight whiskey that he brought to the table with him. He had a nervous habit of smoothing out his pencil mustache with the tips of his index fingers after each swallow from his glass. At least he was quiet.

The meal was simple, though plentiful: mashed potatoes and fried beefsteaks, with ketchup and jarred applesauce on the side. There wasn't much discussion while we ate. Wilson barely touched the food he was served. His small fingers twirled the fork around on his plate, rearranging the potatoes and small bits of meat that Hamilton had cut for him. When that grew old he used the ketchup to paint a series of parallel loops with the tines of the fork, forming the red lines over the top of the potatoes. Then he repeated the design with the applesauce as his medium, layering it over the red lines with great concentration.

I ate quickly and had second helpings of the mashed potatoes and applesauce. Neither Hector nor Mary spoke a word after the meal was on the table. The only conversation was light banter between Isaac and Delilah about favorite radio shows. Since I had no opinion about *Little Orphan Annie*, *Your Hit Parade*, or malted milk, I kept my mouth shut. No one else said much at all either.

As we were finishing I asked Murphy if they had thought to look for any ice cream when they were out for the ice. They had not.

I couldn't be sure, but I thought I saw Wilson's shoulders drop a bit in disappointment.

Chapter Three

After supper, as the old couple began to clear the table together, Isaac gave a slight head jerk. I followed him out onto the back porch and down to the dock. There was no moon out, just a wide smear of faint chalk and the blinking, indifferent glitter of the universe spread out above us.

"Don't smoke yet," he said in a heavy whisper. "We should talk first."

I parked the Chesterfield behind my ear and nodded. With dark-adapted eyes we would be better aware if anyone from the house tried to come up on us.

"What gives?" I asked quietly. My teeth were clenched and only my lips moved. "This wasn't the plan I agreed to." I didn't actually say it as nicely as that sounded.

"Relax, okay. I don't like it either, not any more than you do."

"No one could like it less than me."

"Okay, I hear what you're saying."

"So?"

It was too dark for me to see Isaac's face well enough to judge his mood. "So what? It wasn't my idea. I didn't have anything to do with it and I'm sorry about it. Murphy was already here with the girl when I arrived yesterday morning. You think I like sleeping out in the barn, having to listen to the two of them? And I didn't know about the kid, honest, I didn't. Or about Hamilton being in on it until Murphy sprung it on me this afternoon. By then it was too late to do anything – couldn't have warned you if I wanted to. Murph said he worked it out with Hamilton a few weeks ago. It was Hamilton's scheme all along. The kid is supposed to add a little urgency to the ransom plot in case anyone gets a bright idea about not paying up. What can we do about it now?"

"For one, we can't put the banana back in the peel."

"Yeah ..."

"But we better make sure the child gets back to his mother in one full piece."

"Surely, you don't—"

"No, I don't. But are we going to trust those other two?"

"Hamilton wouldn't kill his own son."

"Let me correct you there: the boy is his stepson. There's no blood connection between them. Don't underestimate what that means. Blood means everything in this life. If he was willing to bring the boy along on his own kidnapping, to knowingly put him at risk, then what else is he willing to do to the boy? No ... blood means everything, which means we have nothing here that we can count on."

"Dutch Sawyer didn't say anything about this twist."

"I doubt he knew about it."

"He's the big fixer in the Twin Cities, how could he not know?"

"I think Hamilton played us all, all the way across the board."

It was still too dark for me to read Isaac's expression, but the sigh he released was palpable. "I'll follow your lead," he promised thinly. "We'll watch out for the child. It'll be okay."

"We put his survival above all else. I don't want another child's death hanging over me."

Isaac paused as the past came back to him, as it had for me. "Aw ..." he started. "I almost forgot about Kansas City."

"I didn't, I never do."

"I know, it comes to me too, mostly at night, in my dreams. I still see his face."

I nodded. I knew what he meant, because I did too.

"You did everything you could have done for him."

"Except for not robbing the bank in the first place."

"They never should have opened up on us like they did. The law is supposed to be more professional then that."

"They are what they are," I said. "We straight about this child?"

"Yes, we watch over him, protect him if we need to. I will, I swear it."

I nodded in the dark, knowing Isaac could at least sense that motion. "Don't swear it, do it. What about the split-up, how are we figuring that out now?"

"You're not going to like it: I guess Hamilton gets two full shares."

"Two?"

"Yes."

"Says who?"

"It's his money after all. That's how Murphy put it to me. What are we going to do? We can't keep him out now. He knows everything, including who we are."

"We've kidnapped him. What's he going to do?"

"He'll sing."

"He'll sing only if we return him alive."

"I didn't sign on for a murder," Isaac insisted.

"No? Would it be your first." I was angry and taking it out on Isaac. I didn't believe for a minute that he had deceived me, but he'd been careless. By extension then, I'd been careless too. "Why go wobbly now?"

"Come on, Duncan, you know it's not like that, not like that at all."

"Tell me how it is. Do you even remember why I agreed to come along on this lousy job?"

"Hey now, of course. That was for real, and it hasn't changed, we're not backing away from that."

"You said we were doing this for Jimmy."

Jimmy had always been uncomfortable with guns and the life of a criminal hadn't suited him well. He'd been lucky to get out of Kansas alive. Now he tended bar in Chicago and looked after his failing wife with a devotion that we all admired.

"We are, that hasn't changed," Isaac said in response. He took out a cigarette and rolled it between his thumb and forefinger as if were a piece of putty – the short, white pencil shape seemed to glow in the darkness.

"Okay, give it to me again, then."

"You know it well enough: Jimmy's wife needs the operation – and you know she really does, she can't last much longer without it – and then she needs a year or two to recuperate, right? Doctors say she'll do better in warm air, like New Mexico or Arizona. And Jimmy's got to take care of her, right? That's a full time job. Put it together. They need a stake – a good one, maybe three to five thousand, maybe even more with the doctors and hospital costs." After he spoke he put the unlit cigarette to this lips and rolled it around between them.

"What about the gambling debts? You said there were debts to get out from under in Chicago."

Even in the dark I could sense the change in Isaac's demeanor. His head lowered and the angle of his shoulders changed as he rubbed his palms together. "Yeah, I did."

"Jimmy doesn't much seem like a gambler to me."

"He's not, never was … the debts are mine."

I refused to be surprised by this. "How much?"

"Fifteen, maybe twenty."

"That sounds like twenty-five or thirty. Who holds the mark?"

"The Irishman."

I sighed. "Isaac." I said his name and then I stopped while I tried to decide exactly what I wanted to say and how I wanted to say it. "Of all people, of all the grifters, the gunmen, the thieves, *you* should know better then that."

"I know, but the Italians cut me off, they wouldn't let me play any more after I made good with them."

"They did you a favor. That should have told you something."

He nodded slightly. "What can I say? It's my weakness and I know I'll have to pay for it someday if I can't straighten it out."

"You sure it's the only one?"

We were silent for a while. During the lull I could hear Isaac's breathing and it was heavier than it should have been. I knew he wanted to light the cigarette that hung from his lips. When he was ready, he took a deep breath: "He's threatened to kill me if I don't pay off within the month. And I believe him too. His threats are rarely idle."

"That's why you never should have bet money with the Irishman, not at one of his tables. Those are all house games for him."

"I know it."

The Irishman was my enemy. He was a red-haired ghoul from the old country who still talked about his boyhood arrival in the U.S.A., his first sighting of the Statue of Liberty from a ship docked near Ellis Island. That was another era and it was far behind us. His business now was flowers, lavish nightclub entertainment, and the full range of illegal rackets. He was well mannered, well spoken, and typically dressed in a freshly pressed black tuxedo. He liked single yellow roses and if he invited you to visit he would graciously serve you the best imported Egyptian coffee or Irish whiskey available. Yet, when it served the purposes of his business, he callously ordered people to be murdered. A month ago he had killed the woman I loved and he had tried to kill me on more than one occasion. Also he owed me money – a fair sum of it.

"Okay," I said after a while. "We'll get you out of this. Walk me through the math. It seems we need at least fifty large to take care of both you and Jimmy."

"It might not be quite that much," Isaac replied slowly, as if thinking while he talked.

"Isaac, let's be pragmatic here for a moment. We can try that now, can't we? From what you've said and from what I know about both you and Jimmy, I think it comes out to about fifty. The Irishman is holding ten thousand dollars of my money, and with points owed it's probably up to about eleven grand now. I don't expect him to ever pay me back, though we can claim it to shave off what you owe him."

"Thanks, Duncan, that's more than I deserve."

"We're partners. It's what partners do."

"Not everyone has the same view of partnership that you have."

I grinned into the starlight that fell between us. "Well, it's hard to say what the world is coming to. All I can do is stand up for my end."

"It's an old fashion notion you have about partnership, alright, and I'm grateful. Jimmy will be too."

"I know."

"You know I owe Jimmy my life. If not for him, I wouldn't be here." I nodded.

"I'll do anything to pay him back, anything to help his wife. He's devoted to her."

"I know. You don't see it much."

"No, you don't."

"Still, forty or fifty thousand is a lot of moolah. I didn't know we were looking for that much when I signed on to this and I sure didn't know we would be giving a share to Murphy's girlfriend and two to Hamilton."

"Nobody said anything about a share for Murphy's girlfriend."

"We'll have to give her something. She's an accomplice now."

"I say it comes out of Murphy's end."

"No argument from me, but we'll have to see what he says. You can bet he has his own ideas about this."

Isaac sighed. "Yeah, I guess you're right about that."

"And that doesn't even get us to the child or Hamilton's part in this now."

"I know you're sore about that. I'm sorry, I really am. Murphy sprung it on me late. I promise you, we'll take care of the kid and Hamilton won't cause us any trouble."

"Really, you promise? You promise?" I felt the anger rising again. "What's that worth? What's your guarantee on something like that?"

"Aw, Duncan ..."

"Jimmy doesn't know about this, right? He doesn't know it's a kidnapping?"

"Of course not."

"We can never tell him."

"No, we never will. We'll tell him it was a lucky bank score, more

29

than we expected and we're sharing him in."

I didn't say anything for a little while. "You want to smoke now?" I asked presently.

"Yeah," he replied.

We lit up and stood there smoking quietly for a little while without exchanging any words. A shooting star dropped and disappeared. If Isaac saw it he did not comment. It felt good to stand there with the heavens spread above us and to think about how small and insignificant we were, perhaps an odd fact to find comfort in. Crickets made their pulsing noises, but it was still quiet enough that I could hear water lapping gently against the piers of the dock. A loon yodeled, high-pitched and haunting.

"That gives me the willies," Isaac exclaimed.

"It's only a loon," I told him.

"I hate them, I'm a city boy."

"They're one of the few creatures that mate for life."

"Really? Didn't know there was much of that anywhere."

"No."

"Not among the people I've known. My old man left my mother before I was even born. She ran through two more husbands before I was old enough to be out on my own."

"You grew up in New York?"

"Near Five Points, ran with a Jewish gang from the time I was about twelve. You?"

"Twin Cities, Minneapolis," I replied.

"That's right, you and Jimmy grew up together, Colt Rollings too if I recall correctly."

"Yes."

"Old ties, Duncan. It's good to have them, but it raises the stakes, increases the burden."

"Never thought of it as a burden. Man's lucky to have good people to call his friends."

"True enough. I was sorry to hear about Colt's death. I hated to read about it in the papers, wish I could have been there with you."

"Forget about it," I said.

"Life goes on."

"Only for the living," I replied, and then I repeated the line silently in my head.

"He was a right guy, not many like him left now."

"No, there aren't."

"What about his sister. I never met her, but the way he always talked about her, there was something special in her. Where is she now?"

I hesitated before responding.

"She's dead," I told him, but I didn't tell him the story – the Irishman had murdered her with an overdose of laudanum.

"Oh, Duncan … I'm sorry. What happened?"

"Forget about it," I said, working a little to control my voice. "Life goes on, but only for the living."

We were quiet for a moment while we smoked there in the dark. I looked up at the stars and relaxed a little.

Eventually Isaac spoke again: "Maybe Jimmy and his wife are like a pair of loons, mating for life."

"Maybe they are. Let's hope it's a long life. What about the twist?" I asked, changing the subject. "She got anything going on that I need to know about?"

Isaac let a slick whistle between his teeth. "Oh, boy, Murphy's got a hot one there."

"She's just a kid."

"A lot of parts of her are full grown woman."

"Maybe so, but by the calendar she's still a kid."

"She's got a statement to make to the rest of the world alright. She's okay, that one."

To my hot ears the night was murmurous with the tired sighs of girls who had thrown their youth away seeking some distant fire.

"Not saying she isn't," I said. "I'm just worried that we didn't plan for any kids along on this one. And instead of that we got two and each one means a different kind of trouble."

Isaac chuckled softly and his voice, when he spoke, was ugly: "Maybe things will get interesting around here. Maybe Murphy can't handle her?"

"Isaac," I said quietly, but with a voice that was louder than the one I'd been using. "Keep your distance from her. Don't even look her way, you'll turn to stone." My cigarette had burned down. I flicked it out over the water and heard the brief hiss. Without looking at Isaac again I turned and started to walk off the dock.

"Hey, Duncan," he said plaintively behind me. His voice was louder now. It carried a chord of regret. "I'm sorry about this. I really am. I know how you are about setting a plan and sticking to it. I didn't know

31

Murph was going to pull this on us. Honest – I didn't. You're a right guy for sticking by me and for helping Jimmy out. I owe you one, partner."

I stopped and turned over my shoulder. "Just keep an eye on Murphy. Man deceives his partners like this can't be trusted any more than a married Alderman in a whorehouse – and Hamilton's worse because he's a lot smarter than Murphy ever will be and he's got something going on that we can't see."

As I headed over the grass back toward the house the loon cried out again, defending his territory, or perhaps reflecting the floundering of my own innate despair.

Chapter Four

The night was long. It was stirred by an old memory and the bad feelings that came with it. For hours, well past midnight, my eyes stung with a bitter dryness while I watched the shadows creep across the ceiling. At first they looked like giant spiders, slow moving, mingling, and crawling over one another.

I might have drifted off for a few minutes now and again, but real sleep, the bottomless, escaping sleep we seek at night, was elusive. As the sky rotated, the light in the room changed. Paint above me was cracked and peeling. It managed to texture the shadows with the dimension of another living, breathing creature—this time an evil homunculus that might sit on my chest and suffocate me if I slept at all deeply.

Finally, I sat up on the edge of the bed, smoking and turning the dial on my looking glass of recollections to view the past from different angles, through different colored lenses. I was looking at a bank job Isaac and I had been on the year before in Kansas City. A small child had died and he wasn't supposed to. Broken fragments of time came together and then parted in a revolving, shape-changing way. Bits and pieces fell apart from each other and reformed with other bits and pieces to remake the past.

The distortion provided no comfort as I went back to that small room we had huddled in afterward.

*

"Might as well count the take now," Isaac said from the bed where he lay.

"Thought you were catching shut-eye on us," Colt said, grinning.

"I would if I thought I could trust you louses not to steal my share."

"Sure, and you probably need something to cheer you up at that."

The cash was still in the green duffel bag that no one had touched since we had come into the room. Colt picked it up and carried it over to the side of Isaac's bed.

"Do you want to do the honors, you lazy shirker?" he asked.

We all knew Isaac was unable to sit up, but the gallows banter was part of it. Isaac waved his good hand and made clucking noises. Colt pulled a chair over and started laying stacks of bills out on the very edge of the bed.

The piles grew as he counted. I'd learned a long time ago, or what seemed like a long time ago, not to allow my thoughts to advance beyond the count itself. The only thing worse than a low count itself was a low count when you had already spent the imagined fortune in your head.

No one in the room spoke while Colt worked. I leaned forward to sit again with my head down, this time not quite below my knees. Outside, it was eerily quiet. You could hear drops of rain that were beginning to fall as they hit against the window panes and the cheaply constructed roof above us. The browning lawns would receive some of what they needed.

It took twenty minutes for Colt to finish counting. When he was finished he sat back and looked around the room. When his eyes caught mine, he nodded.

"Almost forty-eight thousand," he announced softly. "That's more than we thought. Must have been a payroll."

"It may explain why they were prepared for trouble."

"They were more than prepared. They were waiting for us. No way they get men up on the roof that quickly after an alarm."

"Maybe so, and maybe we missed something. But still and all – divided seven ways it's almost seven thousand each."

The agreement among us was that we always paid out the full share to everyone who started the job, even if they were killed. In that case, their girlfriend or family received the money.

"Now we know," I said grimly.

The rain came down harder against the window, falling in sheets now, and lightning flashed. With the blackening sky, the room had darkened also and we didn't dare turn on a light. I moved onto the floor so that I could lay down with my head on top of my bloodied jacket. There I listened to the rain and the storm that battered against the house.

*

I must have slept.

On the floor, I drifted into my own dark imagination. In my mind, I saw the scene where the law found our apartment hideaway. They would roll up in a caravan of cruisers and trucks, forming a chain the length of the street in front of us. From behind curtains we'd peer out at them, startled and scared, with mouths too dry to speak. Then a bullhorn would croak that they had us surrounded and we had one minute to come out with our hands

34

raised in surrender. With fear and dread we'd look to the eyes of each other for answers that did not exist. The awareness would take hold and each of us would manage it in a different way, a way that could not possibly be predicted before that awful moment. It would only be seconds then before one of the besiegers would panic, maybe a rookie policeman who'd never fired his weapon before or an aging detective whose hands hadn't stopped shaking since the last time he'd seen another man killed in the line of duty. But someone would panic and fire the first shot that would start the fusillade. The sound would be deafening at first, one long continuous role of thunder, until they needed to reload. Then the firing would become more sporadic, a steady beat of shots hitting the apartment, aimed this time for where they thought survivors might be taking cover. First, they'd shoot out the windows; then they'd start on the walls. By that time we would all be on the floor. For those of us still alive the shots would come whistling in over us and shatter lamps, cracking the plaster on the interior wall in the back. Bits of cloth and bed stuffing would fill the air. Light filled holes would appear suddenly and rapidly on the wall fronting the street. Incoming beams of light would quickly brighten the room. The shots, impossible to distinguish individually from one another, would begin to fall lower. Frantically we would crawl on our elbows and knees, searching for a refuge that wasn't there.

Outside they wouldn't stop firing until they were sure. And then there would come the long abrupt silence that we'd never hear.

*

The rain ended as quickly as it had come up and within a few minutes the hazy sun was once again heating the room to a high degree. Slowly, I emerged from my morbid reverie. From somewhere overhead came the persistent, decaying sound of dripping water. It insinuated itself softly.

"We'll have to make a decision soon," Colt whispered, kneeling beside me. Darkening folds in his jaw and neck gave away the internal strain he was experiencing. "He can't speak for himself anymore."

I nodded in agreement. "If it was you, what decision would you want me to make?"

"Easy. Put me down quick, don't let me suffer too much once it's clear I have no chance."

"No hospital?"

"Not if it's to be followed by life in prison. I'd rather die quickly, than

slowly like that."

"That's the choice?"

"It is. You? What would you want?"

"The very same."

"No going back, not ever, no matter what."

"Agreed. But has Tucker been in stir?"

Colt nodded. His eyes shaded gray and I knew well the far off stare they held.

"Six years in Lansing. It's how he met Barker and Karpis."

"Know if he had any fun there?"

"As a matter of fact, he did not. They put him to work in the coal mine for most of that time. He worked underground, with a shovel ten hours a day— it's probably why he has that cough."

I shook my head. "Know if he cares about going back or not?"

"Never heard him say he missed the place."

I managed a dark grin. "Not even the food?"

"Not even."

"So, that's it then."

"Do we poll Jimmy or Isaac?"

I thought about this for a moment. "No," I said finally. "Isaac's out and he doesn't need the burden even if he comes around first. Jimmy … well, he has no experience with this. It wouldn't be fair to ask his opinion."

"Agreed. You think five vials will do it?"

"Yes. It will be enough. Let's get it over with."

Colt held out a hand to help me up off the floor.

*

I had the morphine vials lined up on a small towel, ready to administer in quick succession. But Tucker was already dead by the time I knelt down beside him. His neck muscles had contracted so that his head had rolled back on the pillow. Now his eyes stared up at the ceiling with dilated pupils, a grotesque mask of pain and horror, seeing everything and nothing for the first time.

The three of us stood silently around the bed while above us the water continued to drip on, filling the house and our souls with an inexorable terror. It was the sound of cataclysm that was upon us.

"We should say a few words," Jimmy said after a while. His lips trembled, though he stood straight and he didn't blink. Spiked shapes of light and

shadow cast onto the ceiling above us and down along the headboard to create the illusion that Tucker's body floated in the space between us.

"We don't usually do that," Colt said quietly. "None of us have ever known the right words to say."

"But it's no reason not to if you have the words, Jimmy," I encouraged. I nodded at him to let him know it was okay. Colt nodded too and folded his hands in front of his waist.

Jimmy shrugged and thought about it for a moment. His eyes welled, but he didn't break and his voice held. "Okay," he said finally. "I'll say a few."

We bowed our heads.

"Lord," Jimmy began. "Please take our friend. He's crossed over the river now and he rests with you. Cradle him and hold him to your breast. Soothe him and welcome him home as one of your children. He needs your comfort and your clemency."

Behind us Isaac murmured an unintelligible affirmation.

Jimmy cleared his throat as if to quiet the room from further response. "Now I'll read from the book." A heavily worn Bible appeared in his hands. He opened it to a page marked by a thin red ribbon and I realized he had been preparing for this moment earlier.

"This is from the first book of Corinthians:

'It is the same way with the resurrection of the dead. Our earthly bodies are planted in the ground when we die, but they will be raised to live forever. Our bodies are buried in brokenness, but they will be raised in glory. They are buried in weakness, but they will be raised in strength. They are buried as natural human bodies, but they will be raised as spiritual bodies. For just as there are natural bodies, there are also spiritual bodies.'"

"Amen," Isaac said, his voice stronger than before.

"Lord," Jimmy continued. "I have not spoken to you in good while. Forgive me and understand that I have been angry with you for my wife's illness. I repent my silence and I ask you to hear me now. Please show our friend, Tucker, the mercy you hold for all your earthly flock ... And please shine your light on all those who died today and forgive us for being the agents of those deaths. Amen." When he finished, Jimmy closed the Bible and turned away from the deathbed to look at the opposite wall.

"Amen," Colt said quietly.

I said nothing. My thoughts had drifted. I still saw the expression on the boy's face as he lay dying and then the way his eyes rolled up afterwards. No prayer would crease my lips.

*

It was almost seven o'clock in the evening. Isaac was sleeping. He lay on his back with a wet towel folded over the top half of his face. A gentle rhythm carried his breathing, not quite a snore, to outpace the slackening beat of the dripping water.

"It's late and we need to decide on our plan now," I said to Colt and Jimmy.

"Are there options?" Colt asked. "Once it's late enough I thought we'd make a mad dash for the Essex." He grinned as if to show his easy confidence in the plan.

"No," Jimmy replied. "We can't do that. We can't move Isaac. He wouldn't survive in a moving vehicle for long."

"Jimmy could be right," I said. I cocked my head to the side and glanced between them. "The motion and the jostling might kill him. And besides, he'll die anyway if we don't get a doctor to look at him soon."

"We're not leaving him at a hospital," Colt said. His voice was hard.

"No," I agreed. "But we can bring a doctor to him. He can be cared for right here until he's well enough to be moved."

"You know a doctor in this burg, do you, one we can trust for that kind of service?"

"No, but Boss Pendergast does."

"We can't go to him now."

I considered this. Tom Pendergast ran the city from the Jackson County Democratic Club, a two-story yellow brick building, and most of the people in town called him "Boss." Officially, we should have sought his permission for the bank robbery and coordinated it with his machine, but we hadn't done that. That would have meant a generous kickback to him, possibly in advance, as well as a large share of the final take – if he'd given his permission, which he wouldn't have done if the payroll had been his to begin with.

"Yes, we can," I said finally, and then I paused to think about it some more. I moved over to the window and looked out at the street. The light was lower and it was dry again. If you hadn't been there for the storm earlier you would never believe how hard it had rained a few hours before. Even the internal dripping had ceased.

"Alright," I said loud enough to get everyone's attention. On the other side of the small room Isaac moved so that I knew he was listening from beneath the damp towel over his face. "Here's the way I see it. Colt and I have to sneak out tonight as planned – after he fixes the radiator." I looked at Colt

38

for emphasis.

"You may have no doubt about that," Colt replied.

I continued without responding to him. "Jimmy stays behind to tend to Isaac. We take Tucker's body with us so that it does not come to smell worse in here than it already does, and so we have something to give to Pendergast. He owns the police and they'll like a nice clean and simple case. We leave Tucker's body, along with the Buick at our rendezvous spot. Then, we come back into town, say about midmorning when the traffic thins out. By that time everyone assumes the bank robbers are long gone. They've forgotten about us. We walk into Pendergast's office and we make him an offer. We ask for food, provisions, and discreet private medical care for Isaac, including a nurse to stay with him at night, to be provided right here in this room for as long as necessary. Jimmy will stay here with him until he can be moved. Then we'll set them both up in Chicago with a nice apartment so Isaac can recuperate. At that point we'll get one of our usual sawbones in Chitown to look after him. Colt and I will lay low somewhere else. In three or four months you'll both be ready to join the crew again and we'll get back to work."

"Yeah, it's beautiful," Colt said, "but what about Pendergast. What are we going to offer him?"

"He gets ten thousand, plus another five to pay for the medical care, the supplies, and the nurse."

"Think that will be enough?"

I shrugged. "It's his city, he'll probably want more. So we'll negotiate. We also can offer him the location of Tucker's body and the shot-up Buick. Local police can have a field day with all that."

Colt let out a low whistle. "I guess it might help Pendergast at that to have a scapegoat."

"Never met a politician yet who didn't appreciate a dead body to pin a crime on."

Colt looked at Jimmy, studying him softly with eyes that did not appear to focus on anything in particular. "Jimmy," he asked slowly. "It is asking a lot of you. You okay with this?"

Jimmy nodded somberly. "Yes."

"It means staying behind, right here in this room for at least a week or two."

"Someone has to do it."

"Yeah, but it's not without risk."

"Neither is busting out of here or walking into Pendergast's office."

"So, you're okay with it, you're sure?" Colt asked.

39

"Yes. I'm the best one for the job. Anyway, I can't do what you and Ross will have to do."

We were silent for a while.

Then, Colt spoke to me: "Pendergast might not exactly welcome us when he learns we're the ones that caused all the mayhem this morning. Some of those people we killed out there on the street were probably his."

"Maybe he'll explain how they knew to be waiting for us and why they opened fire without regard for the civilians in the bank."

"He won't welcome us."

"Really? Even after he hears the swell deal we have for him?"

"Even after."

I shook that off. "I think he's a pragmatist who knows that ten thousand and a dead body is a better deal than nothing. Killing us won't put anything into his pocket."

"It would give him the dead bodies that he needs. Besides, you never know when a man's pride is gonna interfere with his greed."

"Then we better be ready to shoot our way out of there."

"Might not be easy."

"Oh, nuts. Do you want to live forever?"

It wasn't a great plan. We all knew it, but it was the best we could do. It would be expensive, and wouldn't come out of the shares of our three dead partners. The living would shoulder the cost.

They always did.

Chapter Five

The Kansas City plan had worked well enough, though with a hiccup I tried not to think about. These days Jimmy bartended a run-down neighborhood tavern in Chicago near Belmont and Lincoln called Sullivan's. It was a dark place that never seemed to do much business. The few customers to be found there at any given time were usually old regulars sitting together at the end of the bar nursing their beers.

I'd only been in there a handful of times. The beer was sour, but the Hungarian cook seemed to know what he was doing. The cabbage soup and bread always made for a decent meal if you were hungry. Mostly I went in there because I trusted Jimmy. In fact, he was one of the very few I could trust anywhere. Yes, Jimmy was now my safety net, my bank, my deposit box, and my lifeline if everything went to hell. He kept a metal briefcase for me in which I stored emergency cash, driver's licenses, maps, lists of contacts and phone numbers – even .45 caliber ammunition – the tools of my trade, of my very survival ... just in case.

As I sat on the edge of the bed at the Iowa farmhouse, remembering, with the homunculus hovering above me in the cracked paint on the ceiling, I thought about another conversation I'd had with Jimmy more recently, not even two months ago. It helped make sense of the Corinthians scripture he'd selected to read over Tucker's body and it played out in my mind like a scene from a movie. I looked into the kaleidoscope again.

*

"How's your wife?"

I extended the pack of Chesterfields. Jimmy selected one and lit it before responding. His expression told me nothing. His almond eyes were impassive.

"Good days and bad," he said after he exhaled. "More bad than good. Life's not worth much when you're sick like that. Most days she's in bed, sleeps some, stares at the ceiling a lot, cries through the night – or rather, whimpers, really. Her spine is shrinking, losing bone, they say. There's an operation that might help, but who can afford it? And no one really believes it would help much anyway, might even make things worse. I'd get it for her if she needed it, but

they don't know even if she would survive. If the operation would help her, I'd find the money in a weekend. But they don't know, they just don't know. They say it could as easily leave her in a coma or paralyzed all the way down."

"Rotten choices, Jimmy," I said. I was surprised by the anger in my own voice. I had never met his wife. "Really rotten."

He nodded, though his face remained calm. "It is what it is," he said presently, sipping from a beer he had carried to the table. "What gets me is knowing it's coming and not being able to do anything about it, seeing her like that."

"That would get me too. It would get just about anybody."

"There just ain't nothing I can do. She can't have kids, we haven't even had relations in a year."

Slow tears filled Jimmy's eyes and he leaned back in the booth with his chin tilted up slightly. I thought at first he might cry harder, but he did not. Instead he gazed at me, steadily, without shame, and then he brought the cigarette to his lips and pulled hard on it.

"I'm sorry," I told him. "What's your wife's name?"

"Helen."

"I wish there was something I could do."

He nodded as he exhaled a lungful of smoke. "Funny thing, confessing to you like this. You bear witness ... like a father confessor. Something about your place and our past together – you're a fugitive – oddly makes you safe. Even with the gun. You've seen things and spilled blood, you don't talk, you don't judge, you're outside it all, outside everything. Like no one else."

I mustered a smile. "Brother, a long time ago, for a short time, we knew each other pretty well and we counted on each other. You can call on that if you need to."

"I know. There isn't anything you can do," he said and his voice choked off as he said it.

I sat there for a while with him in silence and we finished our cigarettes. I thought about what he had to face when each day was through. After we finished smoking, we drank a little of the warm and sour beer. We pushed the mug back and forth between us, taking turns sharing it.

"It isn't all that bad," he said finally. "I really do love her, you know." His eyes flashed hot suddenly, and then just as quickly cooled.

"That's something," I said. "It's a lot."

"Huh, hmmm," he replied. "I wasn't sure when I married her, but I'm sure now."

"It's a lot. I'm envious."

"*You have other things.*"

"*If you love her and she loves you, then I don't have half of what you have.*"

Chapter Six

The dream I was having was one of the better ones I ever tended to have, though it was cut short of its ending. I was still in bed the next morning when the Tommy gun started up from behind the house.

There was one long burst and then two more short ones. I rolled over and hit the floor with a crouch, holding my .45 automatic cocked and ready beside my cheek. Beads of sweat formed across my brow and down the small of my back. I was aware of an ache in my lungs as my breathing troughed out like it always did in those moments.

With conscious deliberation I took in as much air as I could, exhaling with my lips pursed in a large "O". I closed my eyes and listened, still breathing. There were none of the usual sounds one would expect in a law enforcement raid: the of breaking glass, men's anxious shouts, cries of those who had been hit or the captain's bullhorn.

It could have been a raid, but something was different about it. Conversational voices filled the pause in the firing, then there was another long burst from the same gun, this one clumsy, followed by a joyous, hollering whoop. Hunched down I maneuvered over to the window and listened with my head below the sill. I took two hard breaths, counted three, and then raised my head up fast and down again.

Nothing.

I took a four-count. Then I rose up again quickly and looked down over the back of the house toward the pond.

What I saw was Murphy and Hamilton taking target practice out on the dock. A line of beer bottles stood at the far end, some of them broken and several apparently missing altogether from the line. Hamilton held the smoking Thompson up on in the air with one hand. With his other, he pointed at the end of the dock and laughed. They exchanged banter, but I couldn't hear the words. I scanned the edge of the woods—saw nothing moving there. It was just a couple of eager fools playing with guns.

I sat up on the bed and thumbed on the safety of my .45. Then I thought about it again and thumbed it off. I had to go out there. I found my trousers and the shirt I'd worn the day before. Dirty clothing in a pinch never bothered me.

Outside, someone was firing again – inexpert, disorganized shooting. I passed Mary in the kitchen as I went through. She was peeling more potatoes and barely gave me a nod as I went by. Her tired eyes didn't seem to notice anything. In the pauses I heard the clock on the wall ticking as though there were no excitement and never had been.

I came off the porch and took several steps towards them. They were still on the dock, standing together with most of the bottles down. No one else was in sight. Murphy held the Thompson now with the lower end of the barrel against his shoulder, pointed toward the sky. He studied the glass shrapnel and chipped wood that was now strewn across the far end of the dock.

"Hey!" I called when I was near enough not to have to shout. I had the .45 held down beside my leg – visible and present, but not threatening anyone in particular yet.

"Yeah," Murphy said, turning slowly to face me.

"Put it down," I told him.

"I could cut you in half," he asserted with a grin on his face.

Maybe he was trying to be funny. I wasn't smiling.

"You'll have to be faster than me. Do you want to find out?"

Murphy froze, momentarily stunned. Then, holding the Thompson so that the barrel never took aim off the sky, he set it slowly on the dock.

"Aw, Duncan," he said after he had straightened back up. "I was only messing around."

There was a dark glower behind his eyes, partially hidden by an attempted smile that never quite formed. The grin he tried was lopsided and empty, ugly even, and a pretty good likeness of his overall character as I was starting to see it.

"You don't mess around with a Tommy gun," I said.

"Hamilton wanted to see it, wanted to give it try."

"Murphy, we aren't doing this for chuckles. We don't need the kind of attention that clatter could bring, not to mention you might scare the kid."

He nodded and looked sullen, staring toward his toes. Hamilton tried to lighten the mood.

"Well hey, let's all be friends again. This is my fault. I've never seen one of these gizmos up close before. Curiosity got the better of me."

I walked over between them and picked up the Thompson. When I straightened up, my face was close to Hamilton's. I looked down into his blinking eyes as I disengaged the magazine from the gun with a

46

hard click.

"Nuts," I said softly, but with enough force that I know he felt the angry heat of my breath.

Murphy stared back at me with a startled, half-crossed gaze. I focused my best yard stare, relaxed and non-committal. Hamilton started to stammer, then his eyes dropped – and he said not a word more than nothing. I waited for a moment, quiet. Then I turned and walked back into the house, carrying the Thompson cradled in the elbow of my left arm.

Behind me I heard only indistinguishable mutterings.

*

After a breakfast of fried potatoes, eggs scrambled hard, and bitter black coffee I went out onto the back porch to read a little. A soft breeze came in behind the sunshine that skirted the eastern edge along the railing. It pushed in with a cooling ease, passing through the shade of a nearby Sycamore. Sparrows chirped from somewhere down wind, but otherwise it was quiet now that the machine gun had been stored away.

Lately, I'd been thinking about Hell more. I was rediscovering Genesis, the first book of Moses – *the Old Testament*. It held none of the Sunday school charm I remembered from a distant childhood, but rather carried newer and deeper relevance. I read silently for an hour, with only my own thoughts of what lay ahead for occasional interruption.

When I finished the book, I repositioned the bookmark at Exodus and walked around the perimeter of the clearing that surrounded the house and the pond. Ash trees and the edge of merging cornfields bound it, separating it from the unknown that lay beyond – probably another farm, another clearing, another pond – and then another beyond that in all directions, many times over.

It wasn't like the city, with its twin brutish forces of violence and corruption. All the same there was something unknowable rooted in deep there in the rural countryside that worried me, some horrific mystery hovering beneath the veneer of the calm, peaceful garden-like state of the countryside. I didn't enjoy the thoughts that came to my mind as I reflected on the situation I faced.

From the side and back, and from across the open space, the house looked different to me now. The disrepair was more evident. Broken

47

screens and chipped paint told the story of a badly neglected home. Cement blocks propped up the back porch at a listing angle. It was a familiar image. Houses were falling apart all over the Midwest now. I wondered if we were in the midst of the "*seven empty years blasted with the east wind, seven years of famine*" that I'd been reading about.

I had a Chesterfield in my mouth, but I wasn't smoking. My eyes were alert as I studied the ground, looking inward towards the house and barn periodically, not sure what I was looking for. Whatever it was, I never did see it. After pacing the territory twice, I headed back toward the house and pumped myself a bit of water from the well.

While I was doing that, Wilson came down from the porch and sat on the bottom step to watch me. He must have been watching from the porch all along, waiting for me to come over.

"Is it cold?" he asked?

"No, but it's cool enough? Want some?"

He nodded and I handed the jar to him. With both hands he held it to his mouth and took a long drink, tipping the jar faster than he drank so that after a moment water spilled out and ran down both sides of his face and onto the front of his shirt. When he was finished I asked him if he wanted some more, and then pumped some for myself when he said he didn't.

"It's getting hot," Wilson observed. His voice did not carry a note of complaint.

"Yes. I think it will bump ninety by this afternoon."

"I don't mind."

"Where's your father?"

"He's in his room with newspapers. Mr. Murphy picked them up this morning, after they finished shooting."

"What have you been doing?"

"Reading."

"What do you read?"

"Huckleberry Finn. Have you read it?"

I said I hadn't.

"Why were they shooting?" he asked then, suddenly, self-consciously, in that way that children can be when asking questions they have been thinking about for a while.

"They were curious. Your father wanted to try it. It wasn't wise to do it here."

"Why does Mr. Murphy have a machine gun?"

Wilson was sitting on the bottom step again. I took a couple steps and sat down beside him. From behind my ear I found the cigarette I'd been worrying in my mouth for most of the past hour. It was soggy and some of the tobacco had fallen out, but it was serviceable. I lit it and shook the match out.

"It's a good question," I said once I had exhaled a neat line of smoke up into the hot sky. "I guess he uses it for protection."

The boy sat very still, thinking. A soft crease came down between his eyes and his nostrils fluttered. It caused him to appear very serious and even older than he was. "Is that why you carry a pistol?"

"Yes."

"Why do you wear it on your shoulder?"

I was a funny question to ask in follow up. I smoked some more and shook my head. "It's more comfortable to wear it there."

"My dad said we're staying here for a few days until our automobile is fixed. I don't understand why. I miss my mother."

I didn't know what to tell him so I changed the subject. "You remind me of another boy I used to know."

"Really?" his eyes were placid, but he seemed pleased. "Who?"

"A boy named Tad," I said, referring to the child of a landlady in Chicago I'd rented from recently. The boy in the bank crossed my mind too, though I didn't mention that. "He's about your age, same height. He liked to play checkers and he had a cat."

"Where did you know him?"

"I rented a room in his house, from his mother. If we can find a board, do you want to play?"

"Okay. Cats scare me."

I stubbed out the cigarette and we went inside to look for a checkerboard, which we found in a cupboard in the front room of the house.

Chapter Seven

In the heat of the afternoon I laid down in my bed, with the shoulder holster looped over the bedpost. It was too hot to think about doing much. The house was quiet; everyone had retired. I read a bit more of the Old Testament and took a short nap.

Swift dreams of an angry God and broken idols ran serially through my sleep. When I awoke I lay still for a while, trying to find meaning in them, but couldn't. It felt even hotter than before. I had sweat heavily in my sleep against the pillow and bottom sheet of the bed. I turned and moved, seeking a cooler, dryer spot. The house was still quiet. A faint breeze rustled the curtains and cooled me just enough to remind me what cool was and how good it would be to have more of it.

I thought about the situation some more. It wasn't what I expected – the child, the girl, the victim's apparent complicity. None of it was according to the scheme Murphy and Isaac had sold me on. That plan had been to kidnap one man, a wealthy financier, against his will and hold him until his wife paid a ransom to obtain his release. When the money was in hand, we were going to send him home unharmed. The whole thing was supposed to take only five to seven days. Now, not only did we have an extra child and a girl along, but the financier was apparently a conspirator to his own kidnapping. That meant the proceeds would need to be split more ways than we'd planned for. It also introduced a wild card in the deck. Who knew what other surprises were in store? Who else had Hamilton told? Who else was involved?

Even with the new Federal statute – the "Lindbergh" law, some called it – kidnapping was supposed to be easier, simpler, and safer than robbing banks. At least that's what the other crooks were saying. Now I wasn't so sure it was any of those things, and we hadn't even started with the ransom negotiation. No one had taken a shot at me yet, but the likelihood of that holding true for long didn't seem strong. And now there was a child involved, *another innocent child*. That didn't square for me. I thought about Jimmy and his wife and the main reason I'd signed on to this job in the first place. I knew they wouldn't have asked for this. I cursed myself for a fool and I thought about my options. None of them excited me.

Maybe it was too hot to think well.

After a while, I heard crashing sounds from the kitchen – someone was vigorously using an ice pick for the very purpose it was designed for. Cold beer wouldn't be far behind. I got out of the bed and pulled the shoulder holster on over my under-shirt.

*

When I entered the kitchen, Murphy was furiously pounding against what had once been a large block of ice in the sink. Kenneth Hamilton stood at the counter next to the sink. His paunch bulged out against a silk dress shirt that was untucked all around and only half buttoned. The sleeves were rolled up past his elbows. He was opening bottles of Schmidt's beer and pouring them into two jars that were half-filled with ice chips.

"Better make it three," I told them.

"Right up," Hamilton said with a cheerful grin. He spoke as if we'd never had a run-in.

Another jar was quickly filled with ice from the sink and two more bottles of beer were opened. Murphy stopped his hard work and sat at the table with us. I took the cold jar when it was offered to me and swirled the chips around in it, exciting a frothy head.

"We had the Schmidt's in the root cellar so it's cooler than room temperature anyway. With the chopped ice it reaches the perfect temperature, that is to say right cold, in about one minute – which is to say right about now," Hamilton said as he hoisted the jar to his lips and drank deeply.

Murphy and I followed suit. When the three jars were back on the table not one of them was more than half full.

"I might have had a more welcome beer at some point," I said, "but damn my eyes if I can remember when."

"Amen," Hamilton replied. He took another long drink for good measure.

"Where is everyone else?" I asked.

Hamilton started to talk, but Murphy cut him off, "Delilah went for a dip in the pond. She's probably floating around on an old tire-tube, working on a sunburn. Isaac is sleeping in the barn. It's not so hot there in the back, between the hay bales if you don't mind the smell. The old

52

couple is hiding out in their bedroom. They have a fan in there."

"And Wilson is sleeping," Hamilton added quickly.

We finished the beer, scooped more ice, and opened more bottles, almost friends now. I took another long drink and thought about lighting a cigarette, but didn't.

"Heard you got papers today," I said. "Any news?"

Hamilton shrugged and said, "Nothing about me. No mention of my auto being found or my disappearance. Just front page stories about Germany."

Murphy guffawed loudly. "You didn't expect the kind of headlines Lindbergh or Urschel got, did you?"

Hamilton shook his head. "But it's too soon," he replied defensively. His ego had been wounded by the lack of attention. "Abigail would be worried, but she wouldn't think I'm missing yet. She probably hasn't even thought of calling the police."

"Of course, she's not worried about you, but what about her son?" Murphy was still laughing, enjoying Hamilton's discomfort. "You don't think you're going to get the kind of headlines that Urshel got? You won't even get what Hamm or Bremer got."

"I will if they think Dillinger's gang took me," he said, looking at me oddly.

Murphy slapped the table hard and said, "Dillinger doesn't pull kidnappings."

"That's what people thought about the Barker-Karpis gang before they did."

Murphy guffawed loudly again, an easy drunk. The beer was affecting him. He stood up and opened another beer, drinking it from his jar without adding any more ice. Hamilton's face was red and he stared hard at the table.

"Okay," I inserted into the gap. Up to that point I'd remained quiet. "Let it lie. Murphy, why not take a jar of cold beer out to Delilah. She'll appreciate it. Maybe she'll even mistake you for a gentleman?"

*

When we were alone I looked at Hamilton. I studied the faint lines around his eyes, the thin lips, and the near missing chin that might have leant him some air of gallantry if he'd had a bit more definition there.

53

For the first time, I noticed that his eyes were a little too close together. While I watched him he fidgeted with his jar, rolling the remaining ice gently around the bottom in a slow circle. He was quickly half drunk – not to the point where his thinking would muddle or his emotions would overflow – but enough so that he was feeling friendly and pleased with himself, basking slightly in a misguided sense of companionate acceptance. It seemed as good a moment as any to get him talking.

"Why do this?" I asked.

His eyes half crossed and his grin was suddenly coy. "Why not? You do it."

"I'm a criminal."

"Maybe we're not so different, you and I."

"Tell me more about that, I never would have guessed it."

"You rob from banks, you rob from people. That's stealing money."

"I'm a professional thief, it's what I do."

"Show me someone with money who isn't a thief in some way."

It was cynical, but I didn't have a quick counter argument. Instead I changed direction by a half step. "So, you steal money too. Perhaps in other ways than I do?"

I was expecting him to confirm that he did. Instead he shook his head vigorously. "No, nothing like that. I've never used a gun, certainly. I take what people will give me willingly. There's no force or coercion. Is that stealing?"

"Investor beware?"

"Something along those lines. As long as you don't break the rules too obviously, there's no risk to the money man."

"So, why do a nasty job like this? Why take the risk?"

Hamilton nodded and replied, "I have my reasons."

"There are only ever two reasons: money or revenge, sometimes both."

He was still shaking his head. There was a doubting thought forming there.

I nodded at him slowly and pulled at the string a little. "You're either desperate for money – maybe in debt, far over your head; or you're getting even with someone – probably your wife, maybe your employer."

"No need to make everything so complicated when simple greed and a little boredom will suffice to explain the behavior of most people."

"Nuts," I told him, laughing a little as I said it and read the patently false expression on his face. "You think this set-up is simple, without risk to anyone? Better reconsider that because none of the rest of us see it that way. This is life or death, and if we screw it up, we're all dead, you included. Think about that for a minute and see how it looks from where I'm sitting. A man in your position, with your wealth and family, you don't go down this dangerous path unless there's a driving reason to send you."

"You seem awful cocksure of yourself."

I shook my head. "Less so then ever, but I know this: as much as you deny it, your reasons are, in fact, complicated – and desperate to a fault. You're on a ledge and you're windmilling your arms in wide circles, trying to recover your balance, trying not to fall off."

"A dramatic analogy."

"I don't think you're going to make it," I said, grinning. "I think you're wavering now, but in the end I think you're going to tip over to take that long fall. The landing will be hard."

Hamilton's expression dissolved. He stopped moving his head and stood up to lean over the sink. From the window he looked out toward the pond and I knew he could see Delilah and Murphy if they were anywhere near the dock.

"She's a fine looking young woman," Hamilton said finally. His tone was somber and distant. "I never had any luck with young ladies like that."

"Not even after you became rich?"

"No. They see something in me that keeps them away – even now, even in these times."

My voice, when I spoke, came out cold: "I wonder what your wife sees."

He didn't answer. He merely stood there with his belly pressed against the sink, staring blankly out the window, toward some unattainable desire that only he could glimpse. I wondered if he was thinking about the fall, and whether he was tempted merely to step off the ledge of his own volition.

*

That evening I stood out on the deck by myself, smoking. The fireflies were out in force: tiny lights, blinking at unrushed intervals, floating in the air. There was no breeze evident now. It was a hot evening; hot enough that my shirt stuck to my back and the cigarette didn't taste good.

Wilson came up behind me, approaching slowly as if in tune with the languor of the fireflies. I heard his footsteps and turned to watch him.

"Mister, are you sad?" he asked when he was standing beside me.

I looked down into his oval face as he squinted a bit against the dim light. There was a certain perplexity behind his worried expression. It pushed his cheeks out and bunched his eyes.

"Not so much," I told him. Maybe it was a lie.

"You look sad. You're standing out here alone. Solitary, with no one to talk to."

It was a big word for a child his age. I mustered a smile. "Sometimes I like to be off by myself. It allows me to think."

"I do that too sometimes."

"It's okay to do that. Other people might not always be able to say what we need to hear. Sometimes the best thoughts come from within."

"What are you thinking about?"

I sighed. I wasn't quite sure myself. "I'm thinking about parents and children, mothers and fathers, love songs, jazz songs, silly girls and sad girls, the earth, the sky, and everything all at once."

It was a stupid response to make, especially to a child, but Wilson's look and the half-smile that formed beneath his perplexed eyes were appreciative.

"Really?"

"Sure."

"I have thoughts like that too."

I took a drag off the cigarette and held the smoke in my lungs.

"What kind of cigarettes do you smoke?" he asked.

I exhaled slowly, at an angle away from the child. "Chesterfield," I replied. "Do you want one?"

He pulled back, surprised. "My mother doesn't let me smoke."

I gave him my best grin.

"Oh, you're teasing me" he laughed. "My father smokes a pipe."

"Do you want to play catch tomorrow?" I asked.

He peered up at me, trying to gauge whether I was serious this time. After a tick he answered, "Is there a ball?"

"Maybe we can find you one."

"You like baseball?"

56

"Sure do."

"What position do you play?"

That caused me to laugh a little. "I don't play any position anymore. When I was your age I liked the outfield, thought I might get a try-out with the Cardinals."

"Did you?"

"No, I never did."

"That's too bad. I like the outfield, but I follow the Cubs."

"Uh, oh. That makes us natural rivals."

"How do you know about them?"

"I listen to ballgames on the radio."

"I wish my father did. We never play catch, either."

"Who's your favorite player?"

"Lon Warneke."

"The Arkansas Hummingbird." I said it slowly and dramatically like they did on the radio when they introduced him.

Wilson grinned from ear-to-ear. "He won eighteen games last year. Twenty-two the year before."

"You know a lot. What did Babe Herman hit last year?"

"I don't know. Do you?"

I said I didn't.

Wilson perked up with a thought, "I know Chuck Klein won the Triple Crown last year for the Phillies. He hit .368, and I bet he'll hit again this year now that he's with the Cubs."

"I bet you're right."

"Who's your favorite player?" he asked.

I had to think for a moment.

"I guess Ducky Medwick," I said slowly. I thought about how he ran the bases, how he fearlessly always took that extra little bit that was allowed him. *Could he ever get the dirt and sweat fully cleaned from beneath his fingernails?*

Wilson smiled and I smiled back at him. We were friends now. In that moment I was taken back to a place in my long-ago past, a time before any of my sins had accrued, to a time before the apple had been picked and eaten, a time where it seemed an honorable future was possible. It had been years since I thought about having favorite players, but when the questions were asked, the answers rose up as quickly as they had so long ago.

"It's the best, you know." Wilson's voice was suddenly hushed.

"Baseball," he added, in case I didn't follow what he was referring to, but of course I had.

"Yes," I said, quieter now myself. "It's getting dark. Maybe we should go inside now. You'll need to sleep soon."

His face fell a little, but he nodded slowly and turned around to move towards the house with me. "I hope we can throw tomorrow."

"We will, if we can find a ball."

"We found the checkerboard."

"We sure did. I bet there's a baseball in either the basement or the barn."

As we walked in towards the house together, I thought about putting my arm around his shoulder, but I didn't. He wasn't my child.

I wondered whose he was.

Chapter Eight

The next day at the Iowa farmhouse was much like the one before: fried potatoes, eggs scrambled hard, bitter black coffee for breakfast; slow and barely discernable progress through Exodus; cool breezes in the morning; unrelenting heat that settled in by mid-day.

I didn't see Delilah, Murphy, or Hector all morning. Mary moved about listlessly in the kitchen, rattling the odd pan and peeling potatoes between cigarettes. Her undisciplined movements made it seem like unfamiliar territory and watching her, I decided it wasn't her house.

At one point Isaac came into the kitchen and had coffee with me while I finished my breakfast. His eyes were red and he hadn't shaved since the day I arrived. There was an air of tired failure in the way he slouched with his elbows splayed out widely on the table. I hadn't seen him at all the day before and I wondered about that. Laudanum or marijuana could have had that effect. We didn't talk much and he left the table before I finished eating.

At mid-morning Wilson and I found three old baseball gloves and a tattered ball on a shelf in the barn. The leather in the gloves was heavily worn and dry, cracking along seams that hadn't been flexed in years. The ball had blackened stitching and was roughly scuffed to the point that it had several small tears in it.

Wilson selected the smallest glove, but even that was far too big for his hand. Interwoven strands of leather formed a web between the thumb and forefinger. He pulled it on and made the best of it. I chose the first baseman's mitt, a longish glove that essentially folded in half over a small cavity to contain the ball.

"This is great!" Wilson exclaimed after he popped the ball into his glove for the first time. He smacked it in there several more times. He grinned up at me and I grinned back.

"Here, let me see." I tapped my own mitt with the back of my right hand. He flipped the ball up and I scooped it. "I bet we can fix these up a bit. Let's look to see if there's some leather treatment."

After a quick search we discovered some neatsfoot oil on a shelf near where we found the gloves. Using an old cloth we took turns rubbing it into our respective gloves. As the leather became suppler it also took on a dark shine. Wilson put two coats on his glove and he rubbed it in hard while I watched.

"Ready?" I asked when I judged him to be at the point of diminishing return on his effort.

He nodded seriously and we went out of the barn to find a good spot. The sun was up over the trees at the eastern edge of the lot. Even at that angle the rays were fiercely hot. At first we threw within the shade of the Sycamore tree parallel to the house. As the shade drifted and slowly shrank, we moved out toward the pond where there was more room.

The heat edged in steadily and it wasn't long before we were sweating hard. Still, we didn't stop. After three quarters of an hour we paused for Wilson to remove his shirt. White stick arms jangled about his sunken chest. The second baseman's glove now looked twice as big and all the more absurd.

For a while I threw grounders to either side of him; sometimes he fielded them. He was better at catching pop flies that I threw underhanded at first, and then over-handed once I was sure he wouldn't be overmatched.

Delilah and Hector came out to the porch to watch. She clapped when he made an especially good catch. Hector watched impassively while he puffed on an old pipe. He never spoke a word to anyone, and he appeared to shrink within the wrinkled folds of skin that enveloped his skeleton.

When the sun was high enough to be in both our eyes at the same time I waved Wilson over. "Hey," I told him. "You play real well."

He looked down awkwardly. "Naw."

"Sure," I said, anointing him on the top of his head with the tip of my long mitt. "Come on, it's too hot now to play any more."

He raised his head up with a reluctant smile. "After dinner, when it's cooler, can we throw some more?"

"Maybe, as long as the light holds."

"Then maybe when it's dark we can catch fireflies?"

"We'll see," I told him.

"They say Dillinger played second base."

I put a Chesterfield to my lips and shook my head. "Forget about him," I said. "Why not jump in the pond now to cool off? It'll do you good to splash around a little."

In the high heat of mid-afternoon we gathered around the kitchen sink again while Murphy worked the ice pick. This time Delilah and Isaac were both there. The old couple were sequestered once more in their bedroom with the fan and Wilson had been sent up for an afternoon nap.

When the ice was chipped we carried it in a bucket out to the barn and found a spot in the back where it was dark and almost approaching cool. The scent of manure and old hay was heavy in the air. We sat on bales and a long wooden bench pulled over to form an L-shaped conversation area and poured the beers into jars over the chipped ice. Nobody said much for a while as we drank.

"The kid has nice form," Delilah pronounced finally.

"He likes to throw," I replied.

Hamilton made snide noises and we all looked at him.

"What?" he said. "Don't tell me the kid can play. He's got his mother's form, which is to say: flat, pale, and unable."

Delilah glared at him. "She's your wife."

Hamilton pretended to ignore her. "A man doesn't elect to have himself kidnapped if his wife has good form. It *is* elementary, right?" He looked around the barn at the other men present. Nobody took his side. "Okay, okay," he said quickly, stringing the words together as if they were one. "So, look at me like I'm a heel. But don't be so sure you'd be any different if you were me."

"Point is," I explained. "One of us might not have married her, if we felt that way."

"Even with all that cash money?"

"Even with."

Without a clear break, Hamilton suddenly looked deflated. "Well," he said finally, pulling himself up again with his shoulders squared. "I'm glad to be in the company of you honest men. Maybe your bank robberies and murders are lesser crimes than marrying a woman for her money."

Isaac slapped him on the back and said, "Surely, you understand there's honor among thieves. We steal our money the honest way – an honest day's pay for an honest day's work – and robbing banks is dangerous, hard work."

"Yeah, but we haven't seen his wife," Murphy asserted, laughing loudly before he finished the second part. "Maybe sleeping with his wife is dangerous, hard work too!"

Hamilton finally grinned himself, but he didn't like the ribbing.

"Anyway," Isaac added. "If your wife is so rich, then why are you kidnapping yourself? Why extort her for ransom when you could simply ask her for the money over the pillow?" His words slurred a little and I noticed his eyes were quite red still. I studied him carefully; searching for some understanding to calm the nagging voice inside me screaming that trouble was ahead.

"Maybe I want to be like you guys," Hamilton said quietly. His bluster was fading quickly.

"You don't know nothing about us," Isaac responded. "Who do you think you are?"

"I've seen how it is in the newsreels. You guys dash in, grab the cash, drive off in fast automobiles, and hit the town with pretty ladies and you're all dressed to the nines. Everyone loves you, including the cameras. The banks and the coppers are the villains now." His tone was resentful. It was a matter he'd been stewing over for some time.

"Oh brother," Isaac said. "You got it so wrong. It ain't like in the newsreels and it sure ain't like in the movies. You don't see Clark Gable standing here among us, do you?"

"Moving cameras filmed the entire trial of Machine Gun Kelly last year – made him a star!"

What Hamilton said was true. It was the first major kidnapping trial after the new Federal law was passed and they had filmed every minute of it.

The law was created in the wake of the public outcry after the kidnapping and death of Lindbergh's baby in 1932. Even Al Capone had come out against kidnapping at the time. His words had been printed in dailies across the country: "Let me hunt Lindy's baby." But kidnapping a financial magnate was different than kidnapping the infant of a national hero. Who would care about a wealthy man who lived so far above the rest of society?

Kelly's misfortune was in his ambitious-shrew wife who bought the machine gun and worked hard to create his nickname, pushing him out in front of the pack. He'd also suffered from a simple case of bad timing with an equally ambitious new Federal agency suddenly looking to create its own legend.

They built us up so they could bring us down.

"What say you?" Hamilton asked, turning his narrow eyes my way.

I thought for a minute and looked around the room. The near dead eyes that stared back at me gave me my answer, the only answer there could be. It wasn't profound. "I say violence leads to angst, not to glamour. The Feds will hunt us to the end of the earth and right into hell if they must, though it's too late to stop now, too late for any of us."

*

The ice was almost melted and Delilah had left to sun herself by the pond again. Murphy kicked at the bucket lightly with his toe, though he didn't speak. Condensation had formed a wide, dark circle in the bits of hay and dirt on the floor around the bucket. Three or four flies nipped about us.

I stood up and straightened my back, with hands on my hips. "We should talk a little business as long as we're all here and the plan seems to have, shall we say, evolved a bit."

For a quarter of an hour we discussed our situation and the options before us. The original plan had been to demand $100,000 from Hamilton's wife, exactly what we understood the Barker-Karpis gang got when they ransomed William Hamm back to his family the previous year. It was also half of what the papers claimed they got for Edward Bremer Jr.

We were modest bandits and there was what the dailies referred to as a Great Depression underway. On the other hand, it was clear that we now had to split the ransom money with Hamilton himself, and there were our St. Paul connections to pay off. Dutch Sawyer and the O'Connor System of the Twin Cities would expect their cut. Hamilton said he believed his wife could pay $150,000 without too much difficulty, possibly more. After some discussion, we agreed that $150,000 would be plenty and that to ask for more posed unnecessary risks, namely that she could not or would not pay it.

The plan at that point reverted to our original scheme: I would take the ransom demand to our contacts in St. Paul. They would handle the negotiations, collect the ransom money, and guarantee safe delivery home for Hamilton and the child. They would also divide up the ransom money and distribute the shares, after taking their rather hefty percentage – 40%. My plan was to hang around the Twin Cities, collect

63

my share as soon as it was available, and then head back to Chicago to see about Jimmy and other unfinished business I had there.

Since I was leaving in the morning, and since my future was uncertain, we had prearranged for all involved to relocate from the house to some other location – to a place that I wouldn't be able to identify in case the police picked me up.

It wasn't a perfect plan, but it seemed as good as it could get at that point and we all agreed on it. At the end of our discussion, Murphy insisted on a making a toast with the warm beer we had left, and then we shook hands all around and wished each other luck as if we were British gentlemen preparing for a hunt.

Chapter Nine

The night was hot and quiet. It seemed too hot to sleep, but I must have dozed without knowing it. She was in the room before I was aware of her presence, and had the sheet pulled back and was in beside me with her head beside mine on the pillow. Her naked thigh was already moist as she snaked it over my hip and wrapped it around my leg, pulling herself up tight against me.

Ancient desire swelled. She kissed me hotly on the mouth and I recoiled as I awoke, instantly aware that it was too late to hide the obvious fact of my arousal. Her hands roamed and found, gently, what they were looking for. Delilah chuckled deep in her throat and arched her back so that her large, soft breasts were pulled up and swung against my chest. Then she pressed hard against me.

"This isn't right."

I held one of her hands firmly by the wrist.

"Shhhh," she whispered. "Don't say anything, just make love to me. I can tell you want to."

"You're not my girl."

"I'm nobody's girl."

"You're Murphy's girl."

"He's passed out drunk from the hooch out in the barn. Anyway, he's no man."

Delilah's eyes gleamed, shiny in the light that came in from the window. I rolled back from the challenge and the urge so that I could sit on the edge of the bed, facing the back window. The half-moon was out and low enough in the sky that it shone like a pale streetlamp into the bedroom. She sat up beside me, naked and with the sheet off her body. She leaned her chin against my shoulder and took my arm, tugging faintly.

I got a cigarette going and then transferred it directly to her lips. She took it, gratefully, holding my hand for a moment to steady it and then took a long drag while I lit another for myself. We smoked silently and looked at each other for several minutes. She made no effort to cover herself. Even in that light her bronzed arms and legs contrasted with the delicate whiteness of her breasts and stomach. The only discernable sound in the room was made by the smoke as it curled upward between us and gathered above our heads. That's how quiet it was.

Presently, she leaned toward me to whisper, "I don't mind it rough, if that's how you like it."

I looked into her eyes and in that shaded light she was almost more beautiful than I could bear. "No," I offered into the aching, tender space between us. "You misunderstand. That's not it at all, not at all."

"What then?"

"You're too young and I'm damaged goods right now anyway."

*

Delilah sat at the foot of the bed with a sheet wrapped around her. Only her ankles and toes showed now. The imploring tone was gone from her voice, replaced by one that was sadness instead. I sat in a low chair that was pushed up to the edge of the bed. I leaned forward, drawn in toward her.

"I'm a man, but we don't all jump to perform on command."

"Is there another?"

"Let it go," I said in response.

"Now what?" she asked quietly.

"In the morning I'll drive up to St. Paul. It's time to deliver the ransom demand."

"Why did you get involved in this scheme?"

"I have debts to repay," I replied, thinking of Jimmy.

"A kidnapping doesn't seem like it would suit you."

"You asked me that before, though you're mostly right about it. I'm a hard working criminal and this appeared to be a decent job. A lot of people are shooting at bank robbers these days, so I thought why not give something else a try."

"Looking for easy work, huh?" She spoke the words with a soft mocking tone.

"Aren't we all, sister?"

"Can I come north with you?"

"I don't need a tag-along."

"Why don't you want me?"

"You know that's not it."

"My sister, Eva, lives in St. Paul. You can drop me off. I won't be any trouble."

"What are you going to do with your sister Eva?"

"She's family. We're close, she and I, and she comforts me when I need it. We do for each other that way."

I mused on that for a minute. "Does she know you're on this little caper?"

"No," Delilah said quietly. "She doesn't approve of the trouble I get into. We're different. She's a pious one. She's the one that goes to church, carries herself right, and sets herself up for the way things are supposed to be."

"And you?"

"Me? I go a different path. I'm not going to wait around and dry up hoping somebody will come along and find me, and save me, and take me off into the wide blue yonder. I know life is no fairy tale, there's no happy ending waiting for us." Her voice was soft and sensual, and far away now. I wondered where she drifted to when she drifted like that.

"You sound so sure," I said, wanting to find out.

"I take my pleasure where I can and let the trouble be damned. It's no sin to be glad you're alive."

"What's the pleasure?"

"Only some of the little things you don't get if you sit back and wait for them to come to you."

"What kind of trouble do you find to go along with it?"

"Usually the kind that has a man attached to it."

"And Eva disapproves?"

"Every time."

"It sounds like this happens a lot for a seventeen year-old girl. Your sister's probably right to disapprove, but there may be resentment festering there. Be careful it doesn't boil over."

In the dark I could see her ambivalent shrug. "We've had some bully rows. Maybe that's our way. It's not so bad, though. Are you going to take me north with you?"

"Are you leaving Murphy?" I asked.

She merely nodded and loosened the sheet so that it hung from her shoulders, open now down the front. I averted my eyes to the floor.

"Are you leaving him for good?" I asked. "I need to know."

"Yes, I will."

"Okay," I said. I looked back up to her eyes. "I'll give you the ride north to big sister Eva. We're going to be three, though. I intend to take

Wilson with me when I go, to return him to his mother. I'm not leaving without him."

"Won't that botch your kidnapping just a teeny, weenie bit?" She said the words slowly, pronouncing each part of every syllable.

"It will. I don't know how much, but I'm not going to have that child on my conscience. I've got enough weight there as it is."

Delilah allowed herself a dreamy yawn while she considered my words. A half-formed thought shaded her eyes and then she smiled without speaking, and took one last drag on her cigarette.

Shadows in the room seemed to shift and lengthen while we sat still. Finally, Delilah let the sheet slip from her shoulders and she arched her back slowly and then stretched to one side and then back to the other. The motion caused her breasts to sway at the periphery of my vision.

I held my eyes on hers and I saw the defiance that was back in the glint of her expression. She sat there, for a moment longer, staring at me with a thoughtful curl to her lips.

"Mister, I think that's okay," she said at length. Her voice was a low whisper, husky in tone, and there was no mistaking the naked desire that belied her innocent words: "Anyway, we owe him an ice cream. I know a soda fountain where they make the best Black Cow in the entire state."

"Is that it?" I asked.

"Yes," she said.

With that she came up on her knees, leaned forward in a virtual crawl, gave me a rough, hard smooch on my mouth and then she was gone. I was alone again in the hot night, perspiring heavily and wondering why the oxygen in the room suddenly seemed so thin. I was left with the hot imprint of her lips upon mine.

Chapter Ten

Gleaming sunlight introduced the dawn. I'd slept little, disturbed by restless footsteps through the house during the small hours, as well as my own haunted thoughts. I had a sense that the pace of everything was quickening, though in what direction I couldn't yet tell.

When I heard the motor start up from somewhere out by the barn, I was too muddled to put it together quickly enough. The sound of crunching gravel jolted me. I threw myself out of bed to the window just in time to see Murphy's Dodge sedan disappearing fast down the lane, kicking up a cloud of dust behind it.

I pulled on my pants, tied up my shoes, threw on a shirt, and grabbed my shoulder holster with the .45 in it. I checked the other two bedrooms first. They were both empty. I raced down the stairs, across the dining room, and out through the kitchen into the back, calling names out loud. Nobody answered me, nobody was there. By the time I got out to the barn, still fastening buttons, I discovered that everyone except for Delilah and Isaac was now long gone.

Isaac was passed out on a bale of hay in the general vicinity of where one would have expected to find him. Bare-chested, he lay on his side with one arm out along his waist. I could see the scars from the bullet wounds he'd suffered in Kansas City last year – they were hard red welts. Sometime during the night he'd vomited on his side and he now lay with a shoulder planted firmly in the semi-solid muck that remained after any liquid had soaked down into the hay. I poured half a bucket of now-dirty water over his face and nudged him at the hip with my foot.

"Get up," I ordered harshly, barely able to contain my anger.

Delilah was in worse shape. I found her trussed and gagged in one of the horse stalls, with red streaks and contusions on her face, neck, legs, and arms. Blood, now dried darkly, had trickled from her nose and lower lip. Her nightshirt was ripped and stained. I worked the knots frantically. She sobbed into my arms after I got her loose and in another few minutes I had the whole story.

It was a simple and unhappy surprise: Murphy had woken her as he fitted the gag on her mouth. It was an old sock that he'd tied in place using a strip of fabric from one of her skirts. He had then beaten her savagely, and it wasn't the first time. She'd struggled, but to no avail. I didn't ask, but from the bruises on the lower half of her body and the condition of her nightshirt, I assumed he had also raped her after tying her down with an old rope.

Tin pins throbbed between my eyes. I knelt beside her and put my arms around her shoulders and pulled her towards me with my cheek beside hers. Warm tears ran onto my lips. Most of them were hers, but not all of them. Her arms clasped around me tightly. I held her and rocked her.

"I should have seen this coming," I told her when my own breath had leveled out. She was sobbing quietly still, shaking minutely within my embrace, and didn't reply. "We need to move quickly now. Can you hold together?"

I pulled away to look at her face. She didn't speak, but she nodded. In the shadowy light of the barn I could see that her eyes were red and moist. A sense of resolve welled there too. It seemed I could trust that. Actually, I had no choice in the moment; there was little time.

I left Delilah in the barn while I headed back in to make another quick search of the house. Hamilton, Wilson, Murphy, and the old couple were nowhere to be found. Most of their personal belongings had been hurriedly packed and now they had a good fifteen-minute head start. I didn't know which direction they had gone or where.

When I came out the back of the house again to see to Delilah, she was already heading down toward the pond. She moved slowly, limping slightly on her left leg. I intercepted her and walked with her to the dock.

"I'll be okay," she told me. "I need to clean myself."

"Fine, but we have to leave within five minutes." Although I wasn't trying to be stern, it came out that way.

"I know. I'm going to plunge in and then out again, rinse his stink off me. That's all, just that little bit. I'll be ready in five. You'll take me north, to St. Paul, to my sister's home?"

I nodded as I was already walking away. There were no other words for me to say and even if there were there was no luxury of time to say them.

By the time I'd packed my two suitcases in the boot of the Ford and got a pot of coffee brewing, Delilah came into the kitchen. She wore a loose sundress and was squeezing her hair out efficiently with a towel.

"I'm ready," was all she said.

Her glance from me to the clock on the wall and then back told me all I needed to know. I knew she hurt everywhere, but she was focused on what we had to do.

"Good girl. Two minutes, then we leave," I told her. "We'll drink the coffee on the road. Pack your things and meet me at the front porch. Tell Isaac to meet us there too."

She nodded.

"Do you need help?" I asked.

"I can manage."

"Two minutes," I repeated as she turned.

In one of the beer cartons I packed three coffee mugs, three leftover pork chop sandwiches on a plate, a large chunk of ice that I hacked off the corner of the remaining block, a jar of water, and a jar of applesauce from the pantry.

I took the box and the coffee pot out to the front of the house. There I packed the box in the back seat of the Ford and poured out two cups of coffee that I set on the driver's side running board. The coffee pot and third mug I carried back to the porch and then I went into the house again. I moved rapidly through the rooms, focusing mainly on my bedroom and kitchen, wiping down every door handle and surface I might have touched.

When I came back out Delilah and Isaac were standing by the automobile waiting for me. He was slouched over, barefoot and still without a shirt on. Protruding tufts of hair over one ear caused his head to appear misshapen. Clawed, empty fists hung down at his side, signaling his own pent-up but impotent rage at the situation.

"Take the two cups of coffee there and get in," I told her. "You'll find a first aid kit under the front seat. Also, there's a block of ice in the box you'll find at your feet. Start with that, under your eye, and then work it around your nose. It'll help keep the swelling down. Isaac, step over to the porch with me."

His eyes were anxious globes of fresh blood and I knew he probably had the worst hangover of his life.

71

"I'm sorry, Duncan."

"There's no time." I poured the remaining coffee and handed the cup to him. "Drink this."

He accepted the coffee and held it with two hands below his chin. Light steam rose up to his face. His blinking eyes held over it. "I don't know what happened," he claimed.

"Drink the coffee and I'll tell you. You were passed out drunk, high, or probably both." I was pretty sure now that it was laudanum or morphine, though I wasn't sure which.

"I'm sorry. I ain't going to lie to you. I know – I have a problem, but I'm still in so much pain, ever since Kansas City."

"What do you take?"

"Morphine, and last night I took more than usual, along with the whiskey. Sleeping in the barn was hard on me."

"They're only gunshot wounds, Isaac. The damage you do to your soul is far worse."

He nodded. "I get you. How bad is it now?"

"They hurt the girl and took the child, left us here to fend for ourselves."

"I don't know why they did that."

"It can't be for the good."

Isaac shook his head slowly. "No, it can't. But we'll get Jimmy the money he needs. They can't cheat us of our split – that happens on Dutch Sawyer's end. He handles the money for St. Paul and he wouldn't do that to us. He never would."

"Dutch would," I said, "if we're in prison and he thinks he doesn't have to worry about us for thirty years. We have to assume Murphy or Hamilton might have made a phone call. The law could be arriving any minute, and they won't come gently."

"Murphy wouldn't do that to us."

"Wouldn't he? Maybe not, but Hamilton would and Murphy wouldn't stop him, especially not after what he did to the girl. Anyway, we're not going to stick around to find out. Are you sober enough to clear out?"

He considered this, nodded, and took his first sip of the coffee, still using both hands. One hand alone would have shook too bad.

"Yeah, I got pretty much nothing to pack."

"Go start your automobile. I'll wait till I hear the engine going before we leave, just to make sure it starts for you. Take the coffee with you, and anything else that might identify you, but get out of here, fast. Put a shirt on, but don't be more than two minutes behind us. We're headed north. You should head east first. Don't try to reach me, I'll contact you a week from now in the usual way."

"Duncan." His voice was brittle. "I'm sorry about the girl. I really am. I let you down. It's good partners that are hard to find."

"Hurry. There is no time for sentiment."

I shook his palsied hand and turned away.

*

The Ford started right up and I drove it away from the farmhouse very fast, over the gravel lane and out to the main road. Once pointed down a flat straightaway the sedan knew what to do. Apart from the powerful V8 growl, we rode mostly in silence for the first tense hour.

Delilah wrapped the ice in an unidentifiable garment that she pulled from her valise. Then she alternated between holding the ice to various parts of her face and taking urgent sips at the coffee. After she finished her coffee, she continued with the ice for a while and then got the first aid kit out and hunted around in it. Using pre-cut squares of cotton gauze she dabbed rubbing alcohol on her face, arms, and legs. There were several bleeding lacerations, but none that would require stitches. Her nose was starting to swell and she was going to have a heck of a shiner in a day or two.

Eventually the ice melted down most of the way, soaking the garment and the front of the dress she wore. She tossed the remaining piece out the window and then wrung out the garment after it.

"Did we get away?" she asked.

"I think we're clear. We'll head right on to St. Paul today, should be there by late afternoon."

"Those lousy punks." Her voice, when she spoke, was angry in a steady, relaxed sort of way that I liked.

"Yes."

"Will you kill him for me?"

I didn't answer.

"Will you?"

"That's not a question you can ask or a promise I can make."

"I know."

73

"Why did Murphy do it, why did he beat you?"

She took a moment to answer, as if there were several possible explanations she could share. "He was jealous of you," she said finally.

"I hadn't given him any reason to be."

That made her laugh. "You gave him plenty of reasons, you're everything he'll never be. That and he knew I'd been with you."

"How did he know that?"

"He asked and I told him," she replied with an edge in her voice. "I didn't tell him everything. I let his imagination fill in the gap."

"That was dramatic and childish."

"He deserved it."

We drove without talking for a few more minutes.

"Are you going to be okay?" I asked.

"Yes," she said tightly. "It's not the first time. I've suffered worse … I'll be fine."

I glanced over at her quickly and saw that she had pulled herself together okay. Her face was going to be a mess for a few weeks, but her hair was where it belonged, her shoulders were squared, and her eyes simmered with brilliant defiance. There was something about her that I liked, maybe it was her undaunted reach forward.

I smiled grimly and reached a hand over to her. She took it without saying anything and held it in both of hers. A few minutes later she moved over on the seat and rested her head on my shoulder. I didn't shrink away. We did not talk again for a while.

*

Late in the morning we stopped at a tourist camp for a short rest. We'd been on the road for three hours. The heat was already stifling. Delilah's dress had long since dried out from the melted ice. Now it was marked with a gradually expanding perspiration stain near the top center where little rivulets ran down her neck and between her breasts. It clung to her in an affecting way. I left my Stetson on the back seat, but I couldn't remove my jacket because of the shoulder holster I wore beneath it.

We sat at a shaded picnic table and ate the pork chop sandwiches and the applesauce, which we poured into the empty coffee mugs. I could tell that Delilah's mouth and face hurt as she chewed her pork chop, but she didn't complain.

When we were finished eating, we rinsed out the applesauce jar at an old well pump and then filled it and the other jar with fresh water. Before we left she retrieved her other garment from the back seat of the Ford and wrung it out several times under the pump. Then she gestured toward me and washed my face with it. Her hands were gentle. After she finished with me she repeated the procedure on herself, though more tenderly, two times and then hung the wet garment around the back of her neck. Not once did she complain about anything.

Back on the road again, the driving quickly became mundane.

"How bad do you hurt?" I asked.

"I've hurt worse. Can we talk about something else?" She was determined to be tough to the core.

"Sure, name it," I said.

"Do you like the movies?"

"No, not particularly."

Gasping, she made exaggerated pouting noises: "Why not?"

"Real life will break your heart bad enough."

"But I like movies. Have you seen 'Manhattan Melodrama'?"

I shook my head. She was talking now just to pass the time and provide distraction. "You should see it. Clark Gable plays a gangster, running against William Powell, the oh-so-noble District Attorney. You see, they were best friends in childhood and now as adults they fall in love with the same woman, Myrna Loy. They cross paths in a murder trial. It's delicious."

"Sounds pretty far-fetched to me. You see yourself in there, do you?"

She pretended to take the question seriously. "Well, I've got a bit of Myrna Loy going on, not so much physically—I'm prettier and I'm a size or two larger—but people say I have spunk. What do you say?"

I could feel her eyes on me. I looked over at her and to myself I agreed that she sure did, and then some. She sat with her shoulder against the door. The top three buttons of her sundress were undone now and her breasts pushed against the fabric. Locks of hair, slick with sweat, stuck to her forehead and cheek.

"Maybe," I said. My throat was suddenly dry and not because of the heat. I didn't think that anyone in 'Manhattan Melodrama' or any other movie would have had the same effect on me.

Her laugh was soft, low, and slightly mocking: "Maybe you'd prefer the 'Lost Patrol': British cavalrymen can't find their way home. They're cut off, under siege in the desert, starving, dehydrated, and then picked off one by one until only their Sergeant is left. Is that more your style, you grump?"

I shook my head, vaguely. "I don't go to the movies."

"What is it with the movies?" I asked after awhile just to get her talking again.

Delilah thought about this and made small clicking noises with her tongue while she thought. "It's a chance to be someone else," she said finally, "a chance to be someone other than who you really are, if only for ninety minutes or so."

I grinned at that and looked over at her. "From where I'm sitting, it seems there's nothing wrong with who you really are."

"Looks can be deceiving."

"Come on …"

"You know what I mean, and they start early, our self-perceptions. When I was younger, movies were the best escape there was around."

"What were you escaping?"

"Oh, nothing so terrible, not really – merely the usual girlhood things, I suppose. But when you're young you don't have much perspective on things. You don't know what's normal, or how bad someone else might have it – or how bad you could have it later. You wonder if you'll be pretty enough, smart enough, tough enough."

I glanced over at her again, thinking she was certainly all of those things. She didn't need me to tell her, though. "You grew up without a father," I observed instead.

"Sure, he was killed in the Great War. I never knew much about him. There were pictures, but I had no memories and my mother never talked about him. His grave was in France, so there wasn't even anything to visit, nothing to lavish with flowers."

"Siblings other than Eva?"

"Nope, just the two of us. And she was more of a mother than a sister, which wasn't fair to either of us really. She took care of everything. My mother never quite climbed out of it—she had some type of weeping depression and spent the better part of twelve years in bed as far as I can tell. A real wilted flower she was. She died of the fever a couple years back and Eva and I moved around a bit. Then we lived with an older aunt in Des Moines, it's still our home, though not a lot of pull to go back there now."

"It's tough to be an orphan."

"No. I never thought of myself that way. Eva made sure of that – she

76

was always there when needed, and I had good aunts and uncles, good cousins too. I never felt alone."

"So when you're not escaping into movies, how'd you otherwise get to be so tough?" I asked.

"Swore I was never going to be like my mother – everything she was, I was going to be the opposite."

When I looked over towards her I saw that her eyes were wide and serious.

Chapter Eleven

We were somewhere just north of nowhere and a few miles yet from Timbuktu. I had the large sedan running down to only 45 miles per hour because of the heat – I didn't want the radiator to overload. Tendrils of wavy light rose up from the baked road before us.

"Look out!" Delilah gasped, coming up a little on her seat even before I could react.

I pulled off the throttle, but it was too late. The small bird flickered up from out of the brush beside the road. In the instant that it hovered before the automobile, I caught a flash of dark-streaked brown feathers down the back, whitish and black under-parts, and flank streaking: a sparrow, probably what we called a Savannah Sparrow when I was a child. Its crown was yellow and its throat was nearly pure white. Then it was down beneath our sightline at the front of the Ford and we both heard and felt the slight bump.

Delilah gasped again, louder this time, and spun in her seat to look back over her shoulder. I had already started to brake.

"No, keep going," she urged. "It's too late. There's nothing we can do for it."

Ignoring her I brought the automobile to a full stop and put it into reverse. The sparrow lay without moving in the on-coming lane. When we were beside it I stopped again and got out to stand on the road next to it.

It was hot and dry. The heat came up through the soles of my shoes. A slight breeze at the highway surface flirted with the sparrow's feathers, but didn't climb higher than a few inches. As I looked down at it, one dead eye stared back up at me. It was a trivial event in the universe, but to the sparrow it meant everything.

I stood still for a moment. There was no other traffic on the road in either direction. The entire ribbon was still. So, a withering pillar, I stood there with my thoughts. They were dark and rapid and fleeting.

The passage from the first book of Corinthians came to me uninvited and floated, line by line, through my mind. *Our earthly bodies are planted in the ground when we die, but they will be raised to live forever. Our bodies are buried in brokenness, but they will be raised in glory.* I didn't say it out loud, though I let it stand as my prayer. Then I turned and retrieved a newspaper from the back seat. Delilah watched without speaking, as I slid the newspaper under the sparrow's body and carried it off the side of the road.

When we were moving again Delilah remained quiet for about five minutes before she spoke.

"Why did you do that? Why did you lay that poor bird out so carefully off the road?"

"Because it's the only thing I could do."

She was quiet for a moment, and then said, "You feel bad that you killed that bird."

It wasn't a question, but rather a statement made with some surprise. I did not reply.

"Surely, you've killed people in the course of your work, yet you feel bad that you accidentally killed a small bird on the highway."

"Every creature deserves some measure of dignity."

"Where did you ever get that notion?"

I shrugged.

"Most people wouldn't think twice about a dead bird."

I had no good words to respond with so I said nothing and after that she let it be.

*

"Now that they've put the double-cross in what happens?" Delilah asked.

I considered the question. It was the same one I'd been asking myself all day. "It's probably not something you should concern yourself with."

"He might come looking for me."

"Yes, he might," I conceded. "Would he know where to find you?"

"Not right away. But if he asks around Des Moines enough he will. People will know where Eva is."

"Is there somewhere else you can go?"

"No. I wouldn't run from him anyway. More than anything I want to be with my sister – she's my family."

I glanced over at her. "He'll have his hands full for at least a week. He won't dare leave Hamilton or Wilson unattended, and he won't trust the old couple. After all, the lot of them double-crossed us, what's to keep

80

them from double-crossing him? He'll have to watch them carefully. So, he won't have time to even think about you until he gets word that the ransom has been paid and it's okay to release the hostages. Then, he's going to have to worry about other things."

"What other things?"

"Me and Isaac. Maybe a few other fellows in St. Paul, depending on far he took the double-cross. You can't betray your partners – or the big city fixers – without worrying about when they'll come after you."

*

As we approached the outskirts of the Twin Cities, we drove past lakes, churches, single story buildings and grain silos. It was approaching three o'clock in the afternoon. Ahead we could see the new City and County Courthouse and the First National Bank, which loomed over the skyline of a city that was otherwise rather flat. Industrial smokestacks emitted thin, white streams of smoke into the air. Viewed from the horizon, the smoke didn't appear to be moving. It looked like thin strings that connected the industrial center to the atmosphere above. I thought about the First National and what a worthy target it would make if only that didn't violate the rules of St. Paul.

I followed Delilah's directions to an apartment house on South Robert Street in West St. Paul. It was an old stone building with brickwork and awnings over the second floor windows that fronted the street. Someone had planted a bedding of impatiens along the short walkway up to the front door. Gentle reds, pinks, and whites mingled to offset the austerity of the old building.

It was quiet on the street at that hour. There was no movement from the apartment building and nobody peered out from any windows. Delilah did not seem in a hurry to get out of the automobile. From the position of her hands and the tiny movements her fingertips made against each other, I knew there was something she wanted to say. I waited.

"About last night … Well, is there someone?" she asked.

"Do you see a ring on this hand?"

She leaned back against the passenger-side door, twisted on the seat, with her head on the window behind her. Bloated purple filled her cheek under one eye. Her lip was swollen badly and would get worse by the next morning. Without seeming aware, she ran the tip of her little finger over it.

"I never met a man who didn't want to make love to me," she complained.

"You still haven't."

"I thought—"

"Wanting to make love and doing it are separate things."

"You wanted me? You did?"

I didn't answer. She moved across the seat and kissed me on the lips with her mouth closed. The kiss endured, and then it continued, hotly, and then her mouth was open over mine and we were pushing against each other. The taste of fresh blood salted my tongue. Her lip had opened up again with the action, but neither of us cared a nickel about that. Before my toes could curl all the way, I pulled back and stared into her battling eyes. They were large dark saucers that promised everything.

"Okay," she said with a lot of throat. "Okay. Just be careful of yourself and get that kid home."

I nodded without attempting to speak, not trusting my voice to work right.

"And then maybe come find me," she finished. "My last name is Rutherford, same as Eva's. I shouldn't be hard to find. Just look for the Rutherford sisters. If it's Sunday, though, you can only find one of us in church."

She got out of the Ford with her valise and didn't look back. I watched her up the walk and waited until the door opened for her before I engaged the automobile and pulled away from the curb with a jolt.

Ahead of me clouds were gathering and once again I was feeling like a fool.

Chapter Twelve

At a quarter to eight o'clock in the evening I met Harry "Dutch" Sawyer at his joint, the Green Lantern Saloon. It had an interesting address – 545½ Wabasha – and was in a part of town I knew well.

Sawyer was the main fixer in the Twin Cities. Everything went through him. Locally they called it the "O'Connor System," after John J. O'Connor who had been Chief of Police in St. Paul until his retirement in 1920. He had run the criminal operations in the city himself. It was an open town, where criminals like me could find shelter and safety – for a hefty price. The other part of the deal was criminals had to behave within the city limits, or at least coordinate their crimes through O'Connor, now Sawyer.

The corruption was systemic. Top to bottom, most of the city police and politicians were in on it. It was a lot like Chicago, though more orderly. I wondered if the rot was really different from any other large city in America. I didn't think it was. Sitting there with the stench almost noticeable in the air, I felt like a virtuous man.

Sawyer sat sideways in his chair, an arm over the back. Across the top of his head, oily strands of hair were combed up and over at an angle. His face was square, with flat ears, a hawk nose, and a ruddy complexion. Only his eyes moved. I didn't like him and I didn't trust him. But he had never quite let me down, at least not yet.

"They gypped me in the Hamm's kidnapping," he said angrily from across the table. "That's why I planned the Bremer snatch. I'm not blaming Alvin Karpis, or any of the Barkers either. I don't think it was their fault. I think it was Ziegler who pulled the fast one. It's probably why he's no longer breathing."

"I didn't hear about that."

"Someone shot him, several times, coming out of a Cicero chop shop."

It didn't mean much to me. I'd never met the man, never heard anything good about him. It was hard to think well of a man rumored to have engineered the St. Valentine's Day massacre. I lit a Chesterfield. "Too bad."

I had loosened my tie and undone my top button. Earlier, at the hotel, I'd changed into a light blue seersucker jacket. It was still very hot in the Green Lantern. Bourbon was slowly aging over small blocks of ice on the table in front of me. It was my first of the evening. I took a sip, swirling the ice. The clinking sound pleased me and I took another sip, a small, careful one this time, mindful of where I was and why.

"Anyhow," Sawyer said, "that's why I handle the money now. Me. It goes through me, and I manage the split-up. This job might have been my idea too, but you don't need to hear more on that."

"Interesting. Hamilton claimed it as his idea."

"Well, somebody had to approach somebody first. In the end, I guess it doesn't really matter who."

I noticed that he didn't appear surprised to hear mention that Hamilton had a role in the scheme. "True enough," I replied, playing it easy.

"I heard there was a raid on a farm down in Iowa this morning. The special agents got a tip that maybe you were there, maybe with Hamilton and his son. What happened?"

Before answering I took my time with another swallow of bourbon and then a drag off the cigarette. "I wouldn't know. It was all quiet when I left this morning."

"That's interesting. I guess the others had left by then too."

I didn't trust him and I didn't know what he knew so I played it cool. "Yes, as planned," I said. "We agreed a relocation that made sense after I left."

Sawyer stared at me with eyes that revealed little. Then he nodded, as if he believed me.

I nodded too and looked about the place. The Green Lantern was practically a hangout joint for celebrity criminals. The manager, Pat Reilly, moonlighted occasionally with Dillinger. He had a wife named Helen Delany whose sisters were both girlfriends of gangsters. One was with Karpis, the other had been with Tommy Carroll when he got it in Waterloo the week before last.

"I'm sorry about Helen's sister," I said to Sawyer. "Tell Pat I asked after her."

"I will, I'll let him know. It's bad business, this."

I held up my glass. "Too bad about Carroll. He was alright."

"Yeah, a regular guy, to be sure. We're gonna miss him around here."

"They're going down with regularity it seems."

"Dillinger's gang is sure running thin. They've been hounded. He'll

84

have to recruit new blood."

"Not easy to find anymore, at least not the kind of blood you might want for that game."

"Maybe you're available?"

"Me? Not I. I'm looking for a way out if I can find it. Anyway, I seem to do best working with my own smaller crews, away from the limelight."

"How's that looking for you?"

I shrugged. "Maybe a few more scores."

"Then retirement?"

"Maybe."

"A quiet little place in Mexico?"

"Maybe."

"Yeah, maybe, or maybe further south even. And maybe it's exactly what they all say ... Well think on it. Let me know if you ever have a change of heart. They could use you."

"I won't," I replied with a certainty I didn't feel. I was a little surprised by his overt recruitment effort and wondered what that meant for Mr. Dillinger.

"Okay," he said. Then, with a frown and an eye movement he added, "It is a shame about Carroll."

"Yeah, although, still, hardest on the girlfriend. I guess it always is, always will be. What do they ever have to fall back on? I hope she'll be okay. From what I hear, she's too young for the life, never should have left home."

Sawyer nodded rightly. His eyes were still moving. "We'll take care of her," he said.

I wasn't sure I really believed that, but I nodded all the same and looked around the room again. There was nobody in sight that I knew. I thought about an evening I'd spent there a few years back with Harvey Bailey and Tommy Holden. We'd gathered right at the same table where I sat now looking across at Harry Sawyer. Jelly Nash had come over to shake hands and we'd shared a bottle of bourbon and a few laughs and then gone separate ways. It had been a regular *Who's Who* of bank robbers and thieves gathered there. Now they were all gone, dead or in prison, and I was sitting alone with Sawyer, a man I did not like or trust. He fronted for the men who ran the city though, and I couldn't tell if he had been part of the betrayal, so I had to work through him.

Sawyer cleared his throat and looked at me sideways.

"There's someone I want you to meet, he's going to take care of my end and get you fixed up. He'll explain and handle the ransom process. He's also got some bonds that we're trying to fence for another friend. He might ask you to make a delivery to a town you know rather well."

"I've never been a delivery boy."

"This is a special case. It might require your unique talents and connections. It pays well and it keeps us all friends too."

It was news to me that we needed to be kept friends. I shrugged and then waited.

Sawyer waved toward the bar and when I turned to look in that direction I saw a heavy man sidling over. Apparently brown was his favorite color, because it was all he wore: trousers, jacket, tie, shoes, and even his Homburg, all brown. Obesity made it impossible for his arms to hang naturally at his side and as he walked, taking short duck steps, I noticed that they didn't swing with his gait either. I guessed his weight was about three hundred pounds.

Even before he reached the table he was smiling too hard. "Hap Johnson," he said, squeezing my hand eagerly. "Hap's short for 'Happy'."

I didn't stand, but I squeezed back and said the name I was using that week. "Glad you clarified that. I might have thought Hap short for 'Hapless'."

That drew only a blank stare as he pushed into a chair. Vocabulary wasn't a strong suit for most of the mobsters I had to work with.

Sawyer rose up stiffly and nodded at me once. "Hap will take it from here. If you'll excuse me now, there's a shipment of merchandise I need to catalogue and store."

"Heard you grew up in Minneapolis, down on Hennepin Avenue?" Hap said to me when Sawyer was gone. He was one of those people who were always eager to please everyone he met, though he never could have explained why. His ears moved when he talked.

I nodded.

"I grew up near there myself, right in the heart of the Gateway District. Of course the vagrants, bums, and day-workers are starting to take over the entire district now. Maybe we knew some of the same people?"

"Maybe we did," I said. I thought about Colt and Jimmy and a few others back before everything had changed. "It was a long, long time ago. What difference would it make?"

"Naw, I'm just saying, maybe we knew some of the same people, maybe we have friends in common."

I nodded. "Maybe so. Half of them would be dead anyway. Let's talk business. What do you have for me?"

I took another measured sip of bourbon and waited for Hap to speak, which he did quickly and in a great anxious rush. Through the flurry of words I thought I understood that he would deliver the ransom demand, handle the negotiations, and make the exchange. It was general outline of the original plan, except for a couple of details. It meant an extra chore for me, an "easy task" as Hap put it. It also meant I was handing off part of my job to him rather than to Sawyer, which might have made some sense given that I may have been compromised, if I'd had a better notion to trust him. All I had to do was deliver some bonds and federal securities to mutual friends in Chicago. By the time I returned to St. Paul the ransom would be collected and I could pick up my share, as well as my fee for delivering the stolen papers. My payment for the latter would be $3,000 and the goodwill of the city of St. Paul. It was a lot of money to pay an errand boy.

I didn't like it, but Sawyer was in control. It was his city, and it was the only way for me to see this job through – to collect some share of the ransom and to have a chance at seeing Wilson brought home safely.

"Why do you need me to go to Chicago?" I asked when he was finished. "That's not part of this deal."

Hap smiled amiably. A shiny thought seemed to cross his mind.

"Sure, I understand. Two reasons, and admittedly we're combining a few things here for effect. We decided it would be best to post the photo from Chicago – so somebody we trust needs to go there. It's a big town, will throw them off any local ideas the Feds may otherwise get. Do you have the photography? Can I have it?"

I slid an envelope across the table to him. It held film that Murphy had taken of Hamilton and his son taken the day before. They were standing together behind the bar, holding up the morning edition of the Chicago Tribune. The purpose was to verify that they were alive and in the custody of the party that approached with a ransom demand.

"We'll get this developed tonight and drop off for you in the morning if you'll tell me where."

I gave him an address in the commercial district for drop-off and pick-up. "You said there were two reasons. What's the other?" I asked.

"The bonds and securities. Obviously they are stolen from a bank and we're trying to fence them. We've got a buyer in New York, via middlemen in Chicago. We need someone reliable to make the delivery to our contacts in Chi-Town."

"Why me?"

"You're perfect for it. First, you're going there anyway." He hefted the envelope with the film as if I needed to be reminded. "Second, we know we can trust you with these – you understand their value and you're a professional, you won't get ideas. Third, you know the town and our contacts there. They were willing to take delivery from you. That's part of it. Trust is always part of it, right?"

I didn't trust him for a skinny minute. "Who are we talking about?"

He shook his head and grinned. "No names. That's part of the deal. But when you get to the meeting, I'm pretty sure you'll recognize the first face you see."

"Not everyone I would recognize in Chicago would be happy to see me."

Hap's laugh was loud and forced. "I don't know nothing about any of that. But these are friends; you can put faith in that. We've been careful."

"Italian or Irish?" I asked.

"Italian. At least they will be Italian, eventually. The first guy will be regular, plain old American, you know." He grinned at me as if that slur would please me somehow.

"Okay," I answered, after some thought. "I'll go. I'll do this for Sawyer. He's always been straight before."

"Sure you will, never doubted it for a moment. We'll leave the bonds for you in a package tomorrow. You'll get them when you pick up the photographs. One thing: don't open the package. It will be sealed in such a way that they'll know at the other end if it's been tampered with. That would not be good." He placed extra emphasis on "good" by dropping his voice to a lower register and then grinned as if he were showing me a dirty picture.

I didn't like him and the interaction with him had me suddenly feeling strange and out of sorts. "Of course."

"Say, let me ask you a question: You keep in touch with anyone from the old neighborhood?"

I shook my head. I was ready for the conversation to be over with.

"No one? Seems to me everyone was close there. Thought you might still have a few old friends from the day."

"Not me, not any more."

"Ever know Jasper Willingham or Petey Compton?"

"Nope."

"What about Johnny Polanski? Everyone called him 'Knuckles'. He shot a mean game of pool."

"Didn't know him either."

"Who'd you run with then?"

"Hap," I told him, "let's cut it out. You didn't know anyone that I knew and I'm not going to feed you names to play with now. Stick to your circle and I'll stick to mine."

Johnson made a face that seemed to chronicle surprised disappointment at my remark. "Hey, are you hungry?" he asked in a reconciling voice. "Maybe you want to try a bowl of spaghetti? They make it swell here."

I didn't answer him. Instead, I contemplated my glass. The remaining ice had melted into thin wafers that floated on top of the now watery booze.

Chapter Thirteen

I had a corner room on the sixth and next-to-top floor of the Ryan, a magnificent hotel that had been built in 1882 and was still well kept. Most of the other guys I knew stayed at the St. Francis when they were in town, but I preferred the Ryan. Whenever I stayed there I felt connected to some idealized frontier past, with its wide open spaces and individual freedoms, that had now disappeared forever.

The narrow trio of windows aligned in the corner cupola drew me over. From there the view looked out over the intersection of Robert and Sixth, a busy traffic crossing. Automobiles and people were still moving about below. They looked small from up high. Across the street, with bright lettering hung down along the corner of the building, was Browning, King and Company Clothing. I had an order waiting there and decided to stop by in the morning before I left town.

I watched the street for a while. Then I closed the drapes at the top of the window, but left them spread along the bottom so the night air could circulate in. Room service brought me a bottle of rye, a bucket of ice, and a chicken dinner, with coffee and a large slice of rhubarb pie. I was hungry enough to eat every scrap of the meal.

While I ate, I studied the design of the ornate gold wallpaper and the glass chandelier that hung over the center of the room. Tiny geometric shaped pieces of glass threaded together, reflecting the light and the wall designs as if they were all part of the same living organism. The table settings were silver cutlery, silk napkins, and crystal. Such luxury didn't surround me often. I thought about Wilson and the games of catch we'd played.

After supper I reviewed my plan for the next few days. The rye helped, or seemed to. I drank more of it.

I didn't know where the double-cross originated, who was in on it, or what the ultimate intent was. They were separate questions and each had its own implications. I went through the list of names and possibilities several times.

Isaac was the only one of those involved who's intent I actually trusted. I didn't know him real well, but I knew him well enough to know that he wouldn't invoke Jimmy's name as part of an effort to manipulate me, or anyone for that matter. At considerable risk to himself, Jimmy had brought him back to health from his gunshot wounds.

I didn't believe Murphy had set out to betray Isaac or me, he didn't think that deep about anything, but he'd gone along with it sure enough. He'd probably been promised a larger share of the ransom and he wasn't smart enough to wonder about what might snap back on him. I didn't need to worry about him any more, though I would deal with him later if he survived, especially on account of the girl. He had to answer for that. It occurred to me that whoever had set me up might now do the same thing to him, especially if they needed a patsy now that Isaac and I had managed to avoid the fall.

Hamilton claimed the entire caper was his scheme. Maybe it was. Did that mean that he'd planned the double-cross? If so, his only motive could have been a larger share of the split-up. There was a standing reward on my head – $10,000 – but that didn't seem like it would be a tempting sum, especially since he would have had to tip his own involvement to claim it.

Of course, there was another question one could wonder about: Why was Hamilton involved in the first place? Did he really need money that badly and wasn't there an easier way for him to get it than to extort from his own wife?

Then there were the two St. Paul players I knew of: Hap Johnson and Dutch Sawyer. Hap seemed weak and greedy. His attempt to reminisce about the old neighborhood, as he called it, was too contrived. None of the names he'd listed meant anything to me. I wondered if he'd really grown up on Hennepin as he claimed. Maybe he wanted the bigger share and a part of the reward for my capture. Certainly he could have had a deal going with the local law enforcement regarding a tip-off.

Sawyer might have pulled the strings too, as he so often did. But again, toward what end? He hadn't seemed surprised to see me show up at the Green Lantern, though he would already have heard I hadn't been captured at the farm. I didn't necessarily trust Sawyer, but it wasn't his style to agree to a plan that double-crossed men like me. He couldn't afford the trouble that might bring him.

What did it all add up to? The answer eluded me. Perhaps the betrayal had nothing to do with the kidnapping. Maybe somebody was angling to get me out of the way – but why? It's possible it had nothing to do with me at all. Perhaps Isaac had enemies I didn't know of. After turning that over a few times I decided it was unlikely. Isaac was a simple man and he came from a simple world. If he had enemies, they would have come at him more directly: a shotgun blast or a volley of .45 slugs on some dark street or down some alley.

No. It was about cash money and it was about me. Someone had targeted me for death or capture.

The Chicago jaunt came into the jigsaw puzzle that was spread out chaotically on the table of my mind. How did it fit with the other pieces? I couldn't see it. The rye didn't help. It wasn't the first time I'd been asked to make a delivery like that. The request itself was not so unusual. It was the timing and the circumstance of it that bothered me. I'd need to be careful.

I drank more of the rye; nothing became clearer. I thought about Wilson. Then I thought about Tad, the boy in the bank, and finally the children I'd known when I was one of them. Where did things go wrong? My thoughts turned to an old man I'd known long ago in the Illinois State Penitentiary.

*

Lars Hansson leaned against the open end of his cage with his elbows on the cross bar. I watched his lips carefully as he talked to me without making any sound. We pretty much all learned to read lips in Joliet because prison rules forbade speaking in most circumstances. Sometimes we used small mirrors to hold conversations with people in adjacent cells, but Lars was across from me and as long as the light was good I could see well enough to understand what he was saying.

He was an old man, at least sixty, with sharp, blue eyes and weather-beaten skin on his face and hands from breaking rocks under the hot sun for the past seven years. Deep grooves of skin converged at the corners of his eyes. He had a bad cough and because of it they didn't let him work anymore. Mostly he was confined to his cell, except for the few hours each week they let him out to sit in the yard.

Some people called him "the lunger" because of his cough. A few of us called him "the professor" because he had a small audience along my side of the cellblock nearly every night. It was a common enough nickname in stir. It seemed every cellblock had someone the inmates called "the professor".

I knew that the other cons for at least three cells on either side of me stood at their cage doors to receive his evening lectures. Yet always, he appeared

93

oblivious of the others, addressing only me and ignoring their efforts to break in with questions or comments. Once in the yard he'd told me the reason for this: he viewed me as the only one with potential.

"Just don't ever believe it kid," he mouthed across to me. "When they come to you as your friend and they're wearing a suit and tie and you can smell expensive aftershave, don't believe it. They ain't your friend, even if they say they are – unless they've already proved themselves three times over."

He had given me advice before. In fact, it was about all he ever did. Playing the mentor suited him now. He'd taught me how to lip-read when I first arrived, showed me how to comport myself inside, and advised me on the best prison jobs to seek out. He also had been working to prepare me for the time after my release.

His lessons had covered nearly everything: how to fit in with a crowd, how not to stand out in a small town, how to case a robbery, how to plan the getaway route using county road maps, how to time yourself in a bank and maintain discipline to leave when the predetermined time was up. He even gave advice on how to hold a fork in a good restaurant and how to treat women, whores and ladies alike. After a while, he had also schooled me on underworld contacts in several large cities across the country. Every time he mentioned a name or an address he cupped his hands on either side of his mouth so that only I would receive the information. Afterwards I had to mouth it back to him to ensure that I had it right. Periodically he would quiz me to see if I still remembered the names and addresses he had shared previously.

"After you get out, go back to St. Paul. It's the best city for you. Find the people I've told you about. They'll put you up and stake you until you get started. Treat them with respect, always, and pay them what they ask, but don't ever trust them. They are responding to forces you won't ever know about. There will always be the guy you see and then, behind him, there will be the guy you do not see. The guy behind will be in the shadows and you will never know who he is or who might be behind him. Those are the real powers and they stay out of sight."

Hansson broke off on one of his coughing jags. They were violent, wrenching hacks that came from some place deep within him and shook his entire body. His knuckles shined in the dimming light as he gripped the bars tightly, bracing himself against them through each spasm.

With his face buried in the crook of his arm, he coughed in rapid series of threes, several times and then stepped away to spit something in his toilet bowl. I waited until he came back to the open end of his cage. There was heavy sweat across his brow and his eyes gleamed with icy resoluteness.

He wiped his cheek against his shoulder and took his time before speaking again. "It is what it is, kid. Just remember what I've taught you. It will serve you well when you are out there."

My parole was likely only a few months off. I brought up the subject, as I often did, of crashing him out once I was settled with his contacts and had a stake of my own.

"No, kid," he mouthed back to me from across the cellblock. "I'll never see it and even if I did I wouldn't be any good to you or anyone. With this cough, I'm done for."

He coughed violently again into his arm and when he lifted his face up I could see the reddish spittle on his cheek and the pleading look in his eyes that now began to replace the resoluteness I must have imagined earlier.

His body heaved as he started to cough again and he disappeared back into the shadows of his cell for the remainder of the night.

*

After I got out I found that his lessons did indeed serve me well. My childhood friend, Colt, was waiting for me with a small gang already formed. We started with grocery stores and gas stations, using the funds to arm ourselves better and practice the tradecraft. Then we moved up to bigger targets and larger scores.

I didn't hear about it right away, but a year or so later I learned that Lars Hansson had died barely two months after I left Joliet. He was buried in the prison cemetery when no one claimed his body.

The cough had taken him just as he predicted it would.

*

Shortly after midnight, I spent ten minutes cleaning my 1911 Government model .45 automatic. The scent of gun oil soothed me – it always did. So did the paired routine of breaking down a pistol into its component parts and cleaning them. Disassembled and scattered across a piece of cloth they appeared mysterious, but harmless, much as a clock or an automobile engine did when taken apart. Not including the mahogany handle plates that I set on the bedspread to keep out of the way, there was a six-inch silver-colored metal tube, an indistinguishable frame of some sort, a long spring, and a few quirky pieces of black metal of various shapes and sizes.

Separated and strewn as they were, they didn't appear likely to hold potential for hurtling a piece of lead with accuracy and deadly velocity. How well I knew better.

I cleaned each part thoroughly and then put them back together. My fingers relished the work and my mind rested: the routine was automatic for me now. When the handle plates were screwed back in place the menace of the finished product returned.

I checked the slide, pulling it down on the spring several times, and then pushed a loaded magazine in. I racked the slide and set the thumb safety.

The heft of it felt good in my hand.

Plumping both pillows I placed the .45 under one and pulled the spread all the way off the bed and climbed under the top sheet. I lay in the darkened room with the windows open and felt my own heart beat thumping along to a slow taper until I was out and the dreams started as they often did.

Chapter Fourteen

My dreams were wet snowflakes falling gently on a barren field late into the spring. They dissolved and were gone as soon as they arrived. I awoke several times during the night, or seemed to, and grasped out for something that wasn't graspable. Maybe it wasn't even there. The sequence of images appeared and disappeared many times over and I was helpless, stranded in their trail.

As the orange dawn crept in to tease and haunt me, I was left with one last unsettling image. It lingered with me long enough to carry over, briefly, to an awakened state: a small, familiar dog barking at me, nipping at the edge of the bed—an over-active terrier. He was looking for his friend, the woman who took care of him and loved him and who was nowhere to be found. I'd long ago promised if anything ever happened to her, I would look after the terrier. She loved him. Now, in this dream world he was distressed, upset that she wasn't there. He wouldn't stop barking and his eager eyes followed me with expectation as I levitated above the room, confused and upset too, unsure in the reverie of what might have happened to her, but I was worried.

Fresh sunshine and a cooling breeze brought me out of it with a vague scent of lemon in my nostrils. My eyelids were moist with tears. The sheets around me were tangled.

When I opened my eyes I was alone.

*

I lay in the big, wide bed and listened to the muted city street sounds that came in through the open windows.

Six stories below delivery trucks and peddlers set wares up for the rest of the world to buy. Horns tooted impatiently, truck breaks screamed and released, and the entire world went on with its business as it always did. The sounds were rhythmic and mundane and modern.

Thin streamers of light snuck in beneath the curtains that were partially drawn over the windows. From the cupola there was gentle movement as air from outside played into the room. I lay without moving, my eyes open, observing what I could. Time seemed irrelevant.

Slowly my breath returned to me and then, almost gradually, I found I could move again. From the edge of the bed I sat for another long period of time with my bare feet on the floor.

Eventually, I stretched out a little bit, undulated my shoulders in slow circles, and turned my head from side to side. I looked at my watch on the nightstand: almost 6:45 in the morning. Then I checked the .45 and placed it on top of the pillow. It sunk down into the soft whiteness of the pillow and formed a small bowl around itself that was rimmed on one side by a narrow shadow.

Reminded again of who I was, I stood up and readied myself quickly, including a freshly laundered shirt.

*

On the ground floor of the Ryan, I had my first decent shave in five days. The barber was crisp and efficient in his movements. His towels were hot and his straight blade was sharp. He didn't make conversation and neither did I.

After the shave, I found a newspaper and ordered breakfast in a restaurant near the hotel lobby. There were no other customers evident. The waitress who poured my coffee was older than waitresses usually are. She wore an ill-fitted uniform, one that had been designed for someone younger and lighter. Her hair was thin, straight and was died a heavy black, contrasting sharply with the drawn white skin that covered her face. Gaunt eyes attempted and failed to convey enthusiasm. Moreover, there was something careworn in her stance that told me she'd been on her feet too long.

"New here?" I asked, as if I were a regular, which I was not.

"Yes, sir. I started morning shift here just last week."

"Probably work night shift somewhere too?"

She nodded and gestured with the hand that did not hold the coffee pot. "Whenever I can get it, like I did last night. All these general strikes have practically shut the entire Twin Cities down. I'm just happy to have work in these times," she said.

There was an attempt at a smile, but it was forced and it came out sort of wrong.

I nodded back at her. "How long have you been in those shoes?"

"Mister, far too long. Last night until two, and then from five on this morning. I may as well have slept in them. And then I walked three miles to this gig … What can I bring you?"

I gave her my order and then said, "No need to check back on me today. When you bring the eggs, just bring the check too. I'll leave it on the table and you can catch a quick rest until the next table is seated."

This time her smile was more genuine. For a few seconds she looked like a real live person and then she was pallid again as she remembered herself.

"Mister, I'm not afraid of work, never have been. But I never thought I'd be standing right here where I am at this sorry point so late in my life."

"There's a lot of that going around."

She nodded seriously. "I'll get your order in. You just enjoy that coffee and your newspaper."

On the front page of the *Minneapolis Tribune*, below the fold, was an article describing the raid on the Iowa farmhouse where it was suspected that Mr. Kenneth Hamilton and his son were being held: *an anxious nation followed news of the kidnapping, praying for their safe return*. I grinned. Hamilton finally had the attention he wanted, and I wondered what he'd do with it.

From reading the piece I learned that a convoy of police officers and detectives had arrived from Mason City less than an hour after we had cleared the area. With typical journalistic invention it was suggested that Dillinger and his gang had been spotted in the area. There was no mention of any meaningful clues being found and the police would not explain what information had led to the raid. I smiled to myself because I knew, and it had been close, very close.

When the waitress returned with my steak and eggs, she brought the check as I had suggested. She placed the plate in front of me and set the check on the other side of the table, slipping it between the salt and pepper shakers, as if it were a condiment that did not merit attention.

Her bird-like eyes inspected me from an odd angle. "Sorry about burdening you a few minutes ago. Mornings have been tougher than I realized."

"Don't worry about it," I told her. "It's where we are now and we're all in it."

She allowed herself a pinching nod and then straightened her back self-consciously. "My husband went missing a few months ago. He headed south to look for work and I never heard back from him. I guess

I'm still struggling to deal with it."

I thought about all the men in all the tent camps that had sprung up around the country since the Smoot-Hawley tariff, "Hoovervilles" they were so often called in honor of the previous president who many blamed for the depression that had beset the nation. A lot of words came to my mind, but I didn't say any of them.

"I'm sorry," I told her.

"Thank you for your kindness and may God bless America," she intoned and she managed to force another inert smile.

For a tip I left three dollars and some change, knowing I could never leave enough to replace what had been lost.

*

Before leaving the hotel I sent a telegram to a contact in Chicago, using a series of innocuous-sounding, but prearranged words to let him know what I would need and that I would need it by tomorrow. I was activating my insurance policy. Then I headed out to make a few stops before hitting the road.

At Browning's I picked up a blue serge suit, two white shirts, and a dark patterned tie. There was no need to try them for size. Browning's had fitted me several years before and kept my measurements on file. Everything would pull into place as though I was born into it. They'd taken nine different measurements, including each wrist separately to account for the Bulova watch that I wore on my left arm.

Next I stopped at Edward Dockman's jewelry store on Wabasha Street, which, I knew, from their street sign, offered jewelry for both cash and credit. I picked out a small piece that appealed to me and gave the address for delivery. The serious-faced man behind the counter seemed to appreciate the fact that I dealt in cash rather than credit. He probably didn't see much of that these days. I watched as he wrapped the small box in pink tissue and then fit that carefully into packaging for the U.S. Postal Service. After it was packaged and addressed he held it up for my inspection.

"I'm sure your wife will appreciate this very much," he assured me.

"I'm not married."

"With a gift like this, you may be soon," he said with the first hint of a smile beginning to show.

100

"Not me, brother," I promised him before I turned to leave. "It would cramp my style."

*

Out on the sidewalk I stood in the sunshine with my hands in my pockets and felt the electric mix of pedestrians, automobiles, trucks, and streetcars that rushed along in each direction. With so much activity, it was almost hard to believe there was a depression on.

While I was standing there Isaac approached on the sidewalk from my right. Without saying a word, I turned and walked along beside him. I pulled my hands from my pockets and allowed them to swing naturally at my side. Together we walked for half a block without speaking.

"Right, here's good enough," I said after we crossed over a busy intersection, took a left turn, and moved part way down the block.

Traffic along the street was thinner than it had been on Wabasha. We stood close together, turned away from the street and under the awning of a row of shops, several of which appeared to have gone out of business recently. A large roll of white paper had been unfurled across the inside of the window, criss-crossing several times to prevent anyone from peering in from the street. The effect was demoralizing.

"Are you sober?" I asked studying Isaac's face for clues. At least he'd shaved recently. As far as I could tell, his eyes were bright and clear.

"Swear to God, Duncan."

"Okay. What's the word?"

"You heard about the raid down in Iowa yesterday?"

I nodded. "We got out just in time, the very bare nick of it."

"Thanks to you. It was close."

"Forget it. That's just water under now."

"I know. Still, I played the sap and I'm sorry about that. Somebody wanted us to be caught there. Even if they couldn't connect us to the kidnapping we're both wanted on other charges. It would have put us out of the way for good – either prison or the other. I wonder why?"

"That's what we have to figure."

Isaac shook his head as if trying to shake off a mosquito. "I'm the sap."

"We're not saps yet. We can still turn this around. What about you?

101

Learn anything useful?"

"Nothing hard-fast. There's a rumor going around town about some ambitious guy named Hap Johnson. They say he's been making moves to get ahead. Do you know him?"

"Yeah," I said. "I met him last night over at the Green Lantern. Sawyer introduced us."

"You went in there?" Isaac grinned as he squinted into the light that made it under the awning above us.

With a slight shift of my gaze I could see our reflections in the window beside us, rippled and distorted. Our arms hung down long and narrow over short legs, while our heads appeared oversized and dumb. Maybe the glass-reflected distortion was the truth.

"I had to eventually," I said. "I revealed as little as possible, acted as though we still expected him to run the ransom negotiations. We may be able to salvage something from this mess yet. Sawyer played it off like you would expect. He threw me over to this Hap Johnson who tried to chill me with talk about the old neighborhood and an invite to a bowl of spaghetti."

"That's crummy. Which old neighborhood was he talking about?"

"Hennepin Avenue, Minneapolis. Claimed he grew up there."

Isaac was quiet long enough to stroke his chin. "That smells, alright."

"Tell me about it."

"Word is he came out of New York first, then Chicago. He has Irish friends."

I shrugged, and then followed with a grin of my own. "Good thing we weren't born yesterday – nothing left to surprise us. Anything else?"

"No. You?"

"No," I said slowly and then paused to think about it. "I don't think so. Johnson had a story, sent me on an errand to Chi-town. It's to be a drop-off."

"What's the package?"

"Don't know, yet, at least not all of it. Part of it will be the photos and the ransom demand to mail to Hamilton's wife."

"I trust your judgment. How do you figure the rest?"

"It's something that is either very valuable, or worth absolutely nothing."

"The latter would be the more dangerous."

"Yes," I said through clenched teeth.

"Want me to come along?"

I shook my head.

"I can follow behind, watch your back."

"Thanks, but it won't be necessary."

"I don't mind, I really don't. It would be a small thing and it might make the difference. We know we can't trust these people any more."

"I know. You're a good partner, and I appreciate it."

"It's the least I can do."

"No," I reassured him. "It won't be necessary. You stay here and keep your ears open. See what you can learn in this town. We have to work both fronts now."

"You got cover in Chicago?"

"Yeah. We finished here?"

Isaac nodded and extended his hand. I shook it and our eyes held for a moment. "You watch yourself," he said to me. "Give my best to Jimmy if you see him. He doesn't know about this job, but tell him we're gonna come through for his wife as promised."

"He already knows it," I replied. "It doesn't need to be said."

*

I walked back to my own automobile that I'd parked across the street from the Nankin Café. A cloudless pure blue sky overhead suggested no clues about what the high temperature should be, but the concrete around me was already starting to hold the heat, which told a story.

While I was standing there on the sidewalk a man came out of the Nankin Café, crossed over, and handed me an 8 x 11 manila envelope and a heavily taped package that was about the size of a phonebook as he walked by. No words or eye contact were exchanged between us. It was casual, so casual it was as though it had never even happened at all. The man seemed to disappear before I could turn around.

Back at the Ford I took a look inside the unsealed envelope. Even at a discrete angle the photograph of Hamilton and his son struck me for the obvious lack of affection that was apparent between man and boy – stepfather and stepson. Young Wilson stood leaning away from his father with his head tilted up quizzically, eyes squinting into the sun. The fingertips of both hands held the newspaper delicately like one might hold a sullied diaper.

For his part, Hamilton stood far removed, with his hands in his pockets and one foot angled away from his son. His chinless face was cocked away too with his hat back on his forehead. There was nothing in his expression to suggest he knew or cared about the small boy standing at his side, or the situation they were in. Dark secrets and illicit treasure seemed to be reflected in his narrow eyes.

The envelope was already addressed, with postage, to a one Mrs. Hamilton in St. Paul. I studied the address for a moment, and then I slid the envelope, along with the taped package, under the passenger seat, out of sight, and turned over the engine of the Ford.

*

The freedom of the open road relieved me. Somehow I drove the posted speed limit, though with the windows rolled all the way down and the rush of the wind flying through to blot my thoughts. I was relaxed, alert, well fed, and ready for anything. In the trunk I had two Thompson machine guns, one bulletproof vest, and enough ammunition and grenades to re-fight the Battle of the Somme.

Soon enough the Wisconsin border fell under my wheels and I was immediately in hillier country and on toward Wausau. There I would cut south for Madison, then Rockford, and finally Chicago.

If there were no trouble and no surprises along the way, I might arrive by mid-evening.

Chapter Fifteen

Wrigley Field was some place to be on a Sunday afternoon. Even with a Great Depression going on people would pay good money to attend a baseball game if the Cubs were playing.

I arrived a few minutes before the first pitch of the second half of a double header against the Boston Braves. The Cubs had lost game one by a score of 2 to 4 and were now six and a half games out of first place. My seat was on the aisle, down the first base line, five rows back from the field. The seat next to me was empty.

From where I sat I didn't need binoculars to see the sweat fly off the body of Bill Lee as he released each fastball. A shower of droplets filled the air before him as if from a flicked wet towel. I was close enough to hear him grunt with each effort.

The stands were nearly full and filled with the atmosphere of a large party. It was raucous and oddly formal, even with the heat. Two rows down a woman sat with a fur coat splayed over her shoulders. In the sections around and in front of me I spotted several people I knew from the society pages: a couple of politicians, a notorious gambler, a famous actress and her much younger boyfriend, as well as several entertainers from the local nightclub scene. None of them appeared to be more than half sober—or to be paying much attention to the baseball game that was being played in front of them. Everybody wanted to be seen.

The low sky above was soft with clouds and the sun had moved far enough along that the shadows on the field were lengthening. I was wearing seersucker again and a white straw hat with a light blue striped band around it. A pair of inert glasses changed my appearance and allowed for clip-on sun lenses. I'd shaved my mustache and grown my hair out a bit since my last visit to Chicago. More or less, I was comfortable that I wouldn't be recognized by anyone I did not want to know me.

The seat beside me wasn't empty for long. Two pitches into the second inning, a man rose up from the very front row where he was sitting with a mixed-gender group who appeared to be having a very good time together. He had an athletic frame and moved with a sense of controlled efficiency, quickly covering the handful of steps back to where I sat, though with a trace of a limp.

I recognized him by his sardonic grin and the twinkle in his eye. In fact, he looked a little bit like me, though a few years older, and he also wore a straw hat that was cocked to one side and back a little. He didn't wear a jacket and his sleeves were rolled up to the elbows. It signaled that he was a working man. I moved over one seat so that he could have the aisle.

"Hi," was all he said, as he stuck out his hand.

I shook it and he sat down beside me. "It's nice to see you again," I told him.

"Likewise. Are you a Cubs fan?" His eyes narrowed to study the field, and then he looked back at me.

I shimmered my hand sideways to indicate ambivalence. "I like St. Louis."

"Yeah, they're good too. That Dizzy Dean is really something to watch. When do they come to town?"

I said I didn't know. He held up a scorecard, studied it for a moment and then fanned himself with it while we watched the next batter hit a sharp grounder to short. The play was made and from where we sat we could hear the snap of the ball hitting the first baseman's glove.

The next batter came up and took a first pitch called-strike. The man beside me nodded in appreciation, as if we were children at the sandlot. "This Lee kid has promise, look at the way he throws."

"Not bad effort for a rookie."

"Yeah, not bad at all. Look at that kick. I hit against a guy who threw like that once, long ago."

"How'd you do?"

His grin widened. "One for four, a cheap infield single, but turned a double-play in the ninth to end the game and we won: one-nothing."

"Don't boast on it too hard – as you said yourself, it was long ago."

"Naw, he had the form, although not the stuff this Lee kid has. He could be around for a while if he doesn't get hurt."

"Same might be said of you and me."

He laughed loudly and easily in a way that made me like him all the more. Then I remembered one of the other things that were probably on his mind these days. On impulse, I decided to mention it to him, partly because I doubted that anyone else had.

"Hey Johnny," I said. "I was sorry to hear about Carroll. He was a regular guy, stand-up all the way down the line."

"Thanks," he replied, glancing over at me for a moment. "Tommy was that."

He didn't say anything more and I didn't press the issue.

We were quiet while Wally Berger took his at-bat. He hit the ball a long way. My eyes followed it out to centerfield, 436 feet from home plate. The crowd noise rose as the centerfielder made a nice effort on it. Afterwards my companion adjusted his tie slightly and looked at me with business in his eyes.

"Did Hap send you?"

"Yes," I disclosed.

He flashed a brief rascal grin. It disappeared as quickly as it had formed. "Of course I've never met Hap, don't even really know who he is, but he's Sawyer's man and that's the game we're in. Is he as fat as I've heard he is?"

"I don't know what you've heard, but whatever it is he's a mite fatter than that."

"That makes him pretty fat."

I nodded and looked out at the field. The side was out and the Cubs were coming in from the field. When they were in the dugout and before the Braves had taken the field the man cleared his throat. I took it as signal he had something more serious to say.

"Of course I'm not the main contact here in Chi, I'm just the guy to set you toward the one who is – here."

He handed me a small piece of paper with a street address written on it in pencil.

"What time?"

"Eight o'clock, right there."

"Does he have a name?"

The man shook his head and his rascal half-grin formed again.

"How will I know him, then?"

"First of all, it might not be a 'he.' You're going to meet a broad tonight, and I'm warning you, brother, she's a looker all right. Watch yourself because she's fast and loose." He followed that statement with a knowing wink.

"I don't know this place. What kind of joint is it?"

"Just a regular place … at first. Around midnight it evolves into a Black and Tan club. It's real spiffy then and if you see Hazel, tell her I say hello. She can take good care of you."

"How would I know her?"

"If you walk in the front door, she'll be the one who greets you, even before midnight. It seems to be her place. You like Black and Tans?"

I shrugged and lit a Chesterfield, dropping the still burning match over the edge of the metal seat next to me. Black and Tan clubs were mixed race nightclubs known for their lascivious delights that ran the full gamut. I'd never been to one, but color didn't matter much to me either way.

A warm breeze swirled around the stadium, flaring and snapping the banners that hung around the perimeter. Long shadows added texture and complexity to the expansive park. It retained a bright, pure center and it reminded me suddenly of my childhood and the distance I'd come since.

My companion sighed as though he were reading my thoughts. "We never had a chance in this world did we? With our records and this depression who was ever going to give us a job worth having? They celebrate outlaws, but in the end, they'll shoot us like rabid dogs in the street if they can fix their sights."

I looked away from the field. The Depression never quite seemed like sufficient rationale for armed robbery. Nationwide unemployment was over 25% and industrial production just half of what it had been five years ago. We produced only a third the number of automobiles, and stocks had lost three quarters of their value. Home foreclosures were gaining pace like a runaway train and no one could see an end to it. But none of that was the reason I had picked up a gun.

"Who you kidding?" I asked finally. "You and me, we're not social bandits."

The man looked at me straight-faced as if he were about to explode in anger. Instead, after a moment, he burst out into that loud laugh that I'd kind of learned to like.

"Yeah," he said, still chuckling from deep in his throat. "I guess you got that about right. Maybe it's the romance of the road that called and couldn't be resisted. I'm not looking for any sympathy, and expect to get none. That's just fine with me."

I nodded. "Yeah, I see it something like that."

"What is a social bandit, anyway?"

I snorted. "They're the people who resist the true villainy of the banks, like the vigilante groups of neighbors who gather to intimidate buyers at foreclosure auctions, helping the original owners buy back their farms at decent prices."

"I heard about a gang of masked men down in Le Mars last year who abducted a foreclosure judge and then stripped him, beat him, damn near lynched him."

"Yes. We're not doing those things. The banks might be corrupt, but we don't rob them for the communal good."

"I see your point. I guess I'm just trying to even up the score, take back what was denied, live an entire life as fast as I can."

"It's the only way we can live. Maybe there was a point long ago where we could have taken another path, but you and I are way past that now."

The man's nod was tinged with a sadness I wouldn't have expected. Goose bumps formed on the back of my neck and I tried, but failed, to stifle an accompanying shiver. I'm not quite sure what it was that touched me, perhaps some strange variation of brothers in arms.

We watched the baseball game without speaking any words to each other. After about five more minutes he bumped me chummily on the shoulder with his elbow.

"My friend, I should return to my seat now. Don't want to leave the young lady alone for too long."

I nodded at him, but he didn't move right away.

It seemed he had something to say and it took him a good pause to find the words.

"I guess the thing that worries me is this: you got back up?" he asked. His voice was different now, lower. It was a serious tone and I had to bend towards him to hear the words clearly.

"Probably so," I replied.

"I mean good back up, not someone who's going to get the jimmy legs when lead is in the air."

My nod was tight. "I know what you mean. I'll be covered."

"Good. As I said earlier, I don't know this Hap. He's probably a fine-fellow-well-met, but you never know who might sell you out – especially in Lake County, East Chicago. By the way, I like the glasses – nice touch. Maybe I'll get a pair myself."

After he stood up, he paused to watch a pitch land in the catcher's mitt, and then he turned again and leaned down toward me with his hand extended and his mouth very close to my ear.

"It was good seeing you again," he stated with sincerity. "You get the itch to partner up, then let me know. I'd love to have you with us. So would Baby-Face and the others. Maybe we'll work together some day yet."

It wasn't exactly a question, but not quite a statement of opinion either. I gave him my best grin and shot him the gunner's salute.

"You take care, kid."

"You too, Johnny. You too," I said as he moved off, but my words were lost in the noise of the crowd that swelled at the sound of a bat making contact.

Chapter Sixteen

The club was unmarked and set down half a level below the street. From what I could tell it didn't even have a name. The jazz in my head moved into a slow bluesy vamp as I took the first step. I knew I was walking into a dangerous situation, but I had my own back up plan folded into my back pocket just in case.

A semi-frail elderly black man in a tuxedo and a top hat opened the door for me when I knocked and let me into a tiled foyer. It was so quiet that I wondered if I was in the right place. He asked my name and after I gave it he bowed slightly with a gentle frown and opened a door that led into a brightly lit, carpeted hallway.

Down that hallway I could hear the beginning of actual sounds one expected to hear in a place like this. At the end stood another black man; he too wore a tuxedo and a top hat. He was also much younger and three times the size of the first one. When I reached him, he held the door open for me without meeting my eye or saying a word.

The room I stepped into was in the early stages of forming a party. Hazel was right where the man said she would be, ruling her domain like a beneficent queen. She was a very short, very heavy black woman – about as wide as she was tall. I thought of Jimmy Rushing, *Mr. Four by Four*. Red lipstick and rouge polished her face and a shiny red satin cloth wrapped her entire body from shoulder to ankle. The only accouterments that weren't red were the diamonds she wore – several on each hand, around her neck, and in her hair. She liked the color red and she liked diamonds.

"Johnny says hello," I told her as I came through the door.

She smiled brilliantly with her head tilted back to look up into my eyes. The effect was pleasant, and left me with the sense that I'd be well cared for.

"You must be Mr. Duncan. Next time you see my sweetheart Johnny, you tell him Hazel says to get his rowdy handsome self on back here some night real soon. He hasn't graced us for over two months. My girls miss him! It's been downright too quiet without him coming around with his jokes and his lady friends. You know he does entertain the ladies. Here, let me take your hat."

I handed it to her.

"Come to think of it," she said, laughing, "you look rather like him. I bet you hear that all the time, don'tcha loverman!"

"Usually they tell me how I'm much better looking than he is."

She winked at that. "You may be at that, younger too. Can I take your raincoat?"

"No thank you, I'll keep it."

"Awful warm in there for a raincoat."

I didn't disagree with her, but I shook the question off.

After she handed my hat to a hatcheck girl, Hazel led me back to a table along the wall in the back, tucked into an odd corner. The room was half filled, mostly with small groups of young to middle-aged white men in dark colored suits. More or less, they all looked the same. Some of them were thugs and politicians, others were simply curious men, perhaps visiting from out of town or stepping out on their families to find out what happened in joints like this. Most of the servers were male too.

Hazel might have picked up on my thoughts. "Honey, don't you worry. We're not one of those kinds of clubs. The girls don't usually start to arrive for another hour or so, but they'll be along in good time. What can I have one of my guys bring for you, perhaps something from the bar?"

I ordered a gin martini and sat back to study the room more carefully. It was an old sub-basement that had been hollowed out to form one large room. Support beams and three small room-like structures – probably coal bins – jutted out along the exterior walls to give a sense of character and break the room into smaller zones. Part of the effect was to instill coziness.

My table was next to one of the coal bins, giving it the feel of a corner table, with an obscured view of about one third of the room. I didn't mind that – it meant that if something happened I had only two fields of vision to worry about and nobody could come up behind me.

Other aspects of the room drew my attention. It was an old room with a painted white concrete floor and a low ornate pale green tin ceiling. Dim lighting emanated from wall sconces that ringed the room at six-foot intervals, mounted at shoulder height. There were only three points of egress – the door I had come through, a door that led to the kitchen from the other side of a long wooden bar, and a side door that was situated thirty feet from where I sat. I couldn't tell where it led to or whether it was locked.

Set across from that door, on the other side of the room, also tucked beside a coal bin, was an elevated wooden platform upon which a pair of musicians were preparing for the evening. A stand-up bass, piano, and drum kit was set up for them. A trumpet player stood off to one side, tuning his instrument to middle C and then he drew a slide to flatten it to a B. Hazel was waiting nearby as if expecting to sing. A few moments later, the other two members of the quintet arrived and began to tinker with their instruments. They were a mixed race group. The bass and trumpet players were white and the others were black.

The bass player ran a few arpeggios in a variety of keys and then called over something to the drummer who grinned and responded by hitting the foot-pedal on the bass drum about five times. That went on until he suddenly struck up a slow deliberate hi-hat, and after a couple of bars the tall bass walked in. When Hazel finally opened her pipes she filled the room with *C. C. Rider* and the sad, sad story that it told.

*

Her eyes arrested mine the moment she entered the room. They were powerful magnets that drew every man to her, and I was part of the flotsam that began to stream her way.

The band was on a break, so she had the full attention of every eye in the house. She was a platinum blonde with a wide cut bob high up the back of her neck and the tightest, shiniest curls I'd ever seen. They practically glowed in the dark in the way that no man would actually complain about.

She had that certain Va Va Voom. It wasn't only the shape of her hips and bust or the way her white silk dress clung, but also the way that she moved, the way that she walked, the way that she held a cigarette aloft at shoulder height. I felt it in the pit of my stomach and even from across the room she knew it instantly as her eyes caught mine and it reassured her. A confident smile gleamed abstractly my way. It was the way she affected men, all men. I knew that; I was just the next one in her line as she headed towards me.

At the table she paused to stub out her barely smoked cigarette – a light wrist motion and two inches of wasted tobacco. Standing next to her I realized that in addition to a favorable shape, she was also quite

113

tall – in her heels even taller than me.

"I'm Evelyn, Evelyn Bays. Light me up." They were the first words she said to me after I'd held the chair for her and she'd taken it. Her voice reminded me of fresh blown glass from the French Quarter.

I angled across the table with a match and my hand was almost steady. She leaned in too with a fresh cigarette, mostly to allow her cleavage to billow, which it did nicely. White pearls around her neck swung out a little too and then she leaned back with the cigarette going, again held just off her shoulder. Green eyes studied me quietly for a long moment.

"So, Mr. Duncan," she said, "how do you do?"

Instead of responding I took a good pull at the second gin martini I'd had the foresight to order for myself. "Perhaps you would like a drink too," I replied presently, hoping the gin would have quick effect.

"Indeed I would, Mr. Duncan. I'll have what you're having." She spoke slowly, with a lilting twang that carefully pronounced every syllable.

I made a motion towards a waiter who was standing near the bar watching us. Actually, he was watching her, but his eyes caught my movement and then understood the need.

"You're from New Orleans," I predicted for her.

Her smile gleamed brighter and her eyes were merry. "We say 'Nawlens' down there and that was a long time ago, Mr. Duncan. I give you credit for detecting what I thought had smoothed out into a more general accent with only a hint of the fine Southern hospitality."

"I'm sure it is exactly as smooth as you want it to be."

She beamed as though I'd presented her with a long stem rose. That was her gift: she could make any man feel appreciated. I finished my martini just as the waiter arrived with two more for the table. Fresh lace napkins and a clean ashtray also appeared on the table a moment later. As long as I was sitting with her, my table would never want for attention from the male waiters.

Without appearing to move, Evelyn used her left hand to pick up her glass by the stem with a thumb and two fingers. It was graceful and delicate all in the same motion. "Mr. Duncan," she said to me, allowing a little bit more of that fine Southern hospitality to fill her voice, and then she said something in French that I didn't comprehend.

"Cheers," I replied. "Here's to hot nights and cold drinks."

"And fine, handsome company," she added.

"Also to white pearls and platinum curls."

We sipped from our glasses, and though she didn't appear to swallow anything, her glass was somehow empty when it was set back on the table. I gestured toward the waiter, but he was already procuring the next round of martinis. Maybe he'd seen her drink before. When they were before us, we skipped the toast this time and went straight to the drinking.

Again she finished her cocktail without the appearance of effort. I set mine, virtually untouched on the table and lit myself a cigarette. At least my hands were steady now and though my mouth was dry I got it going and exhaled a stream of smoke up toward the pinpoint lights in the ceiling.

"Shall you tell me about our business here tonight?" I asked.

Dimples creased her smile and her teeth were whiter and straighter than before. "I think I shall."

I took a hard drag on my Chesterfield and waited.

"Mr. Duncan," she started to explain slowly. "This is really very simple. There are few pleasures in this town, few real pleasures, that is. I rather think you might be one of them and I would like to conclude our business here this evening as quickly as we might so that you and I can move on to other activities."

I shrugged my best noncommittal shrug and waited for her to elaborate.

"Don't feel pressured to respond," she told me, with her wide smile. "Strong and silent is a welcome type these days. Most men talk entirely too much. In a moment, I'm going to introduce you to a couple of my other friends, not the kind of friends I spend much time with, but the kind we can do a little business with. They are going to ask you for something and after you give it to them they will give you an envelope with money in it, real folding money. And then you and I can go for a ride and you can tell me what it would take for me to get closer to those pale baby blues that you shield so carefully."

"Sister," I replied carefully. "Let's bring those friends over and get on with this before the trumpet starts to gust again."

"I will summon them."

Evelyn turned in her seat without appearing to twist and gestured with the back of her hand, sallying with her cigarette in a slow figure eight.

Two men who were leaning against the bar responded in unison.

115

They were middle-aged hard-boys, both wearing dark-blue double-breasted jackets, narrow ties with very thin and tight knots at the top, and brown angled Stetsons that they had not left with the hatcheck girl for some reason. I'd already spotted them and wasn't surprised to find that they were the next act.

One fellow was clearly the leader of the pair and he lurched over to our table first, with the other directly behind him. For several minutes now I'd been waiting for them to plug in an orange neon sign that said "police officers". They never did plug in the sign, but it didn't matter because every cynical eye in the house had already pegged them for what they were.

"Join you?" the first man asked, using his foot to hook out a chair from the next table over. He held an unlit cigar in one hand and a glass of whiskey and chipped ice in the other. There was a lot of white space showing around the small pupils of his eyes. "I'm Detective Del Vecchio, and this is Detective Quinn. We're East Chicago."

His suit was neatly tailored and up close, with help from the track lighting above, I could see the blueish sheen of woven silk. A carefully folded pocket square peeked over his breast pocket at me. I wondered how it was that so many big city detectives seemed able to afford clothing like that while down at the corner of Monroe and Sangamon three thousand unemployed Chicagoans had been protesting economic and living conditions in the city.

Quinn pulled a chair over from another table and sat down too. He set his glass on the table and yawned. Even from where I sat I could smell the rye on his breath when he exhaled. It was sweet and bitter, like he'd been drinking too much coffee and rye, maybe rock-and-rye cocktails, and chain-smoking through the evening. An intelligent demeanor did not mar his modest good looks, though the bulge of a revolver did disturb the lines of his suit. I assumed he was pleased with that particular effect.

I placed both detectives in their mid-thirties. They looked the same: stout, angry men, who drank and strutted too much, and had little perspective of their own limitations. I'd known too many of the type in every city I'd visited. They had wives and small children somewhere and spent their off-duty hours drinking with each other and grumbling about how little they were appreciated by the society they served. They cheated on their wives whenever they could with the hookers on their beat, and they took small graft in just about every interaction.

Yet they viewed their badges with pride because they represented the fraternity they were a part of and they convinced themselves that the petty corruption was just part of what it took for them to do their big city jobs and keep the social order. Something about these two set them apart, however and I wondered if they might not have been a little more ambitious than usual.

Del Vecchio sat with his elbows planted on the table and his shoulders hunched. The tight collar of his shirt dug into his chin. He looked at me through squinting eyes, studying me with a tribal mistrust. After a moment, he fished out a badge and flipped it open briefly to show me he really was a detective. It was a well-rehearsed motion and I knew he felt good about himself when he did it. He probably practiced it every morning in the mirror before heading out for the day. I wasted no time studying the badge.

"Maybe you guys are music lovers," I suggested. "Maybe you come here for the jazz that goes down after midnight?"

Del Vecchio stared for a long moment and then ignored my question. "Maybe you have something for us," he said. His voice came out as an intentional growl. I assumed he practiced that too.

Evelyn didn't seem to notice their manners. Her fingers tipped the stem of the martini back towards her lips and she finished the drink, again without appearing to swallow. An expression of aloof half-interest covered her face. She might have been witnessing a conversation between two produce stockers trying to agree on where to stack the eggplants.

"Maybe I do," I told him. "Tell me why I would give it to you."

"Because we're Hap's contacts."

"East Chicago police detectives work for Hap Johnson?"

Del Vecchio didn't smile and neither did Quinn.

"No, smart-alec. Hap works for us. As do you. Let's not fool around any more than we have to. Do you have the package?"

"More or less."

"Meaning?"

"Meaning that I have it. I don't have it here with me here in this club."

"Why would you not bring it with you?"

"Because I didn't just this evening fall off the turnip truck."

"Where is it?" Del Vecchio's voice was angry.

"Very nearby."

"Where?"

"On the backseat floor of my automobile."

"Is it parked on the street out there?"

I nodded. Evelyn's eyes watched me with serious intent now. She didn't spare a glance for either of the detectives.

"Give me the keys," Del Vecchio demanded.

"That makes no sense."

"Give them to me."

I pushed the keys across to him. "It's a late-model Dodge. Want me to show you where it is parked?"

Del Vecchio looked at his partner than back at me and nodded. "Lead on," he said.

We all stood. Quinn finished his rock-and-rye and dropped the glass onto the table with a little too much force.

*

We passed through the room in single file, with me in the lead and Evelyn right behind. The jazz quintet was just returning to the stage for their next set. Hazel waved at me as we passed. I noted the room had filled with a new type of customer, though perhaps they weren't really customers. They were tall, beautiful black ladies who all seemed to wear lots of sequins and show ample amounts of bare skin, both high and low. They had quietly started to fill the edges of the room and crowded around one end of the bar. Several tables had been moved aside to create a dancing space.

At the exit, before ducking through, I looked back over my shoulder. Evelyn was right behind me with her hand on my arm, gripping tightly. She gave me a naughty wink and leaned forward to whisper sugared words in my ear.

"We shall come back here, Mr. Duncan, after we have concluded our business and slipped these two oafs. Then we will have some real fun. I hope you are not so much of a puritan as you seem at first blush. Later we might want to invite one of these pretty ladies to join us."

*

We stepped out into the night and onto a wide sidewalk of concrete squares. Traffic had picked up and so had the heat. The city was a steamy marsh and I felt the sweat forming immediately in the small of my back.

It may have been more than the heat that caused me to sweat. Del Vecchio uttered a vile epithet to describe the night, the city, and its denizens. Laughing, Quinn added a few choice words of his own, as well as a rude promise for how he planned to spend the remainder of the evening after the job was finished.

The sinners of Gomorrah had nothing on these boys.

Evelyn continued on my arm, though she did not speak now. Her grip seemed tighter and more anxious than it should have been. I lead us all a block down the street and then turned into a side street that was little more than an alley, with a sidewalk on only one side.

Automobiles were parked along the sidewalk. The other side of the street was unlit and lined with dumpsters, trashcans, and overhanging fire escapes from the backside of a four-story apartment building. There were a few lights showing in windows above the first floor, casting uneven light and muted shadows down upon us as we walked toward the far end.

The Dodge was parked beneath an out-of-order street lamp about forty yards down the narrow street. I was driving it on a special arrangement I'd made for the evening so that I wouldn't expose my Ford. As we approached, I pointed toward it and Del Vecchio stepped quickly around me with the keys jingling as he worked them between his fingers.

"It's in the back seat, on the floor," I said, stopping beside the front end of the sedan.

Del Vecchio paused, as if thinking it over and then held the keys out to me. "Here, you might as well do it."

"Sure," I accepted.

I reached for the keys, but he pulled his hand back.

"Never mind," he told me. Instead he handed the keys over to Quinn who had moved around me and now stood behind the Dodge with one foot in the street. "Hurry, and see if it's really in there." Del Vecchio added a few more of his favorite words to move Quinn along.

Evelyn was drifting now, moving away from me along the edge of the sidewalk next to the building without stepping between me and Del

Vecchio, as if she was curious herself about what was in the backseat. She came around behind Del Vecchio and stood with a hand on her hip, very near Quinn as he bent into the Dodge. A relaxed smile carried her face and I found myself staring at it with soft eyes that took in the entire scene.

"Here it is," Quinn exclaimed louder than he needed to.

"Hey Quinn," Del Vecchio murmured. "Remember the night a few years ago when we got the call and found Hymie Weiss murdered down on State Street? He was straight on his back with his ankles crossed by the time we got to him."

Quinn made an ugly noise that could have been a chuckle. When he stepped around from behind the rear door of the automobile he held a revolver in his left hand. He shot me in the chest, twice in rapid succession. The first slug knocked me back a step. The second spun me around and I fell over hard onto the street between the Dodge and another parked automobile.

For a long moment the shots echoed in the tight space of the narrow street and nobody moved or spoke.

*

Time had stopped and I could not breathe. The air had been knocked from my lungs and everything ached.

"He's down," I heard a voice say.

"Better check on him to be sure."

Then I heard the kick of the shotgun. It exploded twice from somewhere very nearby. A third shell was ratcheted into the chamber and then I heard nothing. A moment later, a hand was tugging at my elbow, pulling me up, trying to turn me. That helped get the air moving through my lungs again, just enough to groan.

"Are you alive?" It was Gordon's voice and he was standing over me.

I nodded and he helped pull me all the way to my feet, where I tottered for a moment and then I took a step towards the curb and peered over the hood of the Dodge at the two bloody puddles that now covered the sidewalk.

The powerful stench of feces was in the air. I felt no pity as I stared down at the lifeless forms and spoke over them, "The shooter who got Hymie Weiss was smart enough to put one in his head."

120

"Jeez, I thought they'd killed you," Gordon said behind me.

I pulled off the raincoat and showed him the two holes in my new white shirt from Browning, King and Company Clothing. It had been a special fitting, and it went right over the bulletproof vest that I wore. He rubbed his fingers quickly over them and a slow Cheshire grin formed. It was all I could see of his face beneath his fedora.

"The lead's still fire-hot," he observed. "Good thing you had a vest on."

"I knew you wouldn't shoot quick enough."

With his thumb, Gordon pushed the fedora back so that I could see his eyes. They were not smiling. "You bastard. I'm glad you're alive. What about the enchantress?"

Evelyn was on the sidewalk, resting on one hip. Her white silk dress was splattered with deep red blots. They covered her face, arms, and legs too. Her pearls were a mess. At first I couldn't tell if she had been hit or not. There was no expression at all in her far away eyes. She might have been in shock. I walked stiffly over to her and knelt down so that my face was very near hers. She moved her head so that her cheek was touching mine. In that half moment I couldn't be sure which one of us was trembling.

"I can't walk," she whispered. "I think I broke a heel."

Leaning back so I could look at her, I studied her face. "Evelyn."

"Don't leave me like this."

"You set me up."

She shook her head with some desperation. "I didn't know. I'll make it up to you, I promise."

Tears welled in her eyes, reflecting the ambiance of the darkened street, causing her green irises to glow yellow. Slowly I rocked back and then I stood up, staring down at her, studying the contours of her body. It was full and still perfectly formed, untouched by stray buckshot.

"You're fine," I said.

"Don't leave me like this," she whispered again, though louder this time. "I can't go back to him after this. I'll do anything you want." She looked up at me with her lips parted slightly and her eyes open wide, focused on nothing.

I didn't ask who he was because I already knew. Instead, I dropped a twenty-dollar bill onto her lap where the bloody white silk was stretched by her splayed legs in a way it was never intended to be.

"Anything I want? I want you to take a taxi," I told her. "Just get the hell out of here."

Silvered pieces of the night began to rain down around us and something inside me fell into ruins.

*

Gordon had the Dodge started by the time I climbed into the passenger side. Lights began to appear above us from the apartment building across the street where somebody opened a window. I could hear the voices muttering indistinctly. We drove away from the scene followed by nothing more than our own long, rolling shadow and the haunting thoughts that would come later in the night.

Chapter Seventeen

For three nights and two days I'd cooled it at Gordon's apartment in Evanston. He had it on a three-month summer lease, which was as long as either of us had lived anywhere since prison. It was a two-bedroom second-story walk-up on a quiet street near the university.

I had to stay off the streets for a couple of days, maybe three, until things cooled off a little. Then I had business with Jimmy to attend to, and I'd pay a visit to a man named Gino Torresi. He was my connection with the Chicago Outfit, and I figured he'd know a thing or two about what was going on.

The front windows looked out on a row of withering Elm trees and shallow lawns covered with grass that was mostly brown. I watched as a crew of lawn boys did their work – cutting, raking, and sweeping – with leisurely precision. Across the street a sprinkler ran, creating swathes of green as it was moved slowly from point to point during the day.

Most of the tenants in the building and surrounding confines were students or faculty and many were away until the fall semester began. The entire street had an air of neglect and the misfortunate about it, as did so many neighborhoods across the country these days.

I'd only known Gordon since the early spring, yet I trusted him as much as I could trust anyone any more. His face was earnestly shaped and he had the fidgety hand mannerisms of a perfectionist. He had grown up on a farm in Ohio and he carried a lot of extra weight, but much of it was in his shoulders and I knew how tough he was in a pinch.

Since discharge from the Army he'd worked as a professional jug marker – the guy who cased the banks for the professional thieves who robbed them – and he'd run hard and fast with Eddie Bentz and Harvey Bailey in the 1920s. Before being caught they had been one of the most professional, most successful gangs of bankrobbers. That was before being sent up for a good stretch in McAllister, where he'd served time with Doc Barker and a few other thieves I knew. Earlier in the spring we had run out a spree of carefully planned bank jobs together. The last one had ended badly, but Gordon had held up his end and it is often in coarse circumstances that you learn who can be counted on.

He was one of those few.

After receiving the telegram I sent him from St. Paul, Gordon had stocked the apartment well – well enough so that we wouldn't have to go out for at least a week. For two days hysterical chatter about the late-night murders of two East Chicago police detectives dominated the radio waves.

The dailies had their fun too. The *Tribune* ran the story on page one, along with a gruesome crime scene photograph and groundless speculation that maybe they had caught up with John Dillinger, who out-gunned them. No one thought to ask why he would have done that. The police had formed a special task force and were rousting the usual sorts across town. Also noted were sympathetic personal details of the dead detectives: Quinn's young wife was expecting their third child in two months and Del Vecchio had recently received a mayor's commendation for courage in the line-of-duty.

There was no mention anywhere – radio or newspapers – of the two detectives' corrupt moonlighting ambitions, a lady in white silk, or anything that would lead anybody my way. The reporters made a joyous romp out of it, as they always did. Exclamation points and not-so-subtle inventions filled the lurid stories they told.

The joy ride lasted until the next replacement story happened along. On the morning of the third day the subject was abruptly changed: Kenneth Hamilton had been released from captivity. Honeymooners from Minneapolis had picked him up on a rural highway in northern Iowa.

A statement from the St. Paul office of the Bureau of Investigation provided information that Hamilton was in good health and good spirits. His nine-year old stepson, Wilson, had not yet been released and there was no word on where the boy might be. There were no clues as to who the kidnappers were or where they might be. An unnamed source was quoted speculating that they may have taken the child to South America.

*

We were sitting in Gordon's narrow kitchen nook, with coffee and cigarettes. Sections of the *Tribune* were spread out over the table. When I finished reading about Hamilton's return, I set the newspaper on the

124

table in front of Gordon's breakfast. While he read the story, I gave the situation a little thought.

Technically, I'd already played my full part in the kidnapping scheme. I'd made the abduction, watched over the victim, and then delivered the proof of his safety and the fact that somebody had him to Sawyer and his people. They were the negotiators now and it was up to them to work out the ransom payment and collect it. I didn't have any involvement in that anymore. Presumably money had changed hands at this point. That meant I was simply supposed to collect my share in several week's time. Now I wondered if I ever would.

Hamilton was the wild card in the deck. I wondered why he was free, but the child wasn't. It could have meant that payments were coming in installments – a confidence building measure. Yet that didn't sit right. It should have been the child who was freed first. I wondered what that meant and couldn't see that it possibly meant anything I liked.

When he finished reading the newspaper in front of him, Gordon looked up at me and then poked at it with his thumb.

"Looks like another couple of unsolved homicides to add to the city's books." Gordon didn't speak much. When he did speak, his words were direct and to the point. "With the dailies focusing on Hamilton now, they'll forget all about the two dead cops in East Chicago, and with the public heat off them the local police will ease up. I guess we're in the clear now."

I shook my head. "Maybe, but don't count on it going quite that way. Eventually they'll find some fall guy to take the rap. They can't let a police murder go cold."

Gordon nodded without blinking. "You're probably right. But it won't be us."

"No, I don't think so. You losing sleep?"

A small sigh escaped my friend's lips as he sat back in his chair and eyed me cautiously. "I killed a man only once before, a hick-town parole officer in Oklahoma who tried to violate me, back when I wouldn't pay the bribe he demanded. That was last year, before we met up in Reno. But no, I'm not losing sleep on this. Maybe it's easier when they seem to deserve it so keenly."

I shrugged. So far, we had talked little about the ambush. "Easier maybe," I replied. "But not easy. It never is and it doesn't leave you quite like you think it will."

Gordon wet his lips. "Agreed, though they didn't leave me any choice."

"No they didn't, but then that's what we always tell ourselves afterwards."

I took a drag off my fifth cigarette of the morning. I usually went through them faster when I was sitting still somewhere with little to occupy me.

"Doesn't make it any less true," Gordon replied.

He had saved my life the other night and yet I still found myself making fine moral distinctions with him. To make up for it, I grinned and made a gesture of capitulation with my right hand. The burn from the cigarette drifted up between my fingers, creating the appearance that I was offering a handful of lazy smoke.

"Right," I said. "It doesn't make it any less true. You did what you had to do, and I wouldn't be alive if you hadn't. Now we each live with it."

"It's the price we pay."

"Its more than that. It's the burden of sin we accept when we pick up the gun, and we'll carry that for eternity."

Gordon was silent for a moment and then he changed the subject: "You haven't said anything about Hamilton, but if Hap Johnson and Harry Sawyer sent you out here, I have to figure there's a connection to the kidnapping of this St. Paul financier."

I pursed my lips around the Chesterfield and drew beautiful smoke into my lungs. Gordon was a friend and I was indebted to him, but he didn't need to know everything there was to know. I phrased my words so as to be intentionally vague: "If Hamilton has been released, then it means somebody paid the ransom."

"That's the way I figure it – most certainly his rich wife. I wonder how Sawyer will split the cash?"

I ignored the challenging look in his eyes. "I wonder too," I replied coolly and took another slow pull on the cigarette.

"I also wonder where the child is and why he wasn't returned along with his father?"

Gordon had read the article carefully and picked up on the one detail that most caught my attention.

"Stepfather," I corrected. "It's the very piece of this puzzle that matters the most."

Gordon stared at me impassively for good bit while he drank some coffee. "I doubt that," he said. "In fact, it probably doesn't matter to anyone other than his mother – and to you. I know how you are about

126

matters of the conscience, especially if a vulnerable creature is involved, like a child, or a wet dog."

"Funny," I said without smiling.

"Not to you. Nothing ever is. If there's a hanging thread you'll pull it until the entire garment unravels. I don't know why, but it's your way. What are you going to do?"

I thought for a moment. "First, I am going to speak with his mother."

"And then what?"

"Then we'll see."

"Know what you're looking for?"

I shrugged. "No, I guess not. I'm trying to understand Hamilton, his wife, and the boy. There's something there that will explain this and when I find it, I think I'll know."

"This is bigger than Hamilton and his domestic troubles. He's connected to someone or some group bigger than he is, much bigger."

"I know. If you have a better suggestion on where to go next, I'll be glad to listen."

With the coffee mug paused below his lower lip, Gordon shook his head and allowed himself a rueful smile. "I know you're going to champion for the boy, but jeez, Duncan, be careful. Don't let your ideas about duty and obligation get you killed."

"They never have."

"What is he to you?"

"For one, he was never a part of the deal I agreed to – I would never have signed on to kidnap a child. For another, he's a sad-eyed kid who deserves something better than some of the rotten breaks he's been handed. He never deserved to be treated like someone's possession. You could see in his face what that did to him."

"Sounds like you became attached."

I shrugged with a nonchalance I didn't feel. "If I can, I want to see him back safely."

"Do you think talking with his mother will help?"

"Maybe."

"So, what are you going to do? You can't simply show up on her doorstep."

"Indeed," I responded as I stubbed yet another cigarette. "That's exactly what I intend to do."

Without being dramatic about it, Gordon repositioned in his chair and looked at me silently. There was something about his eyes that reflected a doubting thought and I knew he had something to say. His lips moved, but no sound came out.

I waited quietly, feeling myself begin to float in that relaxed zone I found every time before the action began. My eyes were soft and my hands calm and ready.

Finally, Gordon cleared his throat to speak and his words chilled me: "This will embarrass you, but I'll say it anyway: I've known plenty of people who thought they walked with God, and not that you think that, but you're about the only one I've ever known who actually just might."

A gust of cold air came in through the window and scattered the newspapers that were spread out on the table, sending many of them gliding towards the floor. Then the air was still and I felt hot again.

Slowly the hairs on the back of my neck began to lie down.

Chapter Eighteen

After breakfast, when the cigarettes were all smoked and coffee was gone, I packed up quickly. Gordon offered to join me, but it was my affair ahead now, not his. I left him with four thousand dollars in cash, which he tried to decline, and an agreement to meet up again soon to set up a couple of scores he had been casing. We agreed to go with a four-man crew on the next run, including Isaac and another reliable man that we both knew. I promised to return with the firearms and ammunition we'd need, obtained through my contact in San Antonio.

"Hey partner," Gordon said at the door with his hand extended. His face was calm, though his eyes held the welling tears of a man trying hard not to reveal emotions felt deeply. A taut gray line quivered between us.

"I'll see you in a few weeks," I assured him. "We'll get back to our work then."

"We've got that business in Kansas City, but you've got something larger standing before you before we get there."

"I'll manage."

"Good luck, and I hope to see you in KC."

"I appreciate what you did for me."

"You sure I can't come along for the ride now?"

"Thanks for the offer, but no. You've already done enough, more than I should ever have asked of you."

"I don't mind."

"I know. You're a true partner."

"I'm a professional with a job to get back to."

I nodded. "But it's more than that."

Our hands were still clasped. "I don't have the words," Gordon said with grit in his tone.

"You don't need them," I replied. "I'll be in touch soon."

Then I took the Ford out of storage and headed down toward Belmont and Lincoln.

The morning was just as hot as the ones that had come before it. Wavy streaks of heat and light reflected off the lake and penetrated into the squared lines of concrete that formed the urban jungle. I drove into the city cautiously, a superstitious native, feeling my way tentatively through the familiar roadways, though traffic was still relatively light at that hour.

Ahead of me a siren blared and then faded as it moved away from me. For just a moment I wondered at its purpose – a fire, a crime, a medical emergency? Somewhere in the city, someone had suffered an unanticipated misfortune, perhaps one that would shatter their life forever, or end it entirely.

*

Sullivan's tavern was practically bustling by its usual standards when I pushed in the door. Three elderly gentlemen sat together at one end of the bar, laughing together over some blue comment one of them had made. Four other patrons were spread along the bar and there were two small groups having early lunches in the rear section of the tavern. Tie knots were loosened and hats were askew.

I took the last table in the back and lit a cigarette while I waited for Jimmy to appear. The joint was hazy with smoke and now I contributed to it. I was almost finished with the first tobacco stick when Jimmy came out through the swinging kitchen door with a polite half-smile on his face. Along with the expression, he wore a short white apron and carried a tray filled with steaming plates of food.

There was a slight ripple of approval from the table he served. After he delivered the plates and cleared dishes from another table, he headed back into the kitchen with the tray. I knew he'd seen me and I waited patiently for his return.

Five minutes later, Jimmy came back out through the kitchen door and stepped over to the bar where he retrieved two mugs of beer. He had a damp towel thrown back over one shoulder. I noticed his stride was shorter on the left side as moved slowly in my direction.

"Hiya," he said, easing into the chair across from me.

"How's the draft today?" I inquired, pulling one of the cold mugs

130

across the table with a finger hooked through the handle.

"Pretty much the same as it ever is. It's a fresh keg, though a bit too much foam and still sour as my grandmother's green apples."

"Sorry for the surprise visit," I told him.

"Not at all, it's always a pleasure – you know that."

His almond eyes looked at me thoughtfully – twin fountains of patience and grace.

"You have customers today, more than usual."

"Relax, they're okay, just regular folks from the neighborhood. They won't gripe any if I sit for a few minutes." The polite half-smile formed again. He wore it for a lot of different occasions and I didn't read much into it.

"Everyone deserves a break now and then," I said.

"Yeah, something like that. How are you?"

"Well enough."

"You've had a tough few months. I've worried."

"Nothing I can't handle with enough gin and .45 caliber bullets."

"With you, that's got to be a lot of gin. Do you need your valise? It'll take me a little while to get it here."

Jimmy kept a locked case for me. It contained emergency cash, contact information, false driver's licenses, and such. It also held a back-up pistol and ammunition in case I ever needed one on short notice. He was my safety deposit box, a necessary element of the life I'd chosen to live. There were plenty of other thieves, robbers, and crooks in my line who didn't keep such a back up. But few of them would roam the streets free for long. Along with the obvious benefits of having the money set aside if I needed it, the money could also be used to pay a lawyer, a bribe, or a ransom if any of those needs ever arose.

I shook my head in answer to Jimmy's question and raised the mug. The foam head had settled somewhat by now.

"Cheers," I whispered and took a long pull off the top. Afterward I had to fight the urge to make a face. "I think you described it right well."

"Only the best for our customers."

"Whose your supplier?"

"This is Chicago. You know well enough who it is. There's not any choice about it in this neighborhood."

I understood what he meant: the tyranny of all those little corruptions kept a foot on our collective throats. "Low quality product," I said, "but at least it's expensive."

131

Jimmy smiled ruefully and raised his own mug again. I took another long swallow and then set the glass down on the table in front of me. Without saying anything more, I found the pack of Chesterfields in my breast pocket. I tapped it once to loosen them and tilted it so that a couple of them leaned out for easy access. Jimmy selected one and I took the other.

We smoked for a while without speaking. Between puffs, he held the butt of the cigarette pinched between his thumb and forefinger, with the burning end pointed back at the center of his chest. The smoke drifted up slowly to his face, teasing his nostrils and irritating his eyes. Maybe it was the only one he'd have time to smoke all day and this was his way of enjoying it.

"How's Helen?" I asked eventually.

Squinting his eyes a little, Jimmy took another drag off the cigarette before he answered. "Pretty much the same as last month, only worse. She's sliding down gradually into a place that she won't come out of if she reaches it."

"Is there much pain?"

His almond eyes filled and he closed them quickly, blinking to hold back a rushing flood. "Yes," he said in a voice that was almost a whisper. "And there's nothing I can do about it."

"It's the hardest part, the helplessness, the watching and the waiting without being able to do anything."

"Yes," he said simply and it sounded like more of a hiss than a word from the English language. When he opened his eyes, I could see the anger there. It smoldered and then receded quickly. But the tears remained and slowly several of them made their way down the cheeks on both sides of his face.

"We pray," he told me. "We pray together, every morning, every night. She can't make it to church any more, but the parish priest visits a couple of times each week and I read the Bible to her—mostly from the Books of John and the Corinthians. It's a comfort."

"It isn't enough, though."

"It's some comfort. Her strength is fading and I worry her faith will fail next. It hasn't dimmed yet, but my greatest fear is that it will. How could she stand it then?"

"How could you?"

"I ask myself that question."

"Is it time to let the doctors operate?"

Jimmy released a long, slow sigh and he put the cigarette out gently into a flat tin ashtray that sat in the middle of the table between us. "It's no sure thing for her. They simply cannot say what it will do."

"But there's a chance?"

He nodded. "And we'll have to take it. This is no life to live, not any more, not broken like this. But—"

"You can you afford it," I said, interrupting him.

He shrugged in a manner that was hard to read and then slowly shook his head from side to side.

I reached out to rest the palm of my hand on the back of his forearm. "Get her the best," I told him. "The best of everything – the best doctors, the best hospitals, the best place to recuperate. Take her south, where the air is warm and dry, or wherever she wants to go – when she's ready. Get her everything she needs. Lavish her."

"All that costs money, Mr. Duncan, and a lot of it. I don't have it, not even close to it, not if I saved for a hundred years."

"Your partners do," I told him. "You'll have thirty thousand coming in a week or so. It's a promise I'll make to you. If you need cash sooner, dip into the valise."

"It's too much. I could never pay you back."

"Brother, you already have, in spades."

Jimmy bowed his head for a moment and then he raised his chin so that it was high enough that he had to look over the end of his nose to stare across the table at me. We didn't speak for a long time. My mind filled with floating blue smoke and lush, sorrowful music – the Fletcher Henderson orchestra was still coming to me.

"Do you ever think about that boy?" Jimmy asked. He didn't specify which boy, but I knew he was talking about the boy in the bank.

"All the time," I told him.

"It haunts me," he said. "It fills my dreams."

"Me too," I said. "I see his face in my sleep; I see it when I look in the mirror; it hovers near me every time I pick up my gun. But there's nothing we can do to undo it."

"You understand why I had to get out?"

"Of course. It never was the right line of work for you anyway."

I finished my beer and lit another cigarette. When I offered the pack of Chesterfields to him again, Jimmy declined. His eyes glistened now. "Do you remember," he started, "the day Colt's kid sister, Elinore, followed you all the way home from the drugstore?"

133

"She was only twelve and she had that silly haircut."

"And you were closing in on eighteen, but you'd bought her an ice cream at the soda counter and she just took to you from that moment on."

"Yes, and it was a mistake on my part. She was only a kid."

"Aw, you were trying to be a nice guy—and she was Colt's baby sister. It was a kind gesture."

"Don't kid yourself. Even then I had a feeling about her that ran all the way down to my toes."

"Not desire?"

"Of course not. But there was this tight connection between us, even then, like our hearts beat together."

Jimmy nodded as though he understood and he probably even did. Without expression now he watched me with a simple plainness. "I remember after that she used to visit you and the two of you would sit on the steps in front of your house in the evening, talking all the while. We all wondered what the two of you could have been talking about."

"Pipe dreams, just silly pipe dreams, and nothing more."

"You waited ten years."

I shrugged. "There were a couple of prison stints mixed in there. Otherwise, maybe things would have gone differently."

"Still, it's remarkable. I'm sorry she's dead now—it must be hell for you."

"Jimmy, we each have our own bit of hell to deal with."

"We have our faith that comforts."

I felt my lips tightening. "I do have my faith, though often it's more of a haunting than a comfort to me."

"You may recall I quoted Corinthians once before," Jimmy said in a voice that had dropped to a whisper. "There is another passage I keep close to me: *'Charity suffereth long, and is kind; charity envieth not; charity vaunteth not itself, is not puffed up.'*"

*

I finished my beer and set a five-dollar bill, folded roughly in half, beneath it. Immediately it curled and changed color from the condensation that was pooled under and around the glass mug.

"I need to leave now," I said. "I have another stop to make."

134

"You don't pay for your beer here."

I ignored this. "There's a guy down on Clark Street," I explained. "His name is Torresi. If something happens to me, you go see him in a couple of weeks – two, or three at the most. He'll have something for you. It will be yours."

"You think he'll just give it to me, with no questions asked?"

"Sure, there will be one question and it will be a very simple question for you to answer."

Jimmy waited patiently, without expression, for me to tell him what that question was.

"He'll ask you what you intend to use the money for."

"What's the answer?"

"Give him the truth – isn't that usually best?"

As I went out the door into the blinding sunlight I remembered how, just a month ago, Jimmy's wife had promised to light a candle for Elinore and for me. *My sweet Elinore* – she was gone now. My heart was still broken, and even with all the cash in my pocket I felt a destitution that words could not describe.

Chapter Nineteen

After I left Sullivan's, I drove over to Clark Street where the usual odors of rotten vegetables and exposed garbage were especially pungent in the high heat of the early afternoon. It was not yet even one o'clock. I looked up at the sky and drew a deep breath before I slid open the door and went in. It was empty and dark inside. The scent of gasoline and motor oil lay heavy in the still, cool air that had collected there.

Gino Torresi let out a low, dropping whistle when I walked into his office at the back of the old garage.

"Man, are you hot," he exclaimed, fanning himself with an old theater flyer.

Torresi was a long-time gunman for the Outfit who had risen up through the ranks and served closely under Frank Nitti now that Capone was pulling library duty in Alcatraz. We had worked together, amiably enough, in the near past.

He was a huge man and his thick facial features contorted into a rare grin as he watched me pull over a chair and find myself a Chesterfield. When I had it lit and balanced well enough on the edge of my lip, I crossed my legs and leaned back in the chair to look about the office.

It was a cramped space, without much furniture and even less sense of style. Cases of booze and cigarettes were stacked two deep along one wall and last year's calendar still hung above them. It featured a very blue photograph, but I didn't study it carefully because I'd seen it before and didn't need to be impressed again.

"Still drinking that Canadian rotgut?" I asked after I was settled.

Torresi gestured towards a bottle that sat nearer to my edge of the desk than to his. The bottle was half empty and the cork was protruding most of the way out.

I shook my head. "Too early for the hard stuff," I told him. "And anyway, I prefer American whiskey."

"It's late enough somewhere on this lonely planet."

"Still with the cynical attitude? Back to where we started when I came in: Why do you think I'm so hot? It's been a while since anyone considered me for a popularity contest."

"Word is those two East Chicago dicks that were found smeared on a sidewalk had gone to a meet with you."

"That's the word is it?"

Torresi nodded and stretched his hands behind his neck. He wore a wrinkled navy blue linen suit. It was the only suit I'd ever seen him wear and I knew he had probably been wearing it since at least the day before. "Mind you," he explained, "the word isn't spread too far and wide, but it's what I heard somewhere. Of course you hear a lot of things in this business, much of it worth no more than a plug nickel. For instance, plenty of folks seem to think it was Johnny Dillinger himself they went off to meet. That at least makes for happy writing in the newspapers, even if it is nonsense of the first degree. Was it your handiwork?"

"I didn't shoot them," I promised.

"Well and carefully phrased, though in truth I didn't think it was quite your style. Anyway, just so you know, there are no tears here at this end. We won't even be sending flowers. Those two boys were dirty as the day is long and they were starting to get ambitions, big ambitions. From what I know, they were on everybody's list."

"Seems you really miss them."

"Their fate was inevitable – just a matter of time."

"Okay, well enough – all that's nice to have as background noise. Now you're going to tell me why I'm so hot? It's not all because of two dead cops."

A bare squint formed at the corner of Torresi's left eye.

"Let me put it this way." He paused to reach for the bottle of Canadian and took his time uncapping it and pouring out a good splash into a tumbler. Some of it dripped down the neck of the bottle and splashed onto some of the papers that were on the desk. Torresi didn't give any indication that he noticed. "Any time Dutch Sawyer and Hap Johnson are mixed up with East Chicago law enforcement, you can bet that something very big and very hinky is in the works. You want to talk about it? I can listen and keep my mouth shut later."

Leaving out most of the names, I gave him the general story, quickly, in very broad strokes. While I talked, Torresi didn't utter a word and his expression did not change. Occasionally, he took small ceremonial sips of the whiskey. There was little evidence that he actually managed to swallow much of the stuff. When I finished speaking, he set the tumbler down on the desk gently and clasped his hands behind his neck again and looked up towards the ceiling. It didn't float away.

For a long while, he didn't speak. Finally he asked me one short question: "Did you bring the bonds with you?"

Nodding, I set the opened package on the table in front of him. "You have a keen mind," I told him.

With just enough motion to reach the package, he thumbed through it quickly with one hand and then looked up at me. "Didn't think you came here merely to swap stories. I know a little about these bonds, where they came from, and who they belong to now."

"They belong to me now," I corrected him.

"Right. I can see that. But you need me to fence them for you."

I nodded.

"How much do you want for them?"

I named a figure.

"A man could retire on that amount."

"I might at that."

"Don't kid a kidder. Anyway, it's high."

"It's not high. Your profit will be more than twice mine."

"This is complicated. More so than usual."

"Tell me about it."

"Uh-uh. I can't. But I can tell you that I can't be known to have fenced these because there are others who would claim them. I have to be more careful than usual and do this through intermediaries, who will also take a share. The risk to me if I'm discovered is not insignificant."

"I see."

It occurred to me that perhaps he was referring to his own bosses within the Chicago Outfit. I countered with a sum that was twenty percent lower than my initial offer.

"It's still too high," Torresi said.

"I don't think so, and it gives you the extra slack you need to pay your intermediaries."

Torresi considered this probability and then nodded. "Okay. We can do business. But I cannot pay you now; you'll have to wait until after we move them and have the cash in hand."

"Acceptable. There's one more thing," I said.

"What now? You want it delivered to you dipped in chocolate on a silver platter with roses?"

"No, those wouldn't mean anything to me."

"I thought you were a romantic."

"You've confused me with someone else," I sighed.

"Confused you? Never. What is this one other thing?"

"I may send someone else to pick up the payment when it's ready."

Torresi's eyebrows notched up a bit. "Really, an intermediary? You mean there's someone else in this world that you actually trust to handle your money."

"That's right. I trust Jimmy. Unless I ask for it first, you're to give it to him. Whether I'm alive or dead, if he shows up you give it to him."

"Does Jimmy have a last name?"

"I'm sure he does, but you don't need to know it."

"How will I be sure he's the right Jimmy?"

"You ask him what he's planning to use the money for."

"And the correct answer is ... ?"

"He'll explain that it's to pay the doctors and the hospital – his wife needs an operation."

"Back to the story of your life, which interests me – you don't know who betrayed you, or why?" Torresi asked.

"What can the 'why' ever be?"

"Usually it's money, and lots of it."

"Yes, and once in a while a little revenge or sex gets mixed in for good measure."

"In either case, there's usually a woman involved. At least that's how it is with Italians."

"That's how it is with everyone."

"You have a point." We sat quietly while Torresi dug out a crumpled cigar from his breast pocket and entered into the usual routine to get it going. Once he had it going, he looked at me as if he had a new idea: "For starters, it's either Dutch Sawyer or Hap Johnson, or both. You didn't mention their names, but the little birdies in the trees out there are singing them bright and loud. There may be others involved, but you can put money that at least one of them is involved in it, though he's probably not the main ingredient."

"Do you have a preference?"

Torresi puffed on the cigar while he considered the question. "I like Hap Johnson. He's the greedier of the two and he might need it more. Word is that he's ambitious, perhaps too ambitious. I understand it's why he had to leave Chicago a couple years back. Sawyer has a pretty nice gig up there, not much reason he'd want to risk messing it up by double-crossing someone as dangerous and potentially annoying as you can be."

"Unless he calculated that East Chicago would take care of me."

"Unless that."

We were quiet for a while.

"Who else is involved?" Torresi asked finally.

"And you won't remember any of this later?"

Torresi shrugged modestly.

"Three others," I told him. "Hamilton – the purported victim in the scheme – Murphy Pendleton, and Isaac Runyon. Their names mean anything to you?"

He nodded slowly while his eyes and the cigar smoke drifted up towards the ceiling. His large eyes might have been tinged with sadness, but I couldn't tell for sure and it would have been out of character for him.

"Give me a minute to think about it," Torresi said, still gazing upwards.

He held the cigar perpendicular to his lips, which were parted slightly. His eyelids bunched in folds and there were rapid movements beneath them.

While his brain was exerting itself, I allowed my eyes to wander around the room. They came to a stop when they reached the calendar on the wall. It was a pleasant enough picture to stare at for a while.

"One of these days you should update your calendar," I said.

"Why is that? What she's doing will never go out of style."

I allowed myself to study the picture more closely than I had previously. It was a professional photograph of a very beautiful platinum blonde who was wearing only her white stockings and a pearl necklace that swung out a few inches from her throat as she leaned forward. Her hair was styled in a high bob, with tight shiny curls. She was on her knees, enthusiastically performing an act with a man that was illegal in most of the 48 states.

"I know her," I said.

Torresi chuckled and sat forward with the cigar held out in front of him now with the back of his wrist flat on the desk. "If you know Evelyn Bays, then you know the very best."

My eyes remained focused on the calendar until I looked away and caught the intrigued look in Torresi's eyes.

"What else?" I asked him.

"If you know Evelyn, then you also know trouble. She's kept regular company with the Irishman for the past couple of years—not so much as a traditional love interest, mind you, but as an employee. She provides

141

him with a range of services."

"The Irishman? Is he back in town?" Hard thoughts jarred through me.

Torresi took a slow puff off the cigar and sidled his head. "No one knows. He's somewhere, and strings are being pulled."

"This gets better at every twist," I sighed. "Is there anything else I should know?"

"Just one more thing. I didn't make the connection right away, but when you started sharing more of the details, it came to me …"

Torresi rummaged around on his desk for something. He had to move the ashtray and the tumbler aside, and then he found it beneath a fanned arrangement of legal-sized folders.

"Did you see this?" he asked quietly. "It's in the afternoon edition of the *Tribune*. Brace yourself for it because it's not pretty."

He folded the newsprint a couple of times to frame the story he intended to show me and passed it across the desk. I took it from his hand and stared at it. My stomach dropped into free-fall.

Another gangland murder in St. Paul had made the headlines. It was a nightmarish image: a pair of vagrants had found the remains of Isaac Runyon stuffed inside a barrel that had been left in an abandoned field behind one of the crummier neighborhoods on the west side. Isaac's throat had been slashed through to the bone and his torso was virtually drained. His body had then been folded in half at the waist and savagely forced into the barrel, possibly even before he was dead. The first thing the vagrants saw when they found him was the near worn-through leather soles of his shoes sticking up out of the top of the barrel. Blood, mixed with other bodily liquids, still oozed from between the staves.

Torresi gave me a moment before speaking.

"This is more than murder – it's a message. It's very Sicilian: revenge and terror. That's the treatment Giuseppe Morello, the 'Clutch Hand', used to give to traitors when he ran New York during the first two decades of this century."

I swallowed. "Isaac didn't betray anybody."

"In that case the message is probably meant for you."

"You said it's Sicilian. Are you sure it's not Irish?"

The Italian mobster shook his large head. "I'm not sure of anything. It could be the Irishman's work. He was in New York during those years and he learned a lot from the Sicilians, even employs a few of them still to this day."

I lit a cigarette and sat smoking it quietly while I thought it over.

"You have a history with the Irishman," Torresi said to me. "After what you did to him and his organization last month, he can't let you have a pass. You killed his right-hand gunman, along with several others, sent him into hiding, and crippled his operations. I know we've encroached. Others probably have too. He has to punish you and it has to be public so that others will know."

"He had a girl murdered."

As I spoke the words the crushing memory came back to overwhelm me once again. A vision of Elinore's still body on the couch where I found her with the empty laudanum bottle nearby cleaved my soul. Shards of existential fury cut me, leaving one half a grieving seeker of redemption, and the other half now one of the detested Others – a remorseless killer, with an unquenchable Old Testament thirst to take the eye in exchange for the one that had been taken from me. Everything blurred before me. I closed my eyes and waited. The voices came and I heard them. When I opened my eyes I was sweating heavily.

"I know," Torresi said to me after a moment, as my focus returned. I looked at him. "He killed the woman you loved, but only after you stole her from him. That too would be an unforgivable betrayal in his mind."

"Where does it end?" I asked, though I already knew the answer.

"With violent death – yours or his."

I nodded and took a last drag off my cigarette.

"What are you going to do now?" Torresi asked.

I handed the newsprint back to him and stood up.

"Tonight I'm driving back to the Twin Cities. I'm going to find the child."

As I left the garage and stepped out blinking onto the bright and reeking street, I realized I had my hand inside my jacket, gripping the handle of my .45 automatic. The cool feel of the metal and ebony grips against my fingers offered little solace against the horror that had gathered around me. The sky burned brightly above and then seemed to drop suddenly, pressing down upon me with its full heat.

Chapter Twenty

At twenty-seven minutes after two o'clock on a hot Thursday afternoon, I swung a large brass knocker against the massive front door of the house where Mr. and Mrs. Kenneth Hamilton lived in Minneapolis. It was a virtual castle, set on a graded hill about a quarter mile back from the street. Granite columns and other quarried stone fronted the structure and ensured its remoteness from the surrounding neighborhood. I'd never been there before and had never met Mrs. Hamilton, but it wasn't hard to find the home of a woman of her wealth and status.

The door was opened by a very tall, bald man with slender shoulders and a face that managed to be serious and intriguingly calm at the same time. He was dressed well, in a dark suit and tie, with polished black shoes. If I'd met him on a train I could easily have believed he was a university dean or some other important position with intellectual gravitas. Cold gray eyes told me he'd seen everything and more in his days on the job. His lips were thin and contoured evenly to avoid the appearance of either a smile or a frown.

I asked to speak with Mrs. Hamilton.

"Whom shall I say is calling?" His voice was low and without any trace of a regional accent or judgment.

"I'd give you my business card, but they don't print them for kidnappers."

He didn't even blink.

"Please wait right here," he said and closed the door lightly in my face.

Two minutes later he was back and I was led through a wide foyer with lacquered parquet flooring, past a spiral staircase constructed of marble, and into a formal sitting room on the shaded side of the house. We stopped together in a square of sunlight on the hardwood floor, just inside the glass-paneled French doors that framed the entrance to the room.

"Mrs. Hamilton will be with you shortly," the butler said patiently. "My name is Northwood. Please let me know if there is anything you need."

"Thank you, Northwood. Maybe you can tell me something. Has

there been any word on the boy? It seems awful quiet for a house with a missing child."

"I'm sorry, sir, I do not have any information regarding this concern."

"Then I may take it that he has not been found?"

"You may, sir."

"What do you know about the child?" I asked.

"Young Wilson is an intelligent young man. He is well-behaved and much loved by his mother."

"You've been educated somewhere."

"I have."

"What about Mr. Hamilton?"

Northwood allowed his lips to form a preliminary smile that told me nothing, while his immobile gray eyes told me even less. "I'm quite sure he loves the child too."

"How is Mr. Hamilton holding up after his own ordeal?"

"He returned to the office the day after he was recovered."

"Takes his work seriously?"

"Yes, sir. His work is very important."

"There's a thing or two about this … I'm puzzled about why Hamilton isn't here to be with his wife, why there aren't police or federal agents here, why there isn't a command post in the house waiting for telephone calls. I would've thought a kidnapped child would evoke more evidence of concern, perhaps more bustle around the household."

The butler didn't reply. The preliminary smile remained in place. It was all I was going to get from him.

"Thank you," I said. "I suppose there's nothing further you can tell me."

Northwood nodded, bowed slightly, and then backed away to leave me quietly to myself.

*

I settled into an upholstered wingback chair and waited with my hands folded on my lap. The windows of the room were opened over a private garden area filled with petunias and delicate herbs, and three ceiling fans managed to circulate the air nicely.

While I sat and looked about, small details caught my attention: a phonograph played Mozart from a distant room; the wallpaper told the story of a nineteenth century British hunting party; cut glass knobs were anchored to the windows and doors; and centering the room was a Persian rug with a crème-colored base and green and red-inflected geometric designs around the edging.

There were no photographs or family portraits. The room was cool enough with the windows open and it pushed cooler with the effect of the interior design. Nothing in the room suggested a nine-year old boy had ever lived in the house.

For ten minutes I waited quietly, enjoying the Mozart and the coolness of the room. It almost seemed that I couldn't remember a time when I'd felt such an absence of heat. When the door opened, I stood up. Northwood came in first and announced Mrs. Hamilton who stepped in right behind him and stood apart for a moment to look at me from across the room. Then she strode in with the purpose of a woman who believes she knows what is right, not only for herself, but also for others.

She was a matronly woman with a square face and large brow, at least six to eight years older than her husband. A wide cheekbone structure held her facial features together loosely, and a large, full-lipped mouth accentuated an appearance of determination. Her eyes were dark green, and not of the piercing quality, but with a sharp tinge of intelligent watchfulness. The way she studied me would have made most people feel small and insignificant. I wondered if she looked at her husband the same way. The birthright vestiges of wealth and privilege hung about her in a way that I suspected made it difficult for her to relate to the other people. Her relations to others would be colored by money and power, leaving her remote and envied.

"I'm Abigail Hamilton, Wilson's mother," she said with her hand extended toward me.

I took it and replied, "Ross Duncan."

"Is that your real name?"

"No, ma'am, it is not."

"Your face is vaguely familiar to me. I presume you are a criminal and your face has been in the newspapers?"

"Yes."

"What sort of crimes do you commit?"

"A swell variety, though bank-robbing is my primary claim to notoriety."

"Are you John Dillinger?"

"No, ma'am, I never have been."

Her eyes refocused after a moment, assessing me further. "Have you seen my son?"

"Yes, Mrs. Hamilton, I have. I'm the man who kidnapped him along with your husband."

"Why have you come to my home?"

"Because," I started, "I want to find your son and bring him back to you, and I believe that speaking with you might help me in that. May we sit?"

She nodded and rearranged two small throw pillows on the divan so that when she was seated it was directly across from me and with her eyes at the same level as mine. A pair of reading glasses hung about Mrs. Hamilton's neck. She perched these on the tip of her nose and looked at me over them and studied me patiently. Above us the ceiling fans twirled quietly, circulating the air.

"Before Northwood leaves us, would you like something to drink?"

Hard eyes of the temperance movement watched me as I considered the question.

"If you have ice, I'd take any cold drink that does not include alcohol."

It was subtle, but I thought I glimpsed the corners of her eyes softening a little. She addressed Northwood, "Bring us each an iced tea, please."

Northwood bowed slightly without further revelation and left the room. I looked at Mrs. Hamilton who was still watching me, though more cordially now, with prayer hands clasped before her.

"I have several questions for you," I started. "But first, I understand that I need to provide you with more explanation and tell you what I know about your son."

"Indeed you do."

I looked about the room before starting. Finding no suggestions there I opened with the statement I'd been rehearsing all the way from Chicago: "Mrs. Hamilton, I am a professional thief and a bank robber. I have not participated in any kidnapping before this one. Someone I trusted convinced me to join a gang on this job after it was already set up. As you probably know from the newsreels, robbing banks has become a bit more, shall we say, adventurous recently."

"By that you mean dangerous."

"Yes."

"It should be dangerous. It's awful business, what you do. The Federal authorities are making a dedicated effort to put all of you out of business. And they will too, eventually. It's high time."

"Yes, ma'am."

"Mr. Hoover is a very serious man."

I didn't express my opinion of Mr. Hoover. Instead, I proceeded with my story: "My partner was killed earlier this spring during a robbery and though I wouldn't do it again, a kidnapping job seemed both safe and lucrative. It also seemed like it would be relatively safe and easy. This one was arranged by powerful people right here in St. Paul and I was persuaded to join them. Here's the thing: we didn't set out to kidnap your child – only your husband. I'm the one who picked them up on the road in Iowa, exactly where their automobile was later found. There was no force or threat involved. Your husband's Packard appeared to have road trouble and I merely offered him a ride, which he accepted quite willingly."

"My husband says you pointed a machine gun at them and forced them into the boot of your Ford."

"Your husband lied. He has lied to you about many things."

Mrs. Hamilton nodded without comment, accepting my statement at face value. I knew she was cataloguing it for further discussion once I was finished with my narrative.

I continued: "Your husband willingly took the passenger seat of my Ford, pretending to believe that I was offering him a ride to the next town over. Wilson, who had been sleeping in the Packard, laid down on my backseat and soon fell asleep again. We drove to a farmhouse where my collaborators waited for us. When we arrived your husband informed me that not only was he participating in his own kidnapping, he had planned it. In fact, he claimed it was his idea to begin with."

"That is preposterous," Mrs. Hamilton declared, though her voice carried little conviction. She removed the reading glasses from her nose and let them hang from her neck again.

"Is it?"

"Why would he do that?"

"That's what I came to talk with you about."

"Why should I even believe you?"

I didn't respond at first. "Mrs. Hamilton," I began slowly. "Obviously I am here at great risk to myself. Why would I take that risk unless I had a compelling reason?"

"Continue."

"We held your son and your husband for several days there at that location. On the third morning I awoke to find that the others had deserted me and another accomplice, taking your son and husband with them. Obviously, this was a surprise, a double-cross, and probably not the first or the last one in their plan. I don't know where they went, but once we realized what had happened we left immediately. Before the hour was out, police and other law enforcement officers converged on the farmhouse. You probably read about it in the newspapers, which is where I learned of it."

"I did. We were very hopeful at first. My son had been there at that house?"

"Yes, ma'am, he had, but there was never any chance that he would've been found there – they were long gone before the Law received the tip that sent them there."

"Then what happened?"

I didn't need to tell her every detail of my movements over the past week. I gave her the abridged version. "A few days went by, and then I heard that your husband had been found, but that your son had not been released with him."

"That is correct."

"I assume you paid a ransom?"

She nodded slowly.

"How much did you pay?" I inquired.

"The federal agents advised me not to reveal that to anyone. They said it would make matters potentially more complicated if it got into the newspapers."

I rubbed the flat of my hand across my chin and considered this possibility. "Yes, it might, but, Mrs. Hamilton, it would help me to know the answer to that question. You don't need to worry about me revealing it to the newspapers, or anyone else for that matter. There's no one I could tell."

"How will it help you?"

"Later today I'll talk to some of the other people involved in this crime, some of them are right here in St. Paul, people who helped plot this kidnapping and who assisted with the ransom end of it."

She nodded. "Of course, and it will help you to know for certain how much they received."

I nodded.

"Mr. Duncan, have you received any share of the money?"

"Not a single penny."

"Are you of a mind to collect any of it?"

I shook my head. "I don't believe I will be paid, and if I am, or if I recover any of the money I will return it to you."

"Then I will tell you. I paid one hundred thousand dollars to have both my son and my husband returned alive. My husband's firm matched it with another hundred thousand dollars. That makes a total of two hundred thousand that has been paid. However, as you know, only my husband was released. We have both been deceived by these men."

"Have you heard any further word from the kidnappers about your son?"

Her head shook in slow, tight arc. "There was only a short note, advising me to break off all contact with federal and local law enforcement. It said Wilson would be returned in a few weeks time, once the kidnappers were convinced that I would not make further efforts to find them."

"How was that note delivered?"

"It was delivered by my husband. He carried it with him when he was released."

"Have you complied with it?"

She looked down at her clasped hands and nodded. "Until you knocked on my door this afternoon."

From somewhere in the house clock chimes struck the hour. As if responding to cue, Northwood came in with a silver tray holding two glasses of iced tea. We didn't talk while he placed them on large silver coasters beside each of us and left the room without uttering a word. As I sipped the cold drink, I noticed for the first time that Abigail Hamilton's hands shook terribly as she lifted her own glass to her lips.

"Mr. Duncan, tell me about my child. Was he hurt or distressed in any way?"

"Not during the three days that I was with him. Wilson ate well, slept late into the morning in a nice room that he shared with his stepfather, and he had free roam of the farm. There was no unpleasantness for him that I could see, apart from the heat, which was beastly."

"My husband claimed they were held in shackles, in a dark basement."

I shook my head. "No ma'am, they were always treated like special guests. We fed them well. They ate supper with us at the dining room table right from the very first evening. In the heat of the afternoons your husband helped us chip ice to cool beer, which he drank."

151

This brought a frown. "My husband promised me he had stopped drinking alcohol."

"Mrs. Hamilton, with all due respect, I doubt very much that was ever true."

"Was my Wilson frightened?"

"He was puzzled by the whole get-up, though I doubt he even understood that he'd been kidnapped. His father told him they were our guests until the automobile was repaired."

"What did he do to pass the time during the day?"

"He took dips into the pond and we played checkers. Also, we found a few old baseball gloves in the barn and played catch and talked about the Chicago Cubs."

"They're his favorite team."

"Yes."

"His stepfather never does anything like that with him. Not ever."

I nodded and sipped my iced tea. "Wilson is a fine boy. He asked a lot of questions. We had several very nice chats about things, lots of different things."

"Thank you for that."

I shook my head. "No, don't thank me. I never intended to kidnap the child and I'm sorry for it. Before my accomplices disappeared with him, it had been my intention to take him with me when I left that very same day. I was going to return him to you myself – along with a ransom note for your husband."

She thought about this, and took a polite sip of her tea, watching me with over the rim of her glass all the while. "Mr. Duncan, what happened?"

"I don't know for sure."

"What do you speculate?"

"Certainly, I was betrayed, as was another man working with me. Someone intended for us to be arrested that morning."

"Perhaps so they would not have to share the ransom with you."

"Perhaps."

"Where is my son now?"

Holding the cold glass against my cheek I just shook my head.

"What do you think has happened to him?"

"The note your husband returned with is a part of it. They want to deter you from trying to find them. Every day buys them time."

"Do you suspect my husband is involved in this part of it?"

152

"He was most certainly involved in orchestrating the kidnapping. I don't know if he shares any further complicity in the fact that Wilson hasn't been released."

"But one might follow from the other."

"Yes."

"What do your instincts tell you?"

I had to consider this carefully, not because I was unsure of my instincts, but because I was unsure of what to reveal to the child's mother. "My sense is that your husband does not love the boy and does not care what happens to him. Indeed, he may even resent the boy and his very existence."

"Why would he?"

"How can I answer that?"

"Surely, you have an idea."

"Mrs. Hamilton, I have no training in marital psychology, but I know something about the greed and appetites of men. Why would your husband arrange for himself to be kidnapped?"

"I do not know."

"Does he need money?"

"He is a successful investment banker."

I set my tea down on the silver coaster. "But does he need money?"

"Not that I know of. He made a small fortune in International Match."

"Are you certain of that?"

"I only know what he tells me."

"That was Ivar Kreuger's company, the Swedish match company?"

"Correct."

"He boasted of that to me as well."

"What do you make of that?"

"Mrs. Hamilton, I'm sure you know that International Match was a virtual Ponzi scheme. They came to a bad end. Millions of dollars were lost when they collapsed. Perhaps your husband didn't get out in time?"

"He always said that he did."

"Who sees to your money? Does he control or invest any of it?"

Mrs. Hamilton sniffed cautiously. "I engage an independent brokerage firm for that. Our finances are separate from each other."

"Do you believe he doesn't resent this? A lot of men would."

She didn't know how to answer this question, so she didn't.

I put it to her another way: "Separate finances – that's an uncommon arrangement for a married couple."

"Yes, but not imprudent, wouldn't you say?"

I nodded and drank the last of my iced tea.

"Would you like another glass? I can summon Northwood."

"No, thank you. I just have a few more questions. Can you tell me about your husband, is he a loving husband to you, a loving father to the boy?"

"You have already shared what your instincts tell you about this."

"Yes, and now I'm asking you directly if my instincts are on the money."

Mrs. Hamilton was quiet. She looked down to study her hands and then she raised her chin up and I saw that her eyes were closed. She might have been praying, though I couldn't tell for sure. I waited without speaking while she let the question hang there between us unanswered. It seemed like an hour or two might have gone by in those few minutes that we sat there.

Before she finally spoke, she cleared her throat twice, as if preparing a hymn. "Mr. Duncan, I cannot see any reasonable way of discussing this question in light of what you have told me."

Through the open windows my eyes were drawn to the tranquility of the private garden. Shadows of late afternoon had grown longer and the air was cooler now. A deep calm lay over the petunias and herbs. Even the small birds were singing languidly from the branches of small trees. The sounds were familiar and comforting, the kind of sounds that connected you to prior moments of quiet contentedness.

"Is there anything I can do to help you find my son?" Mrs. Hamilton asked.

I pondered this. "Who is the federal agent in charge of the investigation here in the St. Paul office?"

"That would be Special Agent Trestleman."

"What's your sense of him?"

"He is a strong, raw man who sees his job in realistic terms. There is no sentimentality about him. He is a former Texas Ranger and he rode out on an expedition to find Pancho Villa in his earlier days. I trust him, and I do not think he would hesitate for a moment to understand his job. If you met him, I think you would understand what I mean."

"Do you think he's honest?"

"He is as straight a man as I've ever met."

"Really, a policeman without corruption?"

She considered this question for longer than I thought she would have needed to. Finally she nodded.

"Yes, I believe so."

"But you hesitate?"

"No. I don't hesitate regarding the literal answer to your question. I believe he would do everything necessary to find my son."

"You lost me on that. What do you mean?"

"Exactly as I said: I believe he would do everything necessary to find my son. However, and do not quote me on this, Mr. Duncan, because I say this just between you and I, I do not believe he would be unduly concerned about breaking certain laws to do so."

I smiled at this and nodded several times. "Sounds like my type of lawman."

"Mr. Duncan, make no mistake about him. Allow me to ask you: do you need to smoke?"

I let my smile widen, slightly. "No thank you, ma'am. I'm okay right now."

"Is there something I might assist you with regarding Special Agent Trestleman?"

"Impossible as it may sound, it might help if I could have a conversation with him."

"That does not sound impossible at all. I can arrange it."

"I would need assurances."

"Of course. You shall have them. I believe he would accept whatever I asked of him in exchange for a quiet conversation with you. I will arrange for it to take place right here, in my house tomorrow, perhaps at about this very same time in the afternoon?"

I paused. "Let me think on it first. I'll get back to you tomorrow after I talk this evening with a guy I know."

"Mr. Duncan, are you a religious man?"

Tenderly as I could, I smiled for her in order to reduce the menace of what I was about to say: "Mrs. Hamilton, I'm a confirmed sinner. In my life I've violated most of the Ten Commandments. I haven't been to prayer service since I was a child. Twice I've been convicted of crimes against the state and each time I served a prison term. These sentences did not rehabilitate me.

"Currently I'm wanted by the Federal government and by law enforcement in at least four states for serious crimes that I've committed over the past year and a half, including armed robbery and murder. Few

155

people familiar with me from the newspapers or police blotters would consider me a religious man."

"That does not answer my question. Have you read the Bible yourself?"

I stifled the urge to shrug. "I am reading it now, very slowly, in small bits here and there."

"Then you know that sinners may be redeemed."

"I cannot see any path for that now."

"With Jesus there is always a path for redemption."

"With all due respect, ma'am, that would require me to make changes I can't make at this point."

"You could accept Jesus as your savior."

While I studied the hunting scenes on the wall, I considered this possibility. "Perhaps, but that would interfere with my efforts to find your son."

"I do not understand."

"Mrs. Hamilton," I started. Then I paused to find the right words. "I believe I will have to continue to break several of the Commandments in order to find your son."

She appeared to consider this and then she smiled firmly at me with a hardness around her eyes that almost surprised me. "Break every single one that you need to break to find him. Do whatever you must do."

"Yes," I told her. "I will, though even then I can't assure you I'll succeed."

She nodded with a vulnerable chin. "I accept that. Will you pray with me?"

We bowed our heads while she began a prayer so softly that I could barely hear it:

"Blessed is the Child of Light
Who doth seek his heavenly Father,
For he shall have eternal life.
He that dwelleth in the secret place
Of the Most High
Shall abide under the shadow
of the Almighty.
For he shall give his Angels charge over thee

156

To keep thee in all thy ways ..."

And as she prayed, her voice trailed out so softly that I lost the ability to make out the words for at least one stanza, until she rose again in volume with a sudden lurch that revealed the passion in her heart:

"And how shall this love be severed?
From the beginning
Until the ending of time
Doth the holy flame of love
Encircle the heads
Of the Heavenly Father
And the Children of Light:
How then shall this love be extinguished?
For not as a candle doth it burn,
Nor yet as a fire raging in the forest.
Lo, it burneth with the flame
Of Eternal Light,
And that flame cannot be consumed."

When she finished I rose from the chair. Mrs. Hamilton rose up too and took my arm. Her fingers were porcelain against the sinews of my muscles. We walked together through the house.

Northwood met us in the foyer and held the door open for me without speaking a word. He blended into the background, silent, near invisible beside the grieving mother. Before stepping through the opened door, I stopped and turned to look at Mrs. Hamilton. Her eyes didn't shrink from mine, nor did she appear likely to speak again. Patiently, she waited for me to speak.

I broke the quiet: "You have not commented on my role in the kidnapping."

She responded without hesitating. "Other men plotted this crime. I believe you were sent by the Lord to watch over and protect my son."

I lowered my chin and my voice. "Then I may have failed."

The look in her eyes was braced with steel. "In which case you shall be his avenger."

Chapter Twenty-One

With the bitter aftertaste of Northwood's unsweetened iced tea still lingering in my mouth, I headed straight for the Green Lantern. It didn't take long to get there. Wabasha Avenue was just starting to shudder as the working day drew to a close for those fortunate few blessed with gainful activities. The humdrum throb of failing aspirations and human need beat about me with a dull, subversive persistence.

I went in hard at the outset, whipping one of the muscle boys posted at the door with the barrel of my .45 straight across his cheek as I went past him. He crumpled to the floor, bleeding heavily. I did not pause.

Once inside I found Harry Sawyer standing behind the bar with his sleeves rolled up to his elbows, surveying crates of recently delivered gin that were half unpacked across the bar. His face was already angry and red in the flat angled light of the late afternoon sun that came in through the windowpanes. And that was before he saw the gun in my hand. Tilting rectangles of light flashed about on the wall behind him. I pointed the pistol at him and called his name out loud in order to ensure his attention. He stopped what he was doing and stared at me.

"Come out from around there," I told him, speaking quickly, with my eyes moving fast to survey the room.

"Duncan, this is a big mistake," Sawyer replied as he stepped around the end of the counter.

I watched him carefully to make sure he didn't come out with a gun of his own. He did not. Instead he carried a clipboard, with delivery invoice sheets on it, and a short pencil.

"No mistake, Sawyer," I told him. "We're going to talk."

Because he was turning sideways I could only see him in profile and his right eye glared against the bright dusky sunlight that came in through the window off the horizon. The orange glow deflected against his ruddy skin and caused me to blink against the intensity of the light.

With a pair of rapid glances, I took in the rest of the room again. Because it was early still, only two tables were occupied. One was filled with six men in uniform, off-duty police officers staring into a binge; the other held four well-painted ladies, preparing for business. It was an awkward mix that I confronted now.

159

"This isn't the way we do business here," Sawyer replied. He set the clipboard carefully on the bar with the pencil on top of it, keeping his hands within my sight.

"It's the way I do business now."

"You'll be finished in this town."

I shook my head. "We both know we're way beyond that."

"Where are you going to go?"

Ignoring his question, I glanced quickly at the policemen. They were frozen with indecision, but I could see the startled expressions on their faces beginning to calm. It wouldn't be long before one of them mustered up the courage to do something foolish.

"You men sit still," I ordered them, swinging the muzzle of the .45 in a quick pass over their heads before bringing it back to bear down on Sawyer.

There was a slight click and from the corner of my eye – I saw the movement. An office door had opened and another one of Sawyer's boys stepped out, restless and inarticulate in his intentions. He was a large man in a brown, plaid suit and small-knotted tie. His face rippled with a nervous tic that started at the outside corner of one eye and dropped down to connect with the slope of his neck just beneath the ear.

I moved three steps to my left so that I had a better angle on him and when he pulled up with a Lugar, I shot him once in the thigh from thirty feet across the room. The impact flipped him around and over so that he landed half on his shoulder and then bounced over onto the opposite hip. Blood spouted up and I assumed I'd shattered his femur bone altogether with the force of my large caliber slug.

I didn't let that distract me any and instead pointed the .45 back at the men and women who were now pushing away from their respective tables. I fired a shot into a near full pitcher of beer that rested on the end of the table where the police officers sat. Beer and glass exploded into the air, raining down into the faces of the three men who sat nearest.

"Don't mistake my kindness," I said into the deafening echo of the gunshots. "The next time I pull this trigger it will be with intent to kill. It's best that everyone hold still right where you are for a few minutes."

"Grab your hat, Dutch," I said. "We're going for a ride."

Sawyer drove my Ford while I covered him loosely with the .45. We didn't make conversation. With my eyes only half on the road on the road behind us, I gave occasional directions. Sawyer followed them exactly. He didn't complain or protest. Nobody followed us. The orderly streets of St. Paul parted easily and we made our way across town to the west side where an abandoned field awaited us. When we were parked with the two front wheels well into an area of knee-high weeds I told Sawyer to get out of the automobile first.

I took a breath. Then, with the two forefingers of my left hand, I pointed the way.

We walked a short way.

"Turn around and face me," I said.

Sawyer's angry eyes squinted into the sun as I pushed him backwards across the vacant lot. When we were standing in the middle of the field, near an area where the weeds were matted down from recent activity, I motioned for him to stop.

"Is this where you kill me?" he asked.

I didn't answer his question.

"Recognize where we are?"

"I've never been here before; don't even know this part of town."

"Think about it for a minute." Nothing beyond the anger seemed to register, so I told him: "This is where they found the remains of Isaac Runyon stuffed down into a barrel."

Slowly, it came to him and his expression changed. The anger melted away and was replaced by a different expression, one that I couldn't quite read. Something less than human, it wasn't fear and there was an edge of defiance in it still. Perhaps it was understanding that was starting to show through the cracks of indifference.

"I heard about that," he said.

"Know anything about it?"

He shook his head.

"No. I don't operate that way, never have."

"Convince me. You've had other men killed."

"Never like that, never with such abasement. Isaac was a colleague in my business and he didn't betray me. I wouldn't have done this."

"You know what I want," I told him. My voice was quiet now. The sun was down below the horizon, but there was still ambient light in the sky that allowed me to study Sawyer's mutinous appearance. "Somebody betrayed me and I want to know who."

"It wasn't in my plan. Think about it. Why would I do it?"

"You schemed the kidnapping, you handled the negotiation, and you received the ransom."

Sawyer shook his head again, more vigorously this time, but still without any apparent expression of fear. "No," he said. "I never planned for the child to be taken, or for you to be betrayed. There was no intention to trick you or anyone else. It was a simple plan: kidnap a rich man and trade him back for a lot of money. No one was supposed to be hurt, no child was supposed to disappear. And I didn't receive the ransom, only a partial cut of it."

"How much did you get?"

His grimace was palpable. "I received five grand. Not a penny more."

"So? What happened then?"

"We were both snookered. I'm still waiting on my next payment, which I expect will never come. We both lost out. It happens. You move on. There are other opportunities, other scores. Nobody can win them all."

"Nobody tried to kill *you*."

"I did *not* betray you."

"If not you, then who?"

"Drop it. Let the System settle the account. It works. It always has. That's what it's for."

"Will the System find the child?"

Sawyer closed his mouth and merely stared at me with inhuman eyes. "Do you mind if I smoke?" he asked finally, without responding to my question.

This insolence angered me and I wanted to hurt him. I wanted to hurt him bad. The rage within me had built up to a point where I felt the ability to contain it slipping away. I held up the pistol and held it pointed at a spot between his eyes.

"I won't plead," he said, as he struck a match to the cigarette. He inhaled deeply and then blew the match out as he exhaled. He dropped it to the earth and ground it under his shoe. The motion reminded me, symbolically, of what he'd been doing to everyone who touched him for some twenty or thirty years. "But killing me solves nothing."

"It would remove one ugly, corrupt blot from this earth – you and your System."

"It would change nothing. Don't play the sap anymore than you already have. You think I matter? I don't."

"You are the O'Connor System."

"I'm not. You think killing me would end the System in St. Paul, or anywhere else for that matter? Wise up. There's an O'Connor System everywhere, there always has been. What do you think the Roman Empire was built on? It's no different from the current government, the one that represents itself as a socialistic movement to take care of the little people, the poor people.

"You don't see any government men sleeping on sidewalks or riding the rails, do you? You don't see their lawyers pan-handling in the streets. Sure, they'll redistribute the wealth, hand out just enough to keep people pacified, but they'll also take their rightful cut along the way as they do it. It's what man's entire social order is based on; it's the natural process of selection for survival, and position, and wealth.

"Every city, every state, every government in the world is based on an O'Connor System, and always has been. The weak fall away. You kill me, and there will be ten more just like me, probably worse, who are ready to step right into my position. Do you think my position is the end of it? No. There's a guy behind me, and a guy behind him, and so on. And none of them will blink or even notice if I'm gone. The system will row on forever regardless of anything you or I ever say or do. This moment, right here in this forsaken field means nothing."

I lowered my .45 and stepped up close to his face. He was right, but that didn't mean I had to like it. "Maybe so," I hissed, "but I'm going to finish this. Give me a name. Tell me who I should talk to?"

"Hap Johnson set this job up with Kenneth Hamilton a month ago and he received the ransom. He paid me just enough of the ransom money to stall me."

"Anyone in it with him?"

Sawyer shrugged and looked away from me. There was no particular calculation in his face, only the arrogant belief that he was justified in his cynicism.

"Give me a name!"

"I don't know," he said quietly, suddenly fatigued.

"What's Hamilton's angle?" I asked.

He considered the possibilities and then gave me the answer I expected from him: "I don't know that either," he said. "I really don't know."

163

"You're not even curious?"

"Nope."

I had one last question for Sawyer: "Are there any police or law enforcement officers in this city you have not bought and paid for?"

It was pretty dark now, but even in the fading light I could see Sawyer's eyes narrow slightly. There was a demon within, stoking the fires below, and he was trying hard to contain it. Maybe I'd reached him in some way.

"Try a Federal agent named Trestleman. I've never met the man, but I hear he won't be owned and he does not care if there is a System in this town or not."

From his tone, I knew that was solid.

"Okay, Dutch," I said. "We're finished here. I'll take you back."

We didn't exchange another word. I dropped Harry Sawyer a block from the Green Lantern and then I headed over to the Ryan Hotel. I'd be safe there for one night, but perhaps for no more than that.

Chapter Twenty-Two

With only the dim light from the street and the sky cast into the room, I stood alone at the window holding a glass of straight rye. The music had stopped and all the chairs were taken. Sawyer's words rang in my ears as I struggled with the imponderable blow they struck against the ideal of a loving creator, so primitively conceived and comforting. Was life itself the result of such an indifferent process as the brutal natural selection that he described? How could I accept that?

Perhaps the evidence was on his side. Certainly, the very fossil record itself indicated a natural history of painful death and extinction for innumerable species throughout the eons. Was the divine plan itself, at best, nothing more than a cruel and wasteful prank? Perhaps humans had evolved only by trial and error, with no direct hand of God in their making at all? And perhaps the aggressive cosmology of The book of Genesis itself pointed to the struggle to maintain a social and political order that broke apart at every turn, twisting grotesquely into an O'Connor System that governed the planet. Where was the goodness, the righteousness, that we take for granted as children? It was too bleak for me to bear.

I drank the rye fast and when the glass was empty I poured more.

My thoughts drifted away from the physical reality of the window I stood before. The glass panes became a looking glass into the past, reflecting not my literal image as I stood there, but an earlier image from a formative moment in my life.

One of those nights in the Illinois State Penitentiary came back to me: Lars Hansson had stood at his cage, across the cellblock from me, without speaking for a long period of time. Down the row I could hear various sounds that told me most of his usual audience had lost interest and drifted away to other diversions. But, knowing his moods by now, I'd kept my eyes open, waiting, with the expectation of something interesting to come. I hadn't been disappointed by the story he told me that evening. It sat uncomfortably with the earlier lessons he had shared.

"*There is something else out there,*" Hansson started, "*another force. It's not all dark, you know. There are points of hopeful light—inexplicable moments of time, rare behaviors so selfless that it's hard to imagine they can exist, but they do. Just when you think you can't bear it any longer, sometimes, but only sometimes, one of them comes along to remind and awe you—and it can put you down low with the shame of your own failure.*

"*I don't talk about this often because it doesn't fit into our lives now as we have chosen to live them, but I wasn't always the same man you see before you. When I was younger, emerging from a foolish and idealistic youth, I did a stint in the militia back in the late '90s. You weren't born then, so you probably can't understand the national mood of that era. We were still a young country, still recovering from the Great War between our states, and just discovering our place in a broader world. Some called it an imperial age for our country.*

"*In the weeks after they sank the U.S.S. Maine in Havana Harbor, war fever was catching on everywhere, driven by the yellow journalism of the day and the business interests they aligned with. 'Remember the Maine, to hell with Spain,' was the rally cry. You heard it everywhere and it affected us in an irrational way that seems difficult to understand now, with the perspective of time and age. I'm not sure it was ever really proven that the Spaniards even sunk the Maine, but that was the story then and we all believed it.*

"*Only President McKinley opposed the public demand for war, but he couldn't resist it for long. I signed up with a volunteer state militia right out of Jackson, Michigan, my hometown, and ended up in the mobilization to Cuba.*"

Hansson paused and closed his eyes, gripping the bars in front of him tightly. I thought he was preparing for one of his coughing jags. He stood for a bit of time without coughing and eventually he resumed mouthing the story across the cellblock to me.

"*They sent three hundred thousand of us there on ships. We were only there for a few weeks before the malaria and the dysentery and the plain heat exhaustion set in. It was a horrible place, especially as the tropical summer set in.*

"*Our canned meat was mostly rancid and the flour had weevils in it. They gave us a few steers and told us we'd have to make the beef last for three months. There was no way to keep the cattle—we didn't have feed or land for*

166

them, so we slaughtered them right away. After the steers were butchered each man was issued his share. Luckily for me there were some men in my company who knew how to smoke meat and we were able to rig up a smokehouse. We pretty much survived on beef jerky and flour mush for the next few months ... Stop me if I'm boring you."

I shook my head and waited for him to continue.

"There was a young man in my company, fellow named Claude. I can't remember his surname, can't even remember his face now after so many years. But I remember him. He was only sixteen years old – had lied about his age so that they would take him in the militia. I think he might have been an orphan, so there'd been nobody to speak against his recruitment. He was a nice boy—and still really a boy, not even shaving yet—among all us older fellows. Most of us were eight to fifteen years older than him. He's the one I'm going to tell you about in a minute, he and the woman who saved him, saved a group of us, so hold on to that, but first, well ...

"We were still using Civil War military tactics then—you know, most of our leaders were Civil War veterans, including fat old General Miles who ran the whole show. He had served as a General in the Union Army, won the Medal of Honor at Chancellorsville, I believe. He was a horrible old cuss and we hated him, but we trusted he'd lead us to victory.

"The early fights were small, when we were still sending out skirmishers ahead of the main columns, but they were bad enough. Turns out Civil War tactics weren't very useful. The Spaniards had learned how to fight on the terrain from the past hundred years of battling the Cuban irregulars. None of them lined up to fight in formation like we expected. Instead, they were masters of concealment—setting up small group ambushes and picking us off with their sniper rifles—bolt-action Mausers. And they used the new smokeless powder, which had a very low muzzle flash, so we had trouble sighting down their locations. None of our lead skirmishers ever survived very long out on the point.

"But we were young and naïve, and though individually we were each scared, none of us admitted it. You didn't do that. We pretended that we were brave and tough in the face of the Spanish resistance. But that entire opening march across the island was merely a small time operation compared to what lay ahead for us.

"By the time we neared Santiago and saw first action, we were all sick. Not a one of us had escaped the runs or the fevers that went through the camps. As we set up around the San Juan Heights, we were on double trench duty: digging one to take cover in and one to crap in. Most of us spent about

167

the same amount of time in each. The stench and the mess were unbearable.

"When the main battle started, it was late morning and we were in support at the base of an easy rise that we called 'Kettle Hill' because someone had found a large sugar kettle there. There were thousands of us – probably about fifteen thousand troops plus a few thousand Cuban irregulars. The Spaniards had positioned only about 800 soldiers up on the heights, but they had solid entrenchments and they had the high ground. Plus, they had their Mauser rifles, and you better believe they were real shooters.

"Teddy Roosevelt and his boys were on the other side of the hill from us. They called his regiment the 'Rough Riders' because they were part of a Cavalry division, but of course, apart from Roosevelt, they weren't mounted – didn't even have horses, because almost none of them made it across the water to Cuba. Later newspapers gave Roosevelt and his boys all the credit for winning the battle, as if it had been easy and none of the rest of us had been there. But they got it wrong, badly wrong.

"It was a hot, messy, bloody day and a lot of men died. After the battle it seemed that every tenth man among us, more in some units, had either been killed or wounded. Taking nothing away from the 'Rough Riders,' because they were brave and fought well, but it was our side of the hill that drew the most fire and took the most casualties."

Hansson paused to consider what he was about to say next. "And there was a colored cavalry unit there too that did more than its share of the fighting and the dying, and they took the highest point on the heights. Nobody ever talked about that and they never received any credit for what they did that day. I guess you can draw your own conclusions about that, but to me it was a shame and a disgrace.

"Anyway, it'd be hard for me to describe it. If you've ever been shot at yourself, then maybe you have a glimmer of what it was like. There's something that happens in that moment – with the fear and excitement. Before action you wonder how you'll respond, whether you'll show fear, whether you'll act with courage or with cowardice. Nobody can predict it for you and afterwards, only the survivors are there to say what happened.

"Once the shooting commenced, all was chaos. The sound of firing – the small arms, the cannon, and the Gatling guns – went up all along the line like the roar of a locomotive as it gets closer to you. You could barely see through all the smoke. The Spaniards were dug in real well up there with a command of the whole field, and boy did they lay down the fire with the Mausers and a handful of field guns. We knew we had to go up that hill, into the fire. It was tough ground we had to take, and we all knew it. But who'd go first? Who'd *be the one to climb out of the trench and lead us?*

"There were false starts. I don't know who he was, but the first man out and over was felled after about four steps from the trench. The rest of us went diving back for cover, with the Mauser bullets kicking up the dirt around us. In the trenches, though it was only late morning, it must've been well over a hundred degrees and some men were already weak from heat exhaustion. In the lull that followed our company's retreat, we peeked up over and saw the one man down in front of us. His boots were kicking against the ground, pushing off against it, as though he was trying to crawl on his back towards cover. Except that, with a head wound and his face covered with blood, he was disoriented and moving in the wrong direction.

"You could hear the shots coming slowly, about one every three seconds, as the Spaniards played with him. One bullet practically tore off his hand at the wrist, while another hit his thigh. The sound they made on impact was horrible. He bellowed and shook each time. And we were helplessly watching the spectacle from the trench, with only our eyes up over the edge.

"I wanted to do something but I was too frightened to act, felt ashamed because I wouldn't move to save him and because I realized I was glad it was him and not me that had been hit. There was a shameful relief in seeing one of my comrades shot down like that, as if his death might somehow reduce the chances that I would be killed in the battle.

"Since the war, I've heard other veterans describe that very same feeling ..."

Hansson's words trailed off and then he stepped away from the cage for a minute to wipe his face on a hand-towel. When he returned, there was a resolute expression set in his jaw. I watched quietly, waiting, from my side of the cellblock.

"It was a brutal business up there on those heights and many of the Spaniards fought to the knife, defending their positions and their blockhouse. We didn't take many prisoners that day. By sundown we'd cleared the field and the siege of Santiago was on. By August everyone, on both sides, was tired of the war. The problem was the *fiebre amarilla*, the Yellow Fever, which spread amongst us so rapidly that it killed more men than all of the bullets did. It paid no respect to rank, color, or nationality.

"After the treaty was signed, they shipped us back to New York and mustered us out right there at the harbor. Literally, they put us out at the dock within a day of arrival. Didn't matter how sick or hungry you were — and we were all sick by that time, most of us little more than skin over bone. They put you out with your papers and maybe a few dollars pay if you had

169

it coming. Some of the men were strong enough to move on from that spot, others weren't.

"A wealthy widow, Mrs. Rosemont, a civilian from the Upper East Side, lined us up right there on the dock, and chose six of us, going straight down the line, pointing out the sickest ones of the group. She had a coachman with her, and he helped get us into the wagon and they brought us back to her house, where we were put into real beds with fresh linens.

"Mrs. Rosemont cared for us like we were her own children. Young Claude was one of the chosen. I don't think he would have survived if she hadn't come for him, for us. She kept us in her home for almost two months. Mrs. Rosemont was strict, and rigid, and tough as rawhide, but she saved Claude. She saved all of us. And she did it because she explained it was the right thing to do and somebody had to help us after what we had volunteered to do for our country. God bless her."

By the time Hansson had stopped speaking, the light was starting to fade out for the evening and soon we wouldn't be able to communicate silently. From my cell, I could see the tears in his eyes, glittering in the light that was left. They overflowed the deeply sunken well in his face and ran through the grooves in his cheeks.

Before he turned from the cage for the night, Hansson had one last thing to tell me: "You think about those things every day of your life and you wonder why they happened. You wonder how they could have happened. And make no mistake: it wasn't a 'splendid little war' as some have called it. Not if you were there in the stinking, hot trenches with your friends dying around you and your own shit in your trousers. You wonder how, if there's a God in Heaven, he can let such rare selflessness exist right alongside the common, brutal horror. You wonder why you had to be the one to live through it. And then you wonder how you can ever live up to it. I've wondered that every day of my life for the last thirty some years.

"There is another force out there, a bright, shining noble light, and it'll shame you to the very core of your soul if you ponder it."

*

The summer sky turned on its axis above me while I stood staring out the window with empty hands well into the callous night. To soothe myself, I quietly whistled a well-remembered melody – *When it's Sleepy Time Down South.* After running through the chorus twice, I wiped my

170

eyes dry and turned to the bed, where I lay exhausted, yet unsleeping, until dawn arrived.

Chapter Twenty-Three

Kenneth Hamilton's executive secretary answered the telephone when I called his office the next morning from a telephone booth near the Ryan lobby. It was a few minutes after nine o'clock in the morning and another scorcher of a day was settling upon the Twin Cities.

From the booth, I watched an elderly floor sweeper in a starched white cap covering his territory, bent at the waist from a lifetime of the work. I wondered if he ever straightened out fully anymore. His expression was blank as he swung his entire upper body, automatically, in a side-to-side motion, brushing the wide broom back and forth in a slow harmonic rhythm.

"Mr. Hamilton does not accept unsolicited overtures," the executive secretary informed me without warmth. Her voice was a controlled iced lemon with a little syrup drizzled over it. She'd been too long on her job and was a little out of touch with the human side of herself.

"I understand. However, this is an unusual situation and I have important information for him concerning a financial venture he's already deep into. I guarantee you he'll be very unhappy when he learns you prevented me from speaking with him."

She led next with a haughty sniff. "Perhaps you would share it with me, and I would pass it along to Mr. Hamilton."

"It's confidential."

"Of course it is. What is your name, sir?"

"Hap Johnson," I lied easily. "I'm sure that if you tell Mr. Hamilton I am calling for him, he'll speak with me."

"I'm looking at Mr. Hamilton's calendar. Might an appointment next Tuesday be convenient?"

"No. It's urgent."

"Can you tell me anything about what this matter concerns?" The floor sweeper had moved out of my line of sight.

"Other investors are making moves he should know about. The window on this opportunity is closing fast."

"Hold, please."

When she returned to the line a moment later her tone was different. A larger dollop of maple syrup had been poured over the sour ice that was her voice. It didn't impress me. "Mr. Johnson, thank you for your patience. Mr. Hamilton will be happy to take your call right now. Please hold for a moment and I will connect you."

My ears were treated to the buzz of static, then silence for a moment, and then a click that was followed by Hamilton's abrupt voice.

"You're not supposed to call me here."

"Hamilton, come off it, they're onto us," I said, determined to carry the charade as far as I could. Static crowded the line, increasing my odds just that much more.

There was a pause, perhaps while he considered whether he recognized my voice. "What are you talking about?" he asked finally. He was too used to giving orders and having them followed. My indifference bothered him – and he couldn't decide whether to be alarmed or annoyed by it.

"Harry Sawyer came to me this morning and he was accompanied by three of his boys. They weren't friendly and they asked a lot of questions – many of them about you."

"What happened?"

"For starters, Duncan knows everything."

"You were supposed to take care of him … Twice now."

"Yeah, and it didn't work out. That's the tumble. Now, we've new work to think about."

"What did Duncan do?"

"He kidnapped Sawyer from his club last night at gunpoint and beat it out of him, left him in a vacant field with his pockets empty. From what I heard it was savage, the kind of beating that changes a man forever, if you know what I mean."

"So?"

"So, he spilled, and spilled good," I said.

"Sawyer gave us up?"

"Yep."

"How much?"

"Everything. He sang like a tenor."

"I thought he didn't know everything."

I paused, recognizing the potential trap. "He knew enough, guessed the rest."

"And he gave it to that Duncan?"

"Yes, and worse."

"How does it get worse?"

"He also gave it to the Special Agent, the Hoover man, who's been

174

on this—Agent Trestleman. He's formidable. You know he was a Texas Ranger for a lot of years, roaming the southern border. We better think twice about going up against him."

Hamilton swore an oath over the line. Then asked, "Why in damnation? Why would Sawyer do that to us?"

"He's assuming we aren't going to share out his cut, and he's angry that we complicated his life by double-crossing Duncan. That guy is downright dangerous."

Hamilton guffawed at this, but his bravado wasn't genuine. "Duncan? He played the sap for us. We almost had him at the farmhouse. If only the law had shown up fifteen minutes sooner. This is your fault. You were supposed to arrange for him to be taken care of in Chicago. We shouldn't even be having this conversation now."

I was quiet, holding the receiver away from my ear while I took a deep breath.

"Hap? You still there?"

"I'm here." I was grinning to myself now. The spider had its prey tangled in a sticky loop of web. Curious now, I put a finger into it and move it in a slow circle.

"What do you think we should do?"

"Well, do what you like, but I'm lamming it. I called you out of courtesy. I figure you have thirty minutes, maybe less, before either Duncan or Trestleman, or both of them, show up at your office. If I were you, I wouldn't be there when that happens. Those aren't Nancy boys we're talking about. They'll bring the kind of guns that men carry. Do you even have one of any size?"

I could hear the sound of papers rustling and being moved around on his desk.

"Okay," Hamilton said presently. "I'm packing up. I'll be out in ten minutes."

"What about the money?" It was a flyer. I had to try. Presumably Hap Johnson knew where the money was, but the phrasing of the question was vague enough that perhaps it would lead to something.

"What about it? I've got it right here, every penny that we haven't given to Sawyer. You know we agreed to divide it later, to keep it safe for now, and not take the risk of letting it surface yet. The serial numbers can trip us up."

I forced an anxious chuckle, trying to imagine how Hap Johnson would sound. "I know you have debts to pay."

175

"I told you, I'm already clear with International Match."

"Maybe I didn't believe you. Anyway, you never returned our investment on it. I'll need to collect that, as well as my share of this to get out of town."

"What about the bonds, the securities I passed to you?"

That almost stumped me, but of course, it made perfect sense. If you already know you're going down Glory Road, why not go full out? The bonds and securities I'd left with Gino Torresi must have been stolen from Hamilton's business partners. He'd stolen them himself before the kidnapping. It suddenly made sense.

"Those will take some time to move," I told him. "I haven't seen any cash from them yet, it'll take weeks. And I'll need my share of the ransom cash today, this afternoon. You know I have people to answer to, and they scare me far more than any renegade bank robber or former Texas Ranger."

Hamilton's voice, when he replied, was humble. "Of course. I'll meet you somewhere."

"Where?"

"Wherever you like. You call it."

"How about the lobby of the Ryan Hotel?"

"Fine. I'll see you in twenty minutes."

I made another forced chuckle that I hoped sounded like a noise Hap Johnson would make, though it didn't really matter any more. "That's good, I'll be waiting there."

*

After I rung off I immediately clicked for the operator to place another call. It took a few minutes to get through, but when she finally came on the line Mrs. Hamilton said she was pleased to hear from me. Her voice was steady.

"No," I told her. "I am not calling with any particular news about Wilson. I'm calling to ask if you can set up that meeting with Special Agent Trestleman."

"How soon would you like to talk with him?"

"The sooner the better."

"I will have him here at one o'clock this afternoon. We'll gather in the garden room."

176

"Better make it three o'clock. There's something Trestleman needs to do first, and he needs to do it quickly."

"Tell me."

"Right now your husband is at his office packing up to leave town. I assume he has a safe in his office that holds the ransom cash. He's leaving with it in a few minutes. I doubt he'll stop by to say goodbye to you or pick up any of his things at the house, although he might. So you should be ready for that just in case. Don't let him leave."

"I'll call Trestleman right now."

"Trestleman should send someone to be with you at the house, but he should get over to your husband's office himself. If he hurries, there's a small chance he'll get there in time. If he gets there too late, he might talk to some of your husband's partners at the bank. It shouldn't take them long to identify the losses he tried to cover for. That's what I think this is about – at least partially about. My bet now is he didn't get out of the Swedish match company in time and that he lost a fortune like most of the others who got involved in that adventure."

"I'll call Trestleman now. He will move fast once he understands what is happening. Did my husband say where he would go?"

"Well, he promised to meet a man named Hap Johnson in the lobby of the Ryan Hotel."

"I'll ask to have a man sent there too."

"Mrs. Hamilton, he won't be going there. That was merely a ruse. Your husband is on the run now."

"What if you're wrong about that?"

"If he shows at the Ryan, I'll be waiting for him."

"Oh," she said, processing the information slowly. "I see. Yes, well … I will see you here at my house at three o'clock."

"That will be fine … Mrs. Hamilton, I *will* need reassurances."

"Of course. We have an understanding. I give you my personal word that there will be no attempt of any sort to arrest you or hold you against your will this afternoon. Will you accept that?"

"Yes," I told her. "I trust you. And, Mrs. Hamilton?"

"Yes, Mister Duncan?"

"I thank you."

I rang off.

After replacing the receiver I looked at my watch. It was early still – there was plenty of time for my next stop. In the hotel lobby I found a strategic location to sit – in a comfortable chair between two tall ferns.

177

It had a good angle from which to view everyone who entered the hotel through the main entrance.

I lit a cigarette and waited out the remainder of the twenty minutes that Hamilton had promised it would take him to arrive. While I waited, I smoked two cigarettes. I gave Hamilton an extra five minutes and then I moved on. There was no surprise. The only surprise would have been if he'd actually shown.

Chapter Twenty-Four

I located the older sister's apartment house on South Robert in West St. Paul easily enough and knocked on the door. While I waited for someone to answer, I glanced about and noticed the bed of impatiens was beginning to wilt in the heat. Brittle stems rode up to shriveling leaves and blossoms that would soon fail.

The woman who answered the door was familiar in a peculiar sort of way. It seemed as if she was someone I had known years before, but who now appeared different in some way that I couldn't quite put my finger on. Perhaps Father Time had worked his usual cruel trickery. Yet it seemed there was something more than that. One eye was smaller and darker than I remembered it being and the shape of the lips didn't have quite the right curvature of the woman I'd known. As I studied her more closely, I realized that her stance held none of the confident defiance I'd expected.

"Yes," she said. Her voice carried a note of annoyance at the bother. Sleepy eyes struggled to assume a hardened veneer against the unwanted advances a stranger might bring.

"Better give them some water soon," I suggested, gesturing toward the flowers. "They're thirsty."

"What do you want? Are you a salesman?"

"No, ma'am, I'm not selling anything. You must be sister Eva. I'm looking for little sister Delilah. Is she here?"

A shadow crossed her face, sinking deep into the grooves beside her eyes. "Buster, I don't know who you're talking about."

I studied her for a moment and I knew she had mistaken me for another—someone who beat up pretty young women and left them tending bruises. While I was considering how best to make my case, the point became moot.

I heard Delilah's voice from somewhere not too far back inside the house.

"Duncan?" she called, and then her face appeared over the sister's shoulder and she pushed through to open the screen.

In an instant I saw the large eyes and the sparkle at her throat, and then she was through the door and her arms were around me. My hands touched the soft comfort of flannel pajamas. We held tight until the sister started making impatient noises from behind her on the doorstep.

"This is my sister, Eva," Delilah said, pulling away from me just long enough to make the introduction with a slight curtsy, and then she was hugging me again, this time around the waist, with her hip against mine. I felt her hand find mine. Our fingers interlocked momentarily, before I pulled away awkwardly. I gave her a long look. There were purple areas on her face, bruises, and contusions – small red areas where the skin was scrapped and had bled. Her lip and one eye were swollen, giving her a cheerful, lopsided appearance to her face. I knew it hurt to smile like she was doing now.

Eva stared at me with a placid look behind her eyes that indicated she felt considerably less joy at my arrival, or maybe she'd already seen it all by now. I pulled away further from Delilah so that I could stand between them with my feet spread at shoulder length. It was an instinctive stance that allowed quick movement in any direction.

"I knew you'd come," Delilah said. There was a note of determination in her voice.

"No you didn't, not like this," I admonished her.

With defiance at the corners of her mouth she stared at me. "What do you mean?"

"Delilah," I told her. "You may not be safe here any longer. The natives are stirring."

Her eyes darkened, but she didn't protest. "Murphy called this morning," she told me. "He said the same thing, more or less, and he wanted to come for me, my protector. Can you believe that?"

"How long ago did he call?"

Delilah looked at Eva. The older sister answered this question in protective fashion. "It was about twenty minutes ago, maybe thirty? We told him he was certainly not welcome here, not after what he did to her."

"*You* told him that," Delilah snapped. "I didn't even have the chance to speak with him."

"After what he did to you, you think I'd let him talk to you now?"

"I'm a big girl, sis."

Eva frowned and took a step backwards, twisting slightly toward one side, as if to intentionally disrupt the geometric symmetry of the triangle we had formed together. She emphasized her remoteness by turning her head to face completely away from us. I read this quietly as

180

a long running behavioral pattern between them. "*Love me, love me not,*" it seemed to say. It wasn't unusual for siblings, with childhood behind them, to allow ever more bitterness to creep between them over the years – even as they stuck things out together.

"Perhaps we might take the discussion inside," I suggested.

"Smart move," Delilah agreed, ignoring her sister's posturing.

Eva didn't turn to look at us again. Instead she made a sullen nod and pulled the screen door open to walk into the apartment ahead of us. She seemed affected and I wondered if she might not speak again. Behind us the screen door slammed and then I hung back to turn the deadbolt on the door.

Inside, we stood in a small sitting room that was sparsely furnished with cheap wooden furniture. Straight-back chairs, strung with yellow cushions, and a low coffee table formed a tight, but orderly U-shape. Well-polished oak floor panels, three inches wide and placed in staggered rows, connected the small room to the slightly larger dining room that was adjacent to it.

A matching set of chairs, with yellow cushions, and a table large enough to seat six were the only furniture in the dining room. The beige walls were bare, forcing the yellow cushions and the polished oak to stand out boldly in a way that they wouldn't have were the room decorated with other colors. It was a die-cut, standard American apartment interior design.

Delilah made small, confident clucking noises with her tongue. I looked at her. She was beaming and twirling minutely on the toes of her bare feet, daring me to rebuke her. With delicate fingers she worried the sparkling something that hung above her breastplate on a silver chain. It was intricate and lovely against her dark skin.

"You sent me this necklace. I knew it was from you when it arrived. It didn't come with a note, but I knew you sent it. It's the prettiest stone I ever wore, and not just another gewgaw."

I nodded my admission. It was the item I'd selected for delivery at Dockman's jewelry store.

"It's just a trinket, I felt bad about what happened."

"No, it's not. It's more than that, and I know it wasn't cheap and you sent it for other reasons."

I moved on. "We only have a few minutes," I said to both of them. "Pack up a few things, nothing too much, just enough for a night or two. We're scramming this place."

Delilah stepped over to her sister.

"Both of us?"

"Yes," I replied. "These people aren't likely to make much of a distinction between the two of you. Even if they recognized the difference, they wouldn't hesitate to use you to get to Delilah. This Murphy's trouble enough, but he's small time and if he can find you, so can the others. And the others will be worse, far worse than him."

"How much worse?" Delilah asked.

"Delilah," I said. "Did you read about Isaac in the newspaper on Wednesday?" I didn't have to say any more.

"Oh, no." She looked at Eva and the posture of her sister reminded me of the impatiens drooping out in front of the apartment.

"Haven't you done enough, already," Eva accused me.

"Yes, I have. Now I'm trying to undo some of those things."

Chapter Twenty-Five

Northwood opened the door before I even set the knocker.

"Come in, sir," he invited me. "They are waiting in the garden room for you now, Mrs. Hamilton and two federal agents with machine guns." His tone was the same tone others might have used to comment on the possibility of light rain on a Sunday afternoon.

I stepped past him and waited while he closed the door behind me. Inside, the air was cool and scented with jasmine. We crossed over lacquered parquet, passed through the house and then paused together at the French doors while he announced my arrival. Then I was in the quiet room with the ceiling fans, looking into the faces of the two large men who stood to meet me.

Abigail Hamilton sat shrinking in one of the wingback chairs and she did not rise. A pair of Thompson machine guns were placed together, off to one side on the edge of the Persian rug. They looked out of place in a curious sort of way, though I half suspected that if they sat there long enough, they'd begin to blend in with the other selected décor. I stared at them absently.

"We missed Hamilton at his office by ten minutes," one of the men told me. He spoke with a sun-drenched drawl. "I'm Special Agent Trestleman and this is Special Agent Harrison." He stepped toward me and extended a large palm, which I shook.

"You'll pardon me if I don't introduce myself."

"We know who you are."

My eyes worked around the details of his face. Abigail Hamilton had told me that Trestleman was a former Texas Ranger who'd once ridden after Pancho Villa twenty years earlier, and he certainly looked the part. A thick brush of mustache hid his mouth entirely, emphasizing a granite block jaw. Alert cobalt eyes formed tight oblongs that seemed to note every detail. They stood out between weathered ridges of skin along a high forehead. There was no hint of softness or good humor to be found anywhere within his gaze—only a direct purposefulness. He wore a simple white shirt, dark tie, brown trousers, and a brown checked jacket. Everything he wore was freshly pressed. I judged his age to be about fifty, though he could have been up to ten years out on either side of that mark.

I shifted my attention to the other agent, a much younger man with bland features. His hair was meticulously combed and his tie was knotted far too tightly at his throat. The impression he gave was that of a young man proudly trying too hard to impress – this notion was accentuated by the sharp crease in his trousers and the hard polished shine of his wing-tipped shoes. He'd returned to his seat without offering to shake my hand. Instead he picked up a notepad and pretended to write something important in it. His fingers moved the pen around on the page like he was working putty, and I assumed he wasn't writing any words that would be recognizably from the English language.

"You can pardon the college boy," Trestleman told me. "He's better than he looks, just a little formal and a little anxious when the line becomes blurred. Law school didn't prepare any of them for this sort of job."

I shrugged this off and found a seat in a chair that was upholstered in burgundy twill and positioned kitty-corner to the wingback where Abigail Hamilton sat. I nodded at her and saw that her eyes, still determined, were edged with a red inflammation that suggested sleep deprivation and profound worry.

"We need to move quickly," I told them all together. "Kenneth Hamilton won't stick around, and neither will his accomplice, Hap Johnson, once he learns the score."

Mrs. Hamilton cleared her throat long enough for us to look her way. "Would anybody like an iced tea?" she offered. Thin slivers of doubt had penetrated her voice, the same way they'd penetrated her eyes and mouth, causing her to appear quite a bit older than the last time I'd seen her, less than twenty-four hours ago.

Trestleman shook his head.

"I'm sorry, ma'am, but we don't have time for the social niceties. We're up against the clock now." He turned his eyes towards me. "Do you know where either of these men would be?"

I shrugged and looked back and forth between the Federal two agents. "I have no idea about Johnson, but it's even odds he's wherever he would otherwise be at this hour. He has no pals left these days, no one to tip him. You can probably pick him up at his home or wherever he spends his afternoons."

Trestleman was the agent in charge and seemed to be doing all the speaking for the two lawmen. My conversation was with him now.

"His office would be in City Hall," he said.

I didn't skip a beat on that. "Then find him there. Hamilton is on the move now and he'll try to disappear. You might luck out at the train station – be sure to look in Fred Harvey's restaurant – though I doubt he'll be waiting for the Northern Pacific, or any other such ride. And just so you know, he's carrying cash, and lots of it, probably in a suitcase or a large valise."

"We've already got men at the station, but I agree, we won't find him there. He took the automobile, left the chauffeur twiddling thumbs at the office."

"Then he's probably halfway to Chicago.

"Or San Francisco."

"Or Dallas."

"I get it," Trestleman told me. "What did he take with him?"

"All of the ransom money; save five grand he spread around town on a stall."

"There's something else," Trestleman disclosed evenly. "According to Hamilton's partners, a large number of securities and bonds are missing from their safe. They just discovered it this afternoon while we were there pawing our way around."

That gave me reason to pause. I stroked the side of my cheek and looked up at the ceiling, then around the room.

"You know something about this?" Trestleman asked casually.

"Yes, I think Hamilton stole them a couple of weeks ago – before he allowed himself to be kidnapped."

"What makes you think a big complicated thought like that?"

"He told me so this morning when we spoke."

My words lay over the room with a pall. Nobody quite reacted. From outside I noticed the sounds of small birds chirping to each other in the garden. Their noises should have been comforting, but they weren't. Abigail Hamilton lowered her head and stared carefully at her fingernails.

"We better pick up Hap Johnson," Trestleman said finally.

I nodded.

"Anybody else we should grab now?"

"Like who?"

"Harry Sawyer, maybe?"

"Never heard of him."

Trestleman sat patiently for a moment while he considered this response. "Sure. Who ran the job with you? You didn't do it alone."

"A few others. You already found one of them earlier this week: Isaac Runyon."

If this surprised him it didn't register in his expression. "Your work?"

"No, not a chance. Isaac was alright with me."

"Then, someone else, cleaning up a mess. Who?"

I shrugged. My lips were closed tight.

"Who were the others in on the score with you? Somebody had to front the house you stayed in."

I shrugged again. "Best leave them to me, and we best cease this chit-chat. The clock is ticking down and Hap Johnson won't wait around forever. You better pick him up. He'll panic if he sees me coming."

Trestleman grunted and looked at his partner. "Go make the call."

Agent Harrison stood up and left the room. He seemed to know exactly where he was going. From some other part of the house I heard Northwood's solicitous voice and then the noises of a telephone call being placed.

Before he resumed with his questions, Trestleman resettled himself on the divan with his large hands spread over his knees. "Do you know where the child is?" he asked.

"No."

"How is that possible?"

At that question, Mrs. Hamilton protested on my behalf, "He has already explained that to me."

"I need to hear it for myself," Trestleman told her.

He held up an open palm to show he meant no intended threat.

"Of course," I replied. I quickly ran through the facts, pretty much exactly as they occurred, leaving out only the names of my partners, other than Runyon, and the existence of the girl altogether. Midway through my account, Agent Harrison returned to the room. His expression was serious. Reluctant to interrupt the flow of my narrative he stood at the edge of the seating area with his hands on his hips, under his suit jacket, until I finished speaking.

"Did Hamilton reveal anything to you about his plan or his intentions?" Trestleman asked.

"Nothing that would help us. If he had, I would have told you already."

"Anything on his motive?"

"I can only surmise the financial motive."

186

"We're listening."Trestleman's words could have conveyed impatience, except the tone of his voice was a calm bucket of fresh white paint.

My gaze found Abigail Hamilton. She sat upright in her chair now with her shoulders pressed back between its wings. It was a brave front, betrayed only by the fact that she didn't appear to be breathing.

I glanced back at Trestleman before answering his question. "I think he lost Outfit money to International Match last year," I told him.

"I don't follow."Trestleman's voice was still calm, but his sharp eyes pricked the air between us.

Agent Harrison spoke up suddenly for the first time. His voice squeaked out – the same pitch as a balloon being abruptly pulled wide and flat: "Krueger and Toll; remember Ivar Krueger, the guy with the world monopoly on safety matches? Only it proved to be a bigger Ponzi scheme than Ponzi ever dreamed of."

"I seem to remember something about that. What's the connection?"

The conversation was between the two Federal agents now. I was merely listening.

"It crashed last year. Krueger committed suicide and his investors lost everything. The financial investigators are still sorting through the jumble, trying to figure out who lost what, dividing up the few bits of remaining assets. It's complicated because so many nations around the world, everyone from Sweden to China, are involved." Harrison's voice had leveled out. He was sitting again, with his notepad ready, but he wasn't writing anything now.

Trestleman nodded with understanding and looked at me. "Do you think Kenneth Hamilton was investing Outfit money?"

"Yes, and I think he lost a bundle of it."

"The Outfit would not accept losses gracefully."

"They don't accept *profit* gracefully."

"Does St. Paul have the kind of money I think we're talking about?"

"Sure, they do. So does Chicago, or New York, and they're not provincial anymore. You don't know it yet because your boss is preoccupied with the small-timers, but they're big business in this country. They spread their money all around—wherever they can control the odds in their favor. Anyway, I wouldn't assume its all from one source—you have Italian money, Jewish money, Irish money … Sometimes they even play together."

Trestleman stared off to the left of my face while his mind strung the pieces and questions together. He was an intelligent, practical, and tough-minded man. Nothing would surprise him anymore and I realized why Abigail Hamilton trusted him as she did. He would've been a good partner for any man to have—in any line.

"So," Trestleman said. "Hamilton was a willing participant in his own kidnapping in order to recoup losses for the Outfit. I follow it so far. But why take the child? And why was the child not returned with Hamilton? How does that square?"

Agent Harrison was quick with a hypothesis: "Maybe the child was collateral. To ensure Hamilton shared out the ransom money after it was collected."

"How can that make sense?" I asked. "In fact, this has been bothering me all day. How did Hamilton glom his own ransom money?"

The two agents looked at each other, then Mrs. Hamilton, then back again at me. Trestleman spoke first: "Mrs. Hamilton's bank wired half the funds, one hundred thousand to Hamilton's firm. They matched it with another one hundred thousand and transferred the entire two hundred thousand in cash to the kidnappers themselves."

"That's a whole lot of money," I said. "How did they transfer it to the kidnappers?"

The silence that followed pulsed throughout the room.

"They used one of Hamilton's safety deposit boxes."

"So, he either collected the money himself or he gave his key to his kidnappers."

"We had assumed the latter ..."

"And now we're assuming the former," I finished. "So he collected the ransom money himself? That's curious."

Trestleman's face was grimly set. "We weren't authorized to monitor or scrutinize any part of the transaction, per the kidnapper's instructions. We were out of it completely."

"Is that standard practice? Do you always do whatever kidnappers say to do?"

"It is when the family requests us to. We always let the family make decisions about how to respond to kidnapping demands."

I looked at the child's mother. She'd sunk into the chair again, even smaller than before. Tears filled her eyes and rolled slowly all the way down to her neckline. A silk thread seemed to hold her from slumping to the floor.

"I feared for my child," she said, shaking her head, as if to deny reality itself.

My gaze found a small spot in the middle of the floor. "That's why the child was taken," I said. "It gave them the upper hand and let Kenneth Hamilton's puppet-masters believe they held more strings than there were to hold."

"Oh, sweet mother," Harrison started and then cut himself off.

Abigail Hamilton was weeping quietly, but steadily now. She covered her face with both hands, dabbing with a silk handkerchief that dropped down from her eyes like a veil.

"It's not your fault, Mrs. Hamilton," I said to her.

I knew the words provided little comfort. It was bad enough that she'd been manipulated into a course of action that now appeared to have endangered her child. Far worse was the fact that the apparent manipulator was her own husband. His callous use of the child suggested not only that he carried no love for the child or for her, but pointed toward something much deeper—an open hostility that bordered on hate or even sadism. I wondered from what well that had sprung and I remembered my own words about dark motives.

When it came to blood, there were usually only two ground water sources: money and revenge. In this instance I already understood the money. Now I wondered about the revenge and what it might be for, and even as I wondered, I knew it could be for something as mundane as resentment, a resentment over the wealth and power that Abigail Hamilton had inherited through the simple coincidence of birth: she had been born to extremely wealthy parents.

The Federal agents sat quietly, though Agent Harrison fidgeted with his notepad, pretending once more to write important notes to himself. From where I sat, I could easily see the meaningless series of connected loops and tiny arrows that he scrawled on the paper. Trestleman was impassive. A lifetime along the Texas frontier would have prepared him for, probably even inured him to, the grief a mother would display at losing a child.

"It is my fault," she said presently, with her air recovered just enough to speak, but not well enough yet to prevent her voice from catching.

"You don't owe us an explanation," I told her.

She shook her head and brought the handkerchief, now bunched up in the palm of one hand, across each eye, in turn, from the center out. "I have been too protective, never allowed him the opportunities other boy's his age take for granted."

"No, he doesn't see it that way."

189

"Yes, well he wouldn't, he's too polite to think anything like that. Because of me he never … My husband, in his most—"

Mercifully, a small bell chimed from the entrance to the room, interrupting whatever it was she was about to say. We all turned simultaneously to see Northwood standing there with a small silver tray. "There is a telephone message for Agent Trestleman," he said without expression in his voice.

"Come in, Northwood," Mrs. Hamilton beckoned.

The butler crossed the room efficiently without saying another word and held the tray out to Trestleman. The Texan swiped a small piece of folded golden paper from the tray and looked at it momentarily, then glanced at Hamilton, and then at me. His eyes blazed with the scent of action to come.

"They've picked up Hap Johnson," he said. His voice carried over with a low growl to it now. "They're holding him down at headquarters. We should leave immediately. Harrison, you take our automobile; I'll ride down with our companion here." He gestured toward me with his chin and his eyes fixed on mine. "I think you should be there when we question him."

I nodded and stood up quickly. Instinctively, I adjusted my jacket around the shoulder holster I wore, and then tapped my fingers against the butt of the .45. Agent Harrison had pocketed his notepad and was already stooping to pick up the two Thompson machine guns from the floor.

*

The two Federal agents went out through the front door and past the Doric columns ahead of me, each now wearing a Stetson and carrying a machine gun pointed straight up in the air. Their facial expressions were somber. Neither of them turned to say good-bye. They took the steps briskly down to the driveway and conferred for a moment with their backs towards us.

Abigail Hamilton stepped out on the front porch with me, leaning her body towards me so that Northwood, still standing inside the threshold, wasn't positioned to hear the determined words she whispered to me: "I will pay you a reward of one hundred and fifty thousand to find my son. And if he is dead, I will pay you three hundred thousand to kill all of the people responsible."

"Mrs. Hamilton," I started to respond.

"Please call me Abigail," she admonished.

I nodded and restarted. "Abigail. I wouldn't accept your money for something I intend to do anyway."

Chapter Twenty-Six

In the afternoon, the late afternoon with the failing light and the glooming sky, Agent Trestleman drove with me to his office in my Ford V8. He didn't comment on the emotional state of Abigail Hamilton or ask what she might have said to me as we parted. He wouldn't tell me where the office was, saying he wanted to enjoy the surprise when we got there. Instead he gave curt two-word directions in a rasping voice.

We approached downtown St. Paul, coming in past Indian Mounds Park and the railroad yards. It was still hot and several tired men stood about the yards with their shirts off, leaning against stacked cargo pallets. Pale white skin hung loosely from their exposed frames as they watched automobiles pass in each direction. Their gaunt, faraway stares made me think of dead sounds in a cemetery.

"It rankles you, doesn't it," I remarked, "driving with me like this as if I'm one of the good guys? You want to put me away."

His denial was gruff. "No, your time will come. For now I'm content to honor Mrs. Hamilton's request that we work with you to find the child."

"Not exactly by the book for one of Hoover's men."

"I'm not one of Hoover's men. I'm a semi-retired Texas Ranger recruited to the Bureau of Investigation for a two-year hitch. Then I'm back in Texas. I'm only there to help keep young men like Agent Harrison alive long enough for them to learn what it takes in this life-or-death profession."

I nodded, my eyes on the street ahead of us. "I guess someone needs to teach the college boys how to become man hunters ... and man killers."

Trestleman grunted. "Too many of them have been gunned down by people like you."

"I never killed a Federal agent."

"Others have."

"Hoover's men make mistakes, they're over eager. They've killed too many innocent bystanders. We both know they, and you as well, have shoot-first and shoot-to-kill orders. That's fine so far as it goes, except they often kill the wrong man, which scotches any sympathy the public

193

might have for them."

"I don't condone it."

"No, but it makes it harder for them. No one trusts them and it changes the rules for everyone. How can you expect a man to surrender when he knows you are likely to shoot him anyway? Where's the honor in that? Is that how you do it down in Texas?"

"I've never shot a man who surrendered."

"It may be hard to hear this, but I'm a professional at what I do, just like you are at what you do. It will be better for everybody when we're all professionals."

"We both know it will never be that way."

I let this comment settle. I thought of Sawyer standing there in the field with the orange-streaked sky behind him. Even with my .45 pointed at his head, he wasn't willing to concede on the O'Connor System. It drove too much, including the ambitious young men from Washington. No one was immune from the fallibility, the essential corruption of man. "No, probably not," I replied.

"It takes grit for you to trust me."

"I put my trust in Mrs. Hamilton."

"Fair enough. I trust her too."

"I'll work with you until we find the boy."

"What is he to you?" Trestleman asked.

I considered this. In my mind I saw the boy in the bank again as he calmly watched me impotently trying to plug his bleeding wound with my fingers. "Same thing he is to you, a chance to make up for mistakes that were made."

"It's more personal for you, you met him. You had the opportunity to feel directly responsible for him."

"True."

"And you saw the way his stepfather treated him, and I think it bothered you."

"Yes – I saw the utter disregard his stepfather had for him."

"What's the boy like?"

I smiled and took my eyes off the road long enough to glance over. "Seems it may be personal for you too if you're asking questions like that."

The lawman looked away, pointedly so, with his head turned at the neck, stretching back around to look behind him as if trying to see the past again from a different angle.

"So, what's he like?" he asked again after a while, facing forward once more. "It's a simple lawman's question. Maybe I'll learn something that will help me find him."

"Sure," I said. "The answer might be there if only you look hard enough for it. It's what we all tell ourselves from time to time. But okay, I'll take your question at face value. Wilson's just a child, a boy, pretty much like any other boy at that age, though he's probably more fragile and a bit of a bookworm. He has sad, hesitant eyes that seek signs of approval from everyone around him. He was overly considerate and he tended to ask a lot of questions. Some of them were the usual questions you expect from a child that age, others were not – some of his questions were surprisingly intimate, inquiring about emotional states or intentions. He tries to comfort others if they need it. I never had the sense from him that he has ever risked displeasing an adult. Nor did I have the sense that he was aware that he'd ever actually pleased one either. There was little awareness of how others might see him, or that they even do."

"What does he like to do?"

"In addition to reading books he likes baseball – both playing it and following it – listening to radio shows, having cold drinks when it's hot, and maybe playing checkers. I don't know what else. There wasn't a wide variety of choices for him during the few days we were together."

"Seems you came to know him rather well," Trestleman said when I finished.

"He was kind to me."

"How about that?"

"One other thing: he didn't really know how to behave when you treated him decently."

"Did you treat him decently?"

I shrugged. I didn't have an answer to that question.

Trestleman ended our conversation with an abrupt gesture. He pointed toward the next corner. "You're going to turn left there, and then it's two blocks down, on the right side. There will be street parking."

*

I *was* a bit surprised, but I made sure it did not show on my face. Trestleman's squad had leased temporary office space, a large suite, in the new City Hall and Ramsey County Courthouse, at the corner of Kellogg and Wabasha. The building was a large art deco structure featuring expensive stone masonry and twenty different exotic woods in its construction. The exterior of the building was made of smooth Indiana limestone.

As I recalled, the city's timing had worked to their advantage when they went to build. Shortly after they'd floated the construction bonds, the stock market had crashed and prices of materials and labor had plummeted, allowing the city of St. Paul extra money to build in grand style, which they had most certainly done.

We entered through the Fourth Street entrance, beneath gentle relief sculptures, and moved quickly down the white marble floor towards the elevators. There we took one of the lifts up to the twelfth floor, riding with only silence between us, though my mind was still finishing the conversation that had been interrupted a few minutes before.

The more I thought about it, the more I decided it was *all* personal, every bit of it, for each one of us. We stared out from our respective corners, assessing our adversaries, weighing the odds, thinking through the angles, and making the calculations at every step. We told ourselves it was only business—the occupation we had chosen—and in our respective manners we were all merely businessmen of one sort or another: *tinker, tailor, soldier, sailor* ... The old child's rhyme floated through my head like a radio jingle. And yes, business interests were always at stake. But so were most of the seven deadly sins, including pride and wrath, which we served with devotion.

*

When the elevator came to its stop, Trestleman held the door for me. I went through it first and then half-turned as Trestleman came through behind me. His office suite was the first door to the left.

We went through that door into a large outer office that held six desks and four doors that connected to additional offices or holding cells. Agent Harrison and three other agents were waiting for us right there, standing together in a half circle beside one of the desks. There were no introductions made and nobody looked directly at me.

One of the men removed his hat before he addressed Trestleman. "He was in his office downstairs. It was easy as pool. We flashed badges and asked if he might come up to chat with us for a few minutes. He's in there, with a cup of coffee, thinking we're all friends, expecting us to come back with a bottle."

Trestleman took off his own hat and dropped it on a nearby desk. "That's just fine," he said. "Harrison will stay with me. The rest of you men can knock off for the day."

"Are you sure?" the first agent asked. A look of disappointment had crept over his face. "We don't mind sticking around for a while."

"Yeah," another chimed, "all the fun is about to start. We don't want to miss it. I've got my brass knuckles shined and ready."

Trestleman's headshake was firm. "Nope. We'll take it from here. Just lock the outer door behind you, including the top bolt. Come back tomorrow reasonably sober."

There was not another word of protest as they followed his instructions and left the suite quietly.

*

Agent Trestleman pulled a chair up close to Hap Johnson and sat forward with his face about ten inches away from Johnson's face. His voice, still course gravel, was whisper quiet: "We're going to ask you questions about the kidnapping of Kenneth Hamilton and his nine-year old son, Wilson. We're not going to ask you if you were involved in the kidnapping because we already know that you were. Do you follow me so far?"

Johnson's smile was amiable enough and he shrugged his shoulders in a friendly way. "I don't know what you're talking about."

"Don't fuck with me, son. We already know."

"Do you know who I am?" Johnson's tone was indignant. He looked about the room, searching for a potential ally.

Trestleman smiled grimly and lit a cigarette, taking his time about it. He drew in almost half the cigarette on the first drag and held the smoke deep in his lungs for nearly twenty seconds. When he finally exhaled he blew a long, thin stream of concentrated smoke directly into Johnson's eyes.

"I do know who you are. You're a low-life piece of dog shit that needs to be scraped from my shoe. The fact that you have an office downstairs means absolutely nothing to me. The more important question in the room is do you know who *I* am?"

Johnson blinked hard against the smoke and you could see that his confidence was suddenly faltering. "You're a college boy G-man," he tried to bluster. "Probably an accountant."

Trestleman chuckled and took another, smaller drag on the cigarette, taking his time about it. Then he leaned in close and exhaled as he spoke.

"Do I *look* like an accountant? I'm no college boy, Son. I'm from *Texas*. Do you know about Texas? Ever been there? We still have a hard, lawless frontier down there. A soft boy like you wouldn't last long with the kind of criminals we rope down there."

Johnson still didn't get it. He tried to force his way through. "We own half your force up here. You better check with your agent-in-charge. He'll set you straight."

"Look around you, son. Do you see any one else in charge here?"

Hap Johnson shook his head and tried the smile again. It didn't quite form as he intended it to and you could see it in his eyes that he was now having doubts about his situation. Beads of sweat began to form along the hairline above his eyebrows. "What's he doing here?" he asked, gesturing towards me.

I grinned at him and winked, but I didn't say anything.

Trestleman sat back and stubbed his cigarette in an ashtray near his elbow. "He's working with us, I deputized him this afternoon."

"You can't do that!"

Trestleman smiled patiently and responded without any sense of urgency. "Son, I can do whatever the *fuck* I want to."

*

"I have three questions for you," Trestleman continued with his second cigarette going. "I'll lay them out so you'll understand our purpose here. Once you've told us what we want to know, and if we decide that we don't need to hold you, we'll give you another cup of coffee and a free ride back downstairs in the lift. No one has to know we had this little chat. Only three questions: Was Kenneth Hamilton involved in his own kidnapping? Who else was involved? Where is the child? You can start anywhere you like, but the last question is the one we care about the most."

"Are you asking me about the Hamilton kidnapping? I don't know anything about that."

"Son, you don't want to do this the hard way."

"I don't know anything about it."

Trestleman looked up at me. His expression was placid. "What do you say?" he asked me.

I found a cigarette of my own and lit it before responding. "Hap," I started, addressing the obese man in the chair, rather than the Federal agent. "You didn't grow up in the old neighborhood, at least not the same old neighborhood I grew up in. You've never set foot on Hennepin Avenue in your entire life as far as I can tell and we don't know any of the same people from there."

"I swear it."

"No," I said shaking my head. "You're from somewhere else, probably New York."

"I swear it," he said a second time with greater urgency.

I ignored this. "Hap, I've already told these men what I know. I told them that you planned the kidnapping and orchestrated it with Kenneth Hamilton. I suspect that you were able to command his attention because of investment losses he incurred with money that you fronted for him, money that you received from one or more of the large criminal organizations here in the Midwest."

"That's preposterous."

I took a drag from my cigarette. It was my next to last one, so I was in no hurry to finish it. "Hamilton took it on the lam today, which, I suspect, leaves you holding the bag – a very empty bag."

"I don't believe you."

"I'll take that as acknowledgement that you were working with Hamilton."

"I never—"

"Save it," I interrupted. "You can talk to us, or you can talk to the man behind you."

"But—"

"Nuts. Just tell us where the child is. That's really all we care about at this moment. Give us that and everything else can go easy."

The sweat from Johnson's hairline was now beading down into his face. He wiped at it with the back of his hand.

"I don't know," he claimed. "I don't know anything about it?"

"Okay, hold that for now. You sent me on a fool's errand to Chicago last week. I wasn't supposed to come back. Who put you up to that?"

"Nobody, I—"

"Whoever it was, I don't believe they were Italian as you told me they would be."

Hap shook his head so hard that his large jowls rippled in a distinctly unattractive manner. I took another hit off my cigarette and leaned off the wall so that I could stretch towards the only ashtray in the room.

"Hap," I said. "I don't think they were Jewish either. So who does that leave?"

"I dunno."

"Sure you do. That leaves only the Irish."

"No. I swear it."

"Besides, I'm willing to give you a pass on that if you tell us where we can find the child. It's the best deal you'll get here today and I'm down to my last cigarette now, so my patience won't run for too much longer."

*

Scared as he was starting to look, Hap Johnson was still not talking. He clamped his mouth so tight his jaw swelled.

The two Federal agents pushed him backwards toward the open window. Trestleman slugged him twice in the mouth and then hit him with a series of body blows—quick short jabs to his gut, just beneath the sternum. Johnson tried to fend them off, but it had been a long time since he'd used his hands. With blood streaming down his chin from a cut lip he began to cry and plead.

Trestleman hit him three more times and then stepped back to let Special Agent Harrison lean in with his fists. After a bit of this they sat Johnson up against the window, leaning him back and out a ways. I decided to help out. I grabbed onto Johnson's tie to hold him in and Trestleman held onto the lapels of his jacket, shaking him for good measure.

"Now you're going to answer our questions," Trestleman told him after he stopped the shaking.

The obese man began to blubber and squirm. Spit mixed with blood and sweat, foaming at the corner of his mouth. It was not an easy sight. As he squirmed, he inched back on the windowsill until he was practically sitting on it.

"Was Kenneth Hamilton involved in his own kidnapping?"

"No! I already told you, no!"

"I don't believe you. We already know he was. Square with us."

Johnson managed to nod his head. "Yes," he said in a near whisper.

"Tell us where the child is," Agent Trestleman demanded next.

"I don't know where he is."

"Tell us," Trestleman shouted.

I could see the spray of saliva hit Hap Johnson's face, but I doubt he noticed it much. "I can't tell you what I don't know," he sobbed.

"Who would know?"

Johnson didn't respond with words. He simply cried louder and shook his head vigorously.

"Give us a name."

"Let me down and I'll tell you."

"We already tried that. You gave us nothing."

"Let me down!"

"You want down? I'll give you down, and it's a long way."

Trestleman thumped Johnson's chest savagely, with the palms of his hands. I was still holding onto Johnson's tie, which lurched perilously in my grip at the force of the shove. I recovered quickly and wrapped the near end of it around my hand. Agent Harrison was beside me, grabbing hold of Johnson's ankles and lifting, taking away his only source of balance and leverage. Now we had him fully up on the windowsill, with the upper half of his body leaning out backwards at a slight angle towards the open air.

Trestleman firmed his hold on Johnson's right arm, just below the shoulder. In the process he elbowed me aside and I stepped back from the fray, releasing my grip on Johnson's tie. Johnson's other arm was stretched out, grasping for a hold at the external spandrel above him. There was nothing much there to grip onto, only the plain, flat surface that ran between the windows. His stubby fingers groped against it with futility. He had no solid leverage against gravity now.

"Look over your shoulder," Trestleman commanded.

Johnson didn't obey. Instead he shut his eyes and tried to lean forward off the window ledge. The effort made little difference. Without leverage and balanced as he was now, his excessive weight could only work against him.

"Open your eyes, I want you to look!" Trestleman's voice was controlled fury. He twisted Johnson's arm at the shoulder to compel him.

This time Hap Johnson complied. He opened his eyes first and turned his head timidly to look down over his right shoulder. Quickly he jerked his head back around and began to heave. The two agents held him in place for a moment while his body convulsed and the sudden scent of feces filled the room.

"He shit himself," Harrison said with disgust, turning his face away from the odor.

"Not so tough now?" Trestleman asserted. His voice was quieter now, but he didn't relinquish his hold. "I'm going to ask you again: Where is the child?"

"I don't know." Johnson's words were clear enough, though he was sobbing as he spoke them.

"Then give me a name of someone who might."

"I can't do that."

Johnson was heavy. I could see the strain of holding him was beginning to mount. Agent Harrison tried to reposition himself to take some of the load off. Stepping back, as he had to do, however, allowed him very little leverage and with an involuntary grunt I heard him release and snap backwards a full stride. He nearly lost his balance.

I saw Trestleman's eyes and it seemed we were thinking the same thing. I lunged forward, but it was too late. Hap Johnson seemed to swing, twisting away from me and then he was falling down toward the hard surface that awaited him ten or eleven stories below.

Trestleman and I stood at the window, staring out after him. Johnson, with his arms still flailing, hit the ledge of a window below us and then landed on the roof of one of the lower floors of the building. Even from that high up we could hear the impact of his body. Parts of him splattered out in a small radius around his head and torso.

The sight jolted me. It would have been even more sickening if you had any sense that Hap was a regular, deserving human being.

I looked down and then quickly stepped away from the window. Trestleman lingered a moment longer and then, unhurriedly, he pulled back into the room, leaving the window open. We looked at each other and then we looked at Agent Harrison who stood close to the back wall now with his hands splayed wide and a look of stunned anguish in his clear eyes.

"What is J. Edgar Hoover going to say about this?" I asked as we recovered our breath, slowly. I got a Chesterfield in my mouth, but didn't light it yet. It was my last one and I intended to go slow with it.

Trestleman didn't hesitate, "He'll say another low-down dirty rat climbed out a window while in police custody. It was a foolish attempt to escape the law. Harrison, you and I will receive commendations."

Agent Harrison nodded and looked down at his feet. His face was bright red and his combed hair had fallen forward over his face. He was every bit as shaken as he should have been under the circumstance.

Trestleman pulled a chair out from the table and sat down. He set his feet wide apart and rested the palms of his hands on his knees.

"Will the newspapers play along?" I asked.

Trestleman seemed relaxed, sure of himself, "Certainly they will."

"I was never here," I added.

"You sure never were." Trestleman replied. He found a cigarette and lit it, taking in over a third of it on the first burn and holding the smoke in his lungs for a long, long period while we all stared at each other.

Finally, I struck a match to my last cigarette and inhaled deeply myself. From far below we heard the sound of a siren drawing closer.

"Special Agent Harrison," the Texan directed, "would you please close the window."

Chapter Twenty-Seven

The front entrance of the City and County Courthouse was around the corner from where Hap Johnson landed. It was no trouble at all for me to walk out that door and cover the half block to where my Ford was parked. Trestleman accompanied me all the same.

The streets were filled with motion: police cruisers, a fire truck, ambulances, and plenty of eager onlookers all rushing to the scene. It was loud and chaotic with the excitement of the crowd that gathered away from us. A light rain was starting to mist, causing small oil rainbows to form in the dirty street.

"Have any good ideas?" Trestleman asked me when we reached my automobile. He stood with one foot on the running board, as if to prevent me from leaving until I provided him with at least one good idea.

The rain, which was starting to fall harder now, didn't seem to concern him. A small river of water collected on the brim of his fedora and dripped down around his face. He gave no sign that he even noticed it.

"Just one," I replied.

Murphy Pendleton and his penciled mustache had come to mind. I needed to look him up anyway: we were past due for a conversation about how to treat a lady.

"I'm all ears," Trestleman said.

"There's a guy in this town that may have a lead on the child. He was in on this right from jump, and he was there with the others when they hauled out from the farmhouse in the early morning, the day the child was taken away. He might know something."

"Care to share a name?"

"No," I said, almost laughing.

"But you know where this guy is?"

"No, though I know a woman who might know, and if she doesn't, he'll come looking for her eventually."

"Would he have the boy with him?"

I shook my head. "No, I can't imagine that he would."

"Although you think he'd know where the child is?"

"Perhaps, its tough to say. He's not the sort to care enough about the child to pay much attention if it isn't part of his immediate job."

"Nice crowd you run with."

"I'm not proud of this one."

"Tell me: who has the child? You seem to have an idea, or maybe you even know."

"An old married couple. By themselves, they're harmless enough. If the boy is alive, he's probably with them and I doubt they would harm him. At least the old man didn't seem to be a bad sort."

"If you give me their names, I'll help you look for them."

"You already know their names."

"Hector and Mary, the Schulz couple? They owned the farmhouse down in Iowa where you held the Hamiltons."

I nodded. "They lammed it that morning too, along with everyone else, leaving me and Isaac behind."

"You sure it was just the two of you left there?"

I didn't answer this question. Instead I replaced it with one of my own: "So you already know their names, which means you're already looking for them. How's that progressing? Are the Schulz's really that hard to find? They didn't seem like the criminal mastermind type to me."

The large Texan nodded and pulled at his mustache. It was a gesture that I suspect he worked hard to refrain from. I took it as the answer to my question.

"Which means," I continued, "that you're not likely to be of much help to me."

"You really want this one, don't you?"

I nodded.

"I have to observe that it's unusual for a professional thief like yourself to care so much about a child who is not his own. Maybe I wonder about that."

I shrugged at this and studied his eyes. "Maybe I already have a child on my conscience. Maybe I don't need another one."

Trestleman nodded at this and removed his foot from my running board.

"I believe you, and it's nice that you have a conscience. Stay in touch," he said. "We'll move quickly if you can get us anything we can act on, anything at all."

"I know," I said, reminded of our earlier conversation in the automobile. "It's personal now."

"Never mind that," he said curtly and then he started to turn.

I watched him take a few steps away from me and then a thought crossed my mind. "Hey, Trestleman," I called softly.

"Yeah?" he replied, half-turning back towards me again, partially twisted now at the waist with one foot still pointing down the sidewalk toward the courthouse.

"Tell me something. Back in the day, how close did you ever come to catching up with Pancho Villa?"

Trestleman squared his body and thought about this question for a moment, studying me as he licked his lower lip. He was trying to decide how much to reveal. Then he moved to turn away again.

"Maybe about a hundred yards," he said finally. "He was on the other side of a deep ravine all by himself, riding a white-maned palomino along the crest, with the sun behind him. I had a Winchester, fired a shot that must have gone far wide. He just waved his hat at me and then disappeared down the other side. Never caught his trail again."

"It eats at you still, doesn't it?"

Trestleman didn't respond. He merely turned his back and stalked off into the rain that was falling harder now, filling the brim of his hat and soaking through his shoes.

Chapter Twenty-Eight

The sisters were waiting where I'd left them, at a downscale motel on the edge of town. It was a double row series of single unit bungalows that had fallen into dilapidation. From the outside you could see the peeling paint from the exterior walls and the twisted gutters hanging from the roof. They were in #6 and I had #8.

Eva, not Delilah, answered the door to #6 when I knocked. Maybe she always answered the door, and maybe she had been doing that since they were little. Maybe Delilah had never learned how to open a door when someone else was knocking on it.

It was nearly half past eight o'clock and I was dog-tired, though lonely and hungry and in need of a smoke. I leaned against the frame after the door was pulled as wide as the chain would allow, and stared into the room.

"I believe you're in number eight," Eva told me, with her carefully framed look of heavy disapproval.

Perhaps there was something about the expression in my face that caused her to take pity, because she pinched the door closed just enough to take the chain off and open the door all the way for me. Behind her I could see Delilah sitting on a metal camp chair with one bare foot on the bed. Her red toenails danced in the weak light of a naked bulb that hung from the ceiling.

The room was hot and a small desk fan in the kitchenette criss-crossed the room, sending out a lukewarm breeze that provided little relief as far as I could tell. I put a foot inside the room, but continued to lean against the frame with my arms crossed. My hat was back on my forehead and my tie was knotted, but only loosely, several inches below my throat.

"Do you have a cigarette, maybe a drink?" I asked into the space between the two women. The tension between them was palpable. All I wanted was a few moments of quiet company and something to numb the swelling anguish within me.

"Sure," Eva told me. "We have all the supplies you bought for us this afternoon. Delilah?" She turned to look back at her sister, but Delilah was already in motion with a scurry and a sway about her.

Before I could say, "jack rabbit" a glass of straight rye was placed in my hand and my hat had been taken from me. Delilah pushed me towards a chair and patted my shoulders. We sat, the three of us, around a small metal counter that folded down from the wall. Delilah and I each had a drink of the rye while Eva got out the fixings to make ham sandwiches.

A package of Chesterfields was on the table and I got it open and lit the first one. When my lungs were filled with the strong, beautiful smoke, Delilah reached across the table and took the cigarette from me, holding it delicately between the tips of her first two fingers. She brought it to her own lips, all the while holding my eyes with hers. It was a sensual gesture. I watched her slowly work the cigarette between her fingertips, seeing the little girl she'd been not so long ago. I wondered how many more of my lit cigarettes she was destined to steal from my lips.

It was a tender moment, though it didn't last long. After she exhaled I looked down toward the table to find another one for myself. I lit it and then swallowed the remainder of my first drink. The sound of dishes rattling came from the kitchenette. Delilah poured me a second drink and freshened her own.

"You could slow it down by having a little something to eat," Eva judged, handing me one of the ham sandwiches on a plate. Her smile was forced, like the smiles of overly responsible people often are.

To her, I suspected, life was a series of tedious obligations. She performed them by rote, like she'd been taught to in school. Rebellion hadn't crossed her mind. It was as foreign to her as a Chinese scroll would've been to me.

I couldn't begrudge her – she was the eldest sister and I imagined that came with certain expectations. With a smile I forgave her dogmatic adherence to the current order and I nodded my head as she watched me for my reaction. If I could play peacemaker between the two sisters I'd do it, gladly enough.

I accepted the sandwich and bit into it. The salty texture of the ham and the bitter tang of the stone-ground mustard was my reward. Chewing quietly, I looked back and forth between them. They were so different and yet so similar. I wondered if either one of them could see it.

"Eva doesn't drink or smoke," Delilah explained to me without expression. "She never learned the habits."

"I don't see the need," Eva responded defensively. Her eyes dipped down, embarrassed to be spoken about that way in front of me.

"I think it's perfectly charming," Delilah said flatly.

Eva rose to the provocation. "Where did it ever take you, anyway? How much of your troubles have been baited with men who wouldn't hold their liquor? You expect me to believe the man who gave you that shiner did it while he was sober?"

Delilah touched the side of her face, self-consciously. "At least I've had my fun. Where have any of your high floating ideals brought you?"

"Okay," I interrupted. "Let's not be mean to each other tonight. I'm too tired for this banter, even if you are sisters."

I meant it. The resentments between them were harmful enough, and they fatigued me in a way that such words rarely managed to do. There was something about the familial nature of their exchange that wearied me all the more.

But Eva wouldn't let it drop: "Delilah fancies herself 'the pretty one' in the family. As if that's an accomplishment she can be proud of. But what is that really? Good looks—simply a coincidence of nature, and one that fades quickly as she'll find out if she keeps living at this pace. Better to develop something that will last."

The bitter envy in her words and tone cut deeply. Delilah's shoulders pulled back and she set her cigarette into the ashtray. For a moment I thought she would respond with her own sharp words, but then she did something expected. Her hands dropped to her lap and she sat still, chin lowered, looking down at the untouched ham sandwich in front of her.

A moment of time skipped over itself and then beat on again, pushing ceaselessly against the vivid past. I noticed a bare flutter of Delilah's eyelids and the corners of her eyes welled slightly, but did not overflow. Her voice, when she spoke was controlled.

"I'm sorry," she said quietly. "Thank you for preparing this supper."

She picked up the sandwich and took a small bite, chewing slowly, deliberately, as if the fate of the world might have depended on it. Eva pulled her hands together and stared down at the table in front of her awkwardly. For a minute she sat without moving. I wondered if she was saying a prayer.

I lit another cigarette and looked back and forth between the two sisters. They were each attractive women in their own way, though Eva's looks would never be conventionally valued, as she might have wished.

211

Delilah was the one. She had a Hollywood figure and style about her, and yet it was her large eyes that snared me, holding me helplessly in a spell that she didn't even seem aware of weaving. If she seemed young and childlike in moments, I suspected it was because as the baby of the family she'd been encouraged to behave that way. Away from her sister, there were hints of wisdom and kindness that suggested a greater maturity than her family was likely to ever see. Like actors reading from a script, it seemed we all reverted to some prior stage when confronted with family manners from our past.

I let the scene play out without comment.

We finished the meal in silence and when we were finished Delilah cleared the plates and food, carrying them over to the kitchenette in three trips. She didn't finish her drink and the abandoned cigarette slowly burned itself out in the ashtray.

I hummed a few bars of a tune to myself. It was a sad melody I'd heard a teenager named Billie Holiday perform at Covan's in New York City some months earlier. Neither of my companions seemed to notice. Maybe they were preoccupied with their own entrenching thoughts, or maybe I'd hummed something that held no meaning for them.

After a few minutes, Eva stood up without looking at me and stepped over to the kitchenette where I heard her apologizing in return to her little sister. They shared a brief embrace and then there was the sound of whispers and contained laughter exchanged between them as dishes tinkled in the sink basin.

Without apologizing for anything, I retired to #8 by myself and sat for a while on the bed, smoking with the lights off. Some time after midnight I got undressed and pulled back the sheets. I was tired and it was a relief to be by myself, away from the push-pull tension of the two sisters.

Passing headlights from the nearby roadway swept across the ceiling at regular intervals like hobgoblins from my own past, keeping me company well into the deepening night.

Chapter Twenty-Nine

In the morning I was awakened early by the whine of trucks downshifting as they approached city limits. Eva was dressed and ready when I knocked on the door of #6. Her hair had dried straight and her face, taut with dry skin, looked eager and slightly confused in the morning sunlight.

She smiled and let me know that Delilah hadn't slept much during the night and that she was still prettying herself for the day. There was no malice in her words. I backed up to wait outside in the shade cast by a nearby sycamore tree, where the slim threads of light filtered down through the leaves.

It wasn't a long wait. Less then ten minutes later, the two sisters emerged with their overnight bags packed and ready to load. Together, the three of us had breakfast in a small diner that we passed on the way back to their apartment. Conversation between us was minimal, which was fine with me.

By the time we got back to the apartment house in West St. Paul, the sun was already hot and the air wasn't moving at all. The month of June was closing out, which meant we weren't even into the hottest days of the summer yet.

I parked on the street behind an old Dodge pick-up truck with rusted fenders and dirty side streaks that indicated it had been used in a field since it had last been washed. It was filled with lawn tools: rakes, shears, a wheelbarrow, two ladders of different sizes, and several other metal contraptions.

A small terrier, leashed to a stake across the street, barked at us as we got out of the Ford. Delilah waved at him. It wasn't clear to me whether that was supposed to quiet him, but if it was, it had the opposite effect. He strained hard against his leash, barking as ferociously as he knew how to in fast, staccato yips and yaps. Eva scowled and told Delilah to "leave the poor thing alone."

I went on ahead, antsy to get in and out.

As I approached the bed of impatiens that lined the walkway to Eva's front door I sensed something was wrong. The door to the apartment was closed, yet it appeared to be tilted oddly within its frame. As soon as I got up close to it, I understood why. The lock had been pried apart and the inside of the apartment had been breached, probably some time under the cover of darkness.

I motioned the sisters to retreat back to the street. Then I drew my .45 and pushed through the door, ready for whatever might wait inside. Nothing inside waited for me other than a royal mess. The place was in complete disarray.

Moving quickly, I went through every room. There were no sounds. Furniture had been broken apart or tipped over, the mattress had been dumped on the floor and cut open, clothing was strewn about near the dresser, and the mirror in the bathroom was smashed. Contents from the medicine cabinet had been dumped into the washbasin. I counted assorted pills, shampoo, eyelash clamps, soap, and a roll of unraveled medical tape. Whoever did it, they'd been methodically destructive.

I holstered my weapon and called out to the sisters with an all clear.

They came in and moved about slowly, stunned, heads turning from side to side, surveying the damage to their home. Nothing of this sort had ever happened to either one of them and they were both shaken by it. I didn't blame them.

"See. Now you understand why we slept in a motel last night."

"Who did this?" Eva asked, a note of despair scratched through her voice. "Was it Murphy?" She held her hands together, wringing them anxiously as if the kinetic energy might help clear the room.

I looked at Delilah, then back at Eva, shaking my head.

"I don't think Murphy did this," I said to them both.

Delilah shook her head and turned to look away from me. I caught a look of hesitancy in her eyes that left me wondering if there was something that she hadn't told me. If there was, I couldn't imagine what it was.

"Why not?" Eva asked.

"It doesn't seem his style and he had no reason to. And, frankly, I think more than one person was involved in this adventure. It was a lot of work to rearrange your apartment like this."

"Who would do this and why?"

I stood still for a moment, trying to understand myself, considering the various possibilities. The danger they faced now was because of me initially, but now they would likely face it whether I was with them or not. The people who were after me wouldn't know it if I left them alone. They might take the sisters to draw me out. At least if I were with them,

214

I could provide some protection.

"Eva, someone has been watching you," I said finally. "They're looking for me and they must have missed us yesterday when I came here. So they were looking for something, or maybe they were sending a message. They came in during the night – it's the only way they could have done it. They ransacked your home, quietly and systematically – and it's not the first time they've done this sort of thing. I think they were professionals. You can't stay here now, it's too dangerous."

"Why?" Eva asked again, her voice edging towards a higher octave. She was growing madder by the minute and I didn't blame her for that either. Her world didn't have an accounting column for the kind of animalistic threat she faced now. She was used to people being nice and asking politely for what they wanted and if they didn't get it, they assumed it was because some rational decision had been fairly made and that their turn would come. The depth of human wickedness was hard to understand, let alone accept, especially when confronted for the first time. I tried to help her with it.

"Eva, it's not about you. They're looking for me. They think I'm with you and Delilah, so they struck what they could here."

"Why?" Eva asked once more. Her voice was strident now, powered by the dogma of her belief in a just world that did not exist and never had.

I took a slow breath and then I spoke bluntly: "Because somebody wants to kill me. It's a haunting from my past. They want to put me in the ground and keep me out of their way forever. The two of you and your apartment are simply a means towards that end."

The room was quiet. Even the terrier across the street had stopped barking. Delilah came around from behind her sister and stood near me with a hand cocked on her hip. She looked angry too, though perhaps for a different reason.

"Who'd want to kill you?"

An image came to me: it was the inhuman face of the Irishman, staring at me with black unknowable puddles where his eyes should have been. He was standing in his wood-paneled office above the Nightingale Club, with the sickly, yellowed lighting and the single yellow rose that sat in a vase beside him on the desk. Dressed in an immaculate black and white tuxedo, with his reddish hair clipped short and combed over to one side, he offered me a vacant ghoulish smile and a generous finger of Irish whiskey, neat, in a crystal tumbler. *He had*

215

taken the only woman I had ever loved.

Now I was angry too.

I didn't describe the image or explain. Instead I stepped away from the two sisters and stood with my back to them, looking out the window towards the small dog across the street. He'd taken a rest from barking at strangers and appeared to be sleeping with his head turned to one side, resting on paws that were straight out in front of him. His tail bounced around behind him, the tip of it flickering with an energy that seemed to be all its own. I knew that at the slightest provocation he would come out of his slumber and be ready to ready to bark at anything that moved or threatened the tranquility of his street.

"Who wants to kill you?" Delilah asked again, louder this time.

"Nobody who matters," I said in response. "Nobody who matters at all, not the least bit."

*

When I turned back toward the room, the two sisters were standing close together now, looking at each other. They appeared to communicate without speaking. I couldn't follow the tender secrets they traded. Whatever they were, they carried a soothing effect. Eva leaned forward and accepted an embrace and a short kiss on her cheek from Delilah. Then they both looked over at me.

"Well," Eva started. "Where do we go from here?" She looked over at Delilah, who nodded, and then back at me with a slight tilt to her face.

"Let's clean up a little bit," I suggested. "We've time to do that. The lock on the front door needs to be replaced."

"We can't stay here?"

"No," I said, though I wasn't sure it had been a question. "Not tonight. This'll blow over soon enough once I move on, but neither of you should stay here for a little while. Can you go back to Des Moines and stay for at least a couple of weeks?"

Eva nodded, but Delilah started to protest. "I want to stay with you," she announced.

She bent over at the waist, with a long, tan leg out in front of her, rubbing her ankle as though it might have itched. To me it seemed a practiced, though possibly unconscious, gesture, and one that was designed to draw attention to the sexual perfection that was represented by her leg.

"We've been through this already," I told her. "There's no good that can come of that."

She brushed her hair back over her shoulders and looked at me with a blaze.

"Says who?"

"It's certainly obvious if you think about it," I said. "With mobsters trying to kill me and law enforcement across the Midwest trying to arrest or shoot me, it's not safe for you to be anywhere near me."

"You're trying to find Wilson, right?"

I nodded that I was.

"Then I can help, if you let me. But you have to let me stay near you."

This made me laugh a little.

"How can you help?"

"I can get Murphy to tell me everything he knows, and he might know where the child is. Right?"

"Delilah, I don't know. And even if he does—"

"Of course he knows. He split out with the old couple, the child, and Mr. Hamilton. Both he and Mr. Hamilton are back in St. Paul now. That means the little boy is with the old couple—and Murphy will know where they are. He's probably not with them, may not even know what they've done since he left, but he'll know where they went, where they are. You know I'm right."

Although I didn't want to admit it, I agreed with her logic. Eva moved into the conversation: "Delilah, you should listen to him. There's no life for you if you stay with him. And you cannot save the child yourself."

"I don't know any such thing. And neither do you. Matter of fact, you don't know what you're talking about."

"It doesn't make sense and it's dangerous. You can't go near Mr. Pendleton. He hurt you once, he'll do it again. If you need to be reminded – then just look at yourself in the mirror. Your face is ghastly!"

"I won't have you throw that at me. My bruises are my own, and I already carry them on my face. I don't need you pummeling me too. For the sake of the child, I have to try. Plus, I owe that son-of-a-bitch, Murphy, at least something for what he did to me."

"What can you do to make him tell you?"

"I'm busted up some, but not broken. I have a few tricks left."

"Well, I just bet you do."

217

Delilah swirled to stare at her sister, angry at the implication of her words. The cycle had revolved again.

"You can't be thinking that."

"And what if I do? Is it such a stretch from how you've already behaved?"

Delilah shook her head vigorously, denying this point. She looked back at me, quickly, and then back at her older sister. "I'm with him now," she said, gesturing with a sideways bob of her head. "He will protect me."

Eva paused before responding. When she did speak, her tone was lower and she spoke slowly. It was an attempt to be persuasive, not damning. "Delilah, listen to me: There is no way you can have a life with him."

"You stay out of this now—just because you've never had a man—"

The words Delilah had started to utter were probably true enough, though insensitive and cruel in effect. She caught herself before actually finishing them out loud, yet she may as well have screamed them from the roof. I moved backwards, out of the circle that now held only the two of them.

Eva's hair had fallen down over her face and she tossed her head back to clear it from blocking her vision. She looked at Delilah steadily from beneath one errant lock that refused to re-perch on top of her head. The look of black resentment in her eyes was palpable. In her own way, Delilah seemed to shrink from it, turning on one heel to present a sideways target for the bitter arrows aimed by her older sister. But she didn't deflate as I would have expected.

"Live your life," Eva responded angrily, surprising even me with the cutting edge in her tone. "Live your own life. Stop chasing some fairy tale that you've imagined is possible. This man will bring you nothing but heartache and trouble. You can choose your man. You can have most any man you want—you've proven that often enough. So, why not choose one who won't bring you such heartache?"

"We both know she's right," I said to Delilah, stepping back into the circle, directly between them. I'm not sure what I was trying to prevent in that moment, but it seemed to be my movement, more than my actual words that broke the angry force that connected them.

Delilah's shoulders dropped and she turned fully around, with her back to both of us, and crossed the room to a chair that lay on its side. Slowly, she righted it and then positioned it to face the window. With her shoulders squared again she sat down and released a small noise that could have been sigh. Then she was still, sitting erect with her hands on her lap. Her lips were moving slightly, with no sound, but I was unable to read them.

Eva went to her and knelt beside the chair. She patted Delilah's neck gently and whispered quiet consolations that I could not hear.

*

I withdrew to another part of the apartment and removed myself further by examining the mess in the kitchen. I thought about the man or men who'd done this. I'd already identified them as professionals. But was I missing something? Had they been looking for something, or merely sending a message? And if they were looking for something, then what was it? As far as I knew, we didn't have anything that anyone would be looking for.

The contents of the cupboards had been pulled out onto the counters and floor. Canned goods were everywhere. Packages of rice and flour had been torn open and sprinkled about. There were no footprints in the flour that was on the floor, indicating that it had been the final act. The vandal must have walked backwards out of the kitchen sprinkling the flour as he walked. There were no traces of flour on the floor in the sitting room or front hallway. So, whomever he was, he'd been careful enough not to get any on him.

The meaning of it eluded me. I waited a few more minutes until I heard the sound of the two sisters laughing together about something. After that resolution, they seemed to have decided upon something.

"Alright," I announced to get their attention, stepping back over to their side of the room, back once more into their circle. "We need to get this place straightened up and then it's time to have a talk with that old boy, Murphy Pendleton."

Chapter Thirty

We spent the rest of the morning and early afternoon fixing up the apartment as best we could. A female neighbor from upstairs came down to visit and stayed to help. She'd heard nothing during the night and was surprised to see the damage throughout the apartment. In the early afternoon, a locksmith came by and replaced the hardware on the front door and added two deadbolts, high and low, leaving two sets of new keys—one for each sister. He did his work quietly, without asking how the lock had been broken. I imagined he saw a lot of that in his work and the reasons had ceased to surprise – or matter.

While the locksmith was doing his thing, Eva announced she was going back to Des Moines and then disappeared into her bedroom to pack and prepare. Sending a dark look my way first, Delilah went in with her and closed the door behind her. They were in there together for the better part of an hour. I sat resting on one of the yellow cushions by the window and stared out at the terrier across the street.

Eventually Delilah came out and smiled.

"I'll be coming with you," she announced, and then she turned away from me before I could respond. Across the street the terrier had raised his head. He'd heard something, but he wasn't sure what it was. He sniffed the air, and then he let his chin fall back to rest on his paws.

Eva came out of the bedroom a few minutes later carrying a medium sized grip, and she smiled at me as if she now approved. "It's decided. You can drop me at the bus depot. I'll catch a ride to Des Moines later this evening. It's an express, with only one stop between."

*

Murphy Pendleton was easy enough to reach. Delilah simply called him at the telephone exchange he'd left the day before and invited him to meet her for a drink at a local watering hole. It was not too far away from where we were.

Shortly after dark, I entered the tavern by myself and found a seat at a table along the wall. Delilah came in five minutes behind me and took a table in the middle of the room, near the bar itself, facing me.

221

From where I sat I could easily watch both the entrance and the table that Delilah had chosen. We didn't have to wait long.

Murphy came in a few minutes later, ten minutes early himself, and pulled a chair out to sit down across the table from Delilah, with his back towards me. As he'd entered, I noticed he was dressed rakishly in a tailored pin-stripe suit and a matching bowler hat. His clothing looked brand-new and was self-consciously worn. He'd trimmed his mustache, thinning it even more now in the pencil style that was so popular in the big cities. Thin and contrived, it carried little of the masculine authority of the mustache Agent Trestleman sported. I smiled to myself at the absurd thought of them meeting each other to compare facial hair.

The tavern was only half full of customers and it was poorly lit by design. Each table had a large, flat candle burning within a tinted glass tube that was shaped like a pear. I nursed a draft beer and waited, watching the table where Delilah and Murphy sat conversing with each other. After about twenty minutes, Delilah looked toward me and gave a concise wave with her first two fingers held together as one.

I stood up and crossed the room quickly to stand next to their table.

"Hiya, Murph," I said.

"Duncan?"

The look in his eyes was one of surprise and fear. I couldn't tell which reaction was primary. He pushed his drink away and squared his shoulders, ready to move if I challenged him.

Delilah stood up to address me. "I know where the child is. Let's go. There's no need to mix it with him now."

"Me and Murph, we're not settled up yet," I said, turning my head to look at Murphy.

Delilah pulled at my arm. "Leave it," she implored. "He doesn't matter. Let's go get the child. I know where he is, and he's all that matters now. Murphy doesn't mean a thing, not a thing to me now."

Ignoring her, I gestured with my hand. "Stand up," I told him.

"I'm not carrying, Duncan."

"I won't draw on you. Stand up."

With an uneasy grin he rose from his chair and moved it forward a few inches, holding it by the back center columns. He stood so that it was positioned between us. A few inches taller than me, he'd have a longer reach. But I probably had five pounds on him and a lifetime of experience. I remembered the fear and the doubt that shaped his eyes when we faced off at the dock that morning after he and Hamilton had been practicing with the Thompson gun. I'd known it then, as had he. If it came to a fight between us, he'd be the one to back down.

"Did you turn over Delilah's apartment last night?" I asked him.

His long nose moved about anxiously and his eyes didn't land on mine. He touched his pencil mustache with the back of his hand, drawing the knuckles of his first two fingers across it and then down in a J shaped pattern. "No," he said evasively. "She told me about it. I didn't do it, and I don't know who did."

"Where is the child?"

"Wilson?"

"Yes, that's his name."

"I don't know. He's probably with the old couple. We split up the same day we left you at the farmhouse. I came back to St. Paul that very day. They all traveled to a hideout I'd set up as backup before the kidnapping. Delilah was with me; she can help you find it—if you really care to. It's only a few hours drive from here, this side of the Iowa border."

I nodded. We had what we'd come for, but I wasn't finished yet. I couldn't let it go. "What happened, Murphy?"

He stood there with his palms out, moving his shoulders in an ignorant up-and-down motion. "I don't know," he said. He added several foul words to the string. "What are you talking about?"

"We went into this together as partners, and you messed it up. Perhaps worse than anything, you violated the code. There's supposed to be an honor among thieves, and we'd agreed on a few principles before this job started. Remember, we have no one else to count on. You double-crossed us all the way down the line."

"It wasn't my idea to," he said defensively. "And by the time they put it to me there wasn't a way out of it."

"What about Isaac? He was our partner."

That stopped him. "I heard about that," he said slowly, trying to gauge my reaction as he spoke.

"Were you a part of that?"

"No, I would never—"

"Did you set him up?"

"No. It was awful business. I would never have done anything like that to him, or any of our crew."

"Did you know what they intended to do?"

"No! And I'm sorry about it. I really am. I didn't have anything to

223

do with it. They never said anything to me. I don't even know who did it or why."

"What's your best guess?"

"Same as yours, probably."

"Spell it," I suggested.

"Goons, Irish goons from Chicago." Murphy looked down at his toes and rocked back and forth slowly, letting his weight shift from one foot to the other. "I didn't know you and him was such good friends."

I shook my head firmly. "Doesn't matter if we were friends or not – we were partners. When you side up with a man you stay with him, you see things through. Otherwise you're no better than a feral animal."

"Okay," he said. "You're within rights to be sore and I'm sorry."

"You still have to answer for her," I told him, pointing towards Delilah who stood on the other side of the table with her hands held flat to her sides. She stood very still.

"It wasn't exactly like I raped her," he asserted.

"How was it not?" I looked at Delilah who'd moved around the table towards me. There was a sad expression of fear in her face that tugged at me, yet I couldn't let it go yet.

"I was drunk and angry. I already apologized to her," Murphy said. "What's past is past."

His tone was defiant and mean now, anything but apologetic. I took a short step toward him, moving slowly with my foot, until it was planted. The punch I threw next exploded from my shoulder and caught him directly on the face, centered just to one side of his nose as he tried too late to turn from it. His body snapped backwards and his arms jerked into the air, a pair of flightless wings. He went down hard, landing on the table behind him. It fell over under his weight and carried him backwards over it to the floor.

Without any hurry, I stepped around the chair and walked over to where he lay on his back. I lingered for a moment, wanting more of what I'd started. From the table, I picked up a beer bottle and, holding it upside down from the neck, I shattered the base of it over the edge of the table. Glass splintered and flew about. It scattered, along with the remnants of leftover beer that was in the bottom of the bottle.

I stood over Murphy and looked down at his broken face. Blood pulsed from one nostril and his cheekbone sagged as though it had been fractured. The pencil mustache had all but disappeared under the blood.

It wasn't me anymore standing there, I'd snapped and become

224

something or somebody else. I was going to finish it. With the jagged piece of glass held in front of me I leaned toward his exposed neck. He was unconscious, and it was in my mind to ensure that he stayed that way. A quick flick of the wrist and the jagged broken glass would severe his jugular or his windpipe. I'd promised Abigail Hamilton revenge, and maybe I owed it to Isaac too.

Behind me Delilah pleaded with me to step away from him. A bartender started to make noises.

I straightened up and stared the bartender down.

"You sure about wanting in on this?" I said to him and he backed away. To Delilah I said simply: "He doesn't deserve to be spared."

"No," she replied. She drew a long breath before her impassioned speech: "He doesn't. He helped take the child away and he raped me. He betrayed us all for greed. I can forgive him for what he did to me, and if I can forgive him for that, then you have to let it go, at least that part of it. As for the child, if it were on him, really on him, I'd say then finish it and let him be damned, but he was fooled too. They played him off just as cool as they played you.

"Then there's the last and final matter: I don't believe he was involved in what they did to Isaac. He's no good, but he's not all that bad either. He said he didn't know about Isaac, wasn't a part of that, and I believe him there. I don't know why, I just do. Perhaps he's simply too stupid for me to believe it was any other way than how he said it was. They never paid Murphy a penny of what they promised, and he never had any idea the child wouldn't be returned when the ransom was paid. Can't you see? He's not the one you need to kill and he's not worth it."

It was a long speech. I took a deep breath and considered her willingness to forgive the man. Her argument was reasoned.

"Okay," I conceded, turning without any haste to look at her. She stood behind me with her hands turned in at the wrists over her hips. Her little fingers moved back and forth anxiously. "If that's how it is then. Let's get out of here."

I dropped the bottle on the floor behind me. It landed with a clunk and I heard it roll across the hard wood floor of the tavern as we made toward the exit.

On the street together we walked for two blocks without speaking. Automobiles flitted past us, whisking towards late night destinations that were almost certainly destined to disappoint. Their taillights shrank quickly, mirage-like, as they receded ahead of us—as though they'd never even existed. The effect was a lonely one.

When we approached the curb spot where we had left the Ford, I stopped walking and pulled Delilah around, gently but firmly. Together we stood under the soft hum and glow of a street lamp. I caressed the side of her face with one hand.

"Do you really forgive him?" I asked her. "Or did you say that only to persuade me not to kill him?"

Delilah's expression was serious and she nodded, looking up at me into the light. "I've forgiven him. I didn't intend to, I just did it and I don't even know why. I guess life's too short to hold onto the hate forever."

I nodded, still touching her face, holding her hair back so that I could read her eyes in the light. Absolution came from mysterious places, often when you least expected it.

"I guess that has to matter for something. Where is the child? Will you tell me now so that I can get on with finding him?"

She pulled her shoulders down and leaned away from me, so that my hand was no longer touching her. "Better then that, I'll show you," she said.

"That's out of the question, Delilah. Tell me where he is and then I will put you on a bus to join your sister in Des Moines."

"Or else what?" she demanded firmly.

I stepped back from her and my voice, when I replied, was softer. "Or else nothing. There's nothing I would ever do to hurt you or pressure you, but I want you to tell me what you know about where the child is."

"No," she said simply. She crossed her arms defiantly and half-turned so that I was looking at her outstretched chin in profile.

"Delilah."

"You want me. I know you do. You wouldn't have sent me the necklace if you didn't."

I shook my head. "That was a mistake. I admired your toughness, and wanted to give you something that would be comforting after what Murphy did to you. I wasn't even going to let you know if was from me."

226

"I knew you sent it. You're going to take me with you. I know where we can find the old couple – but I won't tell you. I'll only show you. You have to take me with you. If you do, I will help you find them tomorrow morning. That's the deal."

I didn't believe she'd really withhold the information from me if it came down to it, but I didn't have the energy to resist her ... and maybe I didn't really want to anymore. Maybe I already hadn't when I sent her the locket.

Something primitive but good had a hold of me.

Chapter Thirty-One

It was Sunday again – the Sabbath for some, a day of worship or a day of doubt, depending on how much one took on faith. A whole week had gone by since I'd attended the Cubs double-header in Chicago with my pal, Johnny. It seemed like a month had gone by, even a year or more, but it was less than two weeks since I'd picked up Hamilton and Wilson in the Iowa countryside. I tried to remember the last time I'd attended church and couldn't.

Delilah and I drove south toward Iowa for the better part of three hours. Eventually, she directed me to a small town near the state line, just before we would have crossed over the border. A two-lane county road fed us right into the middle of it.

Main Street took us past a county seat and a series of shops and businesses, including a bank, a hardware store, a grocery, a barber, an insurance company, and two diners. The centerpiece of the town, recently decorated with American flag bunting, was a drugstore that advertised fresh fountain drinks and peach ice cream. Each end of the street had a service station and a lone stop sign. As we drove down the street, I realized that I'd been there once before—the previous year, when we took down the bank for about $12,000.

Most of the men who rode with me on that job were now either dead or in prison.

We drove the entire length of the street and then made a U-turn to retrace our path back to the focal point of town. On either side of Main Street were residential neighborhoods, three to four blocks deep, which were lined with two-story wood frame houses. A handful of brick houses centered near the town, probably owned by the bankers and wealthier shopkeepers. From somewhere a block off Main Street you could hear a dog barking rapidly.

Delilah pointed out several turns and then we found the house she was looking for. She remembered it because the front porch, which had been propped up on cinder blocks at one time, had collapsed from water damage and neglect.

The only way to enter the house was through a side door off the driveway. The rest of the house was in a similar state of disrepair. Roof shingles were missing and you could see a squirrel's nest peeking out from large cracks in the chimney. We parked at the curb in front of the house and studied it for a few minutes. There was no other movement on the street.

"It's sure quiet here," Delilah noted after a while.

"The whole town's dead or dying fast."

"Seems more like a long, gradual fade away."

"But that's what brought you and Murphy here in the first place, right?" I asked.

"He picked it. I was just along for the ride. Brother, if I only knew …"

"What's inside?"

"Not much, that's for sure. Just a few basics: three or four chairs and a card table in the kitchen, a dresser and bed in the one bedroom over the front. The kitchen has a few pots and pans, along with an old decrepit icebox. The first floor was pretty much empty when we were here, as was the second bedroom on the top floor."

"What about the basement?" I inquired.

"Never went down there. It was dark and didn't seem to have any working light bulbs."

"I doubt the old couple have added much since they arrived."

"It's sure depressing. I don't see an automobile anywhere. You think they're still here with the kid?"

I checked my holster with a quick pat to reassure myself. I had several spare clips on my belt. "That's what I am going to find out," I said.

"You don't think you're going to need that?" Delilah asked.

"Wait here," I instructed her.

"Can't I come in with you?"

"No. I don't expect any trouble, but if you hear gunshots, start up the Ford and drive over to the drugstore. Have yourself an ice cream soda and wait for me. If I don't show up within forty five minutes, drive on."

"I would never do that."

"Eventually, if you stick with me you'll have to. If not today, then some other day down the road."

"Never."

"Then you'll inhibit my ability to do what I need to do. If you refuse to take care of yourself, I'll have just that much more to worry about—and that increases the risk to me. Is that what you want?"

She considered this, looking away from me all the while at the run-down house. "All right," she said finally. "If I hear gunshots, I'll drive down to the drugstore and wait for you. I'll do it, but I won't like it."

"Promise me?"

She nodded slowly without looking my way. I opened the door on my side and climbed out of the sedan into the street. There was a light breeze in the air. It blew into my face and I squinted to keep the dust from my eyes.

Overhead the sky was hazy with gray and charcoal colored clouds. They stretched as far as you could see, layered over one another.

I walked up the driveway, all the way past the house for a quick glance into the backyard. For that effort I was rewarded with a view of knee-high weeds and two rusted poles from which a laundry line had hung once. A blackbird was perched on one of the poles. He swiveled his head to watch me with one unblinking eye.

I stared back.

Turning around, I went back to the side door and stood for a moment examining it. The doorknob was rusted metal. I tried it gently with my fingertips and it turned, so I pushed it open and stepped inside without knocking.

Straight ahead were three steps that took me up to what I assumed was the first floor, while bare, wooden stairs to my left led down to the basement and its darkness. A musty odor confronted my nostrils: it was a heady combination of rot, cigarette smoke, unventilated air, and something else, something much darker than rot. I couldn't quite put my finger on what that something else was.

For a moment I hesitated there, then took the three steps directly ahead of me and found myself in a short hallway spur with light at either end. No sounds came from anywhere in the house to guide me. Since Delilah had said there was no furniture in the front room when she and Murphy had been there, I assumed it was an unlikely place to find anyone. I went to the left, towards the back of the house where I assumed the kitchen would be.

My quick guess paid off. In the kitchen, I found Mary, sitting by herself at a rickety card table. In front of her was an ashtray so full of old butts and ashes that it was about to spill over. There was also a tall washed out highball tumbler with some two inches of dark liquid at the bottom of it. The liquid could have been whiskey.

As I came into the room she turned slowly to look at me. A cigarette hung from her mouth, issuing a small bit of lazy smoke that floated upwards without urgency. Her left eye, sagging badly now, seemed to wink at me in a manner that was neither flirtatious nor suspicious. It was simply evidence of an old and failing woman who'd lost her will to care anymore about her appearance. Her hair, seemingly whiter now, was no longer piled up in the tangled bun she had worn before. Now it fell flat across her shoulders, neck, and back. The effect was that she appeared twenty years older than she had seemed the last time I'd seen her.

"Mary?" I started.

"Who are you? We have the house until the end of the month."

"I'm not the landlord."

"No, of course you're not."

"Don't you remember me?"

She shook her head, oddly confused.

"I visited at your house, your farm in Iowa, about ten days ago. Remember, I stayed with you when Mr. Hamilton and his son Wilson were there."

The cigarette in her mouth, burned low by now, appeared to put itself out. She removed it from her lips and dropped it on the pile of butts in the ashtray. Immediately, she lit another one, and the ridges around her mouth stood out prominently for a moment as she drew on it.

"Are you that preacher man?" she asked once she exhaled.

"No ma'am, I'm no preacher man." I moved into the kitchen and stood in front of her, near the sink, leaning back against it with my arms crossed.

"You read the Bible."

"Yes, I did. That was me, but I'm not a preacher."

"You had a gun too. I thought you were one of those preachers with a gun."

I shook my head.

"Do you still have the gun?"

This time I nodded, watching her carefully. She seemed far more unraveled than I would have guessed possible in such a short period of time. "Yes, ma'am, I do."

"And have you come to shoot us?"

"No," I said, shaking my head slowly again. "That's not why I am here. But I think you know who I am looking for."

"Then you are here, looking for him?"

"Yes."

232

"Not to kill me?"

"That is not my purpose."

"I thought maybe you were an angel of death."

"No. Can you tell me where he is?"

"He's upstairs, resting. It's Sunday, you know."

I took the stairs slowly and paused at the landing to look about. It was quiet. The only sound was the creak of floorboards beneath me as I shifted my weight. Three doors, all of them partially open, confronted me. One was a closet and one was a room that was completely empty. The floorboards were bare and marked with old stains caused by water and who knew what else.

I stepped through the third door, a bedroom that overlooked the street, and glanced around. There were three pieces of furniture in the room: a large bed, a dresser, and a sagging upholstered chair that badly needed to be re-stuffed. The floor was bare and there were no curtains over the windows.

On top of the dresser was the framed photograph of the young woman in the white dress with the wide brimmed hat that had been in the living room of the Iowa farmhouse. The light was better here than it had been in the other house, and I could see that the woman in the photograph was quite pretty. Soft dimples at the corners of her mouth hinted at what might have been a pleasant smile.

Wilson was nowhere in sight. Instead, I found Hector lying on top of the bedspread. He was dressed in what I assumed were his best clothing, as if perhaps he had prepared for church that morning and then instead lay down and fallen back to sleep. The suit, tie, and socks were all black; his shirt was starched white. A pair of freshly polished shoes was set together on the floor beside the bed where he'd be able to reach them easily if he were to sit up. His hands were crossed peacefully on his chest, clasping a folded handkerchief, and his eyes were closed.

He was dead, of course, though he hadn't been dead for long and his body had been laid out carefully. I stood for a minute, poised above him. There were no notable marks or signs of blood or violence. His previously yellowed skin had paled now to take on a whitish pallor and, when I touched his cold cheek gently with the back of my hand, his lips parted slightly and emitted a slow drool of white foam. I pulled back quickly and stared down at him, trying to understand.

The room was too quiet for answers to my questions, but I stood there anyway for a while longer. Eventually, I turned around to look out the window over the top of the collapsed front porch. I could see Delilah sitting in the Ford parked out where I'd left it. From my vantage point she appeared to be praying. Nothing moved on the street.

Before leaving the room, I picked up the photograph and carried it out with me, holding it face up with my thumb on top. I closed the bedroom door behind me as I left Hector to his long, deep rest.

At the landing, before starting down the stairs, I studied the photograph again. The anxious eyes of the pretty young woman staring out at me from some long distant past were Mary's eyes. I had no doubt about that now. Yet there was nothing in them that hinted at the point where fate had taken her some forty years on, nothing at all. It was hard to fathom.

I took the steps slowly and rejoined her in the kitchen, where she sat exactly where I'd left her, finishing another cigarette.

"Hector's resting," she said to me with a sigh after she became aware of my presence.

I stood for a long moment, leaning with my back against the sink again. "No, ma'am," I said finally. "Hector's dead."

"He's resting."

I moved away from the sink and pulled out a chair so that I sat across the card table from her. I set the photograph on the table between us, with the portrait facing up, so that she could see it. She didn't give it even a brief glance.

"He's resting forever," I told her.

"Yes. Isn't it strange?"

"He hasn't been dead long."

"No. He just drank the poison this morning, only a few hours ago."

By now nothing she could say could surprise me. "Why did he take poison?"

She shrugged and inhaled from her cigarette, pursing her lips around it. "Because I gave it to him."

"Why did he drink it?"

"I told you: because I gave it to him." Her tone suggested a note of puzzlement at my questions.

"He didn't know it was poison?"

Mary shrugged again. I couldn't tell whether she was indifferent or unsure of the truth. "He's been sick. I told him it was medicine."

I nodded. "Why?"

"Why what?"

"Why did you do that? Why did you kill your husband?"

"He was sick, and so very tired. It's been so long. I know he needed to rest. All those years of hard work on the farm, it wears on you, you know. He was plumb worn out from it all, the poor man. I loved him once, so long ago. I fixed him up nicely, didn't you see?"

"Yes, I saw."

"It upset him so greatly."

"What did?"

"All of it."

"Ma'am, I have to ask you a question."

She looked at me with eyes that were not fully aware.

"Can I ask you a question?" I asked her slowly.

This time she nodded and made a short movement with her hand.

"Where is the little boy? Where is Wilson?"

She thought about this for a while. "I remember him. He liked baseball."

"Yes, where is he?"

"He's behind the barn." She spoke the words as if they should have been obvious to me.

"The barn? There is no barn here."

"Not here, at our farm. He's behind our barn there. He's been there all along."

"What is he doing there?"

"He's resting."

I shrank from the truth and sat back in my chair to look at the old woman.

"Mister preacher man, will you pray with me?" Mary asked presently. Her eyes were glassy, perhaps from all the smoke that had collected about her, or perhaps from something else.

I shook my head. "I'm no preacher."

"Yes, you already told me that. But you do read the Bible—I've seen you. Won't you pray with me? Is that asking too much?"

"What are we praying for?"

"Peace of mind."

I dipped my head, then looked up at her again and nodded. She set her cigarette on the edge of the ashtray and closed her eyes. With her head bowed she waited for me to say a few words. I didn't know what to say and so I borrowed what I could recall of the prayer that Abigail Hamilton had offered three days before. I could only remember the first few lines:

"Blessed is the Child of Light Who doth seek his heavenly FatherFor he shall have eternal life."

When I stopped speaking, it seemed to be enough. Mary opened her eyes and looked at me. "Am I forgiven?" she asked simply.

"That's not within my power to say."

"Will I be forgiven?"

"I don't know," I replied.

"Will you forgive me? I know you say you are not a preacher. But will you, personally, as a man who knew the child, forgive me?"

It took me a long time to summon up an answer. When I finally did, my voice nearly cracked as I gave it: "Yes," I told her.

Mary lifted up her chin and stared, with seemingly increased clarity, at the photograph lying before her. "She was a beautiful young woman," she said, tapping the frame with her forefinger. "You know? So long ago, so very, very long ago. Who remembers anymore? What happened to her?"

No response came to mind, so I said nothing. The questions seemed to be rhetorical. I watched as Mary took one last drag from her cigarette and then dropped it onto the ashtray. Ash overflowed the shallow dish now, reminding me of fallen sand in an hourglass. Something about it may have prompted Mary. Leaning forward in her chair, she picked up the tumbler of brown liquid that had been on the table in front of her and held it near her mouth, where she paused to look over at me.

"Excuse me," she explained. "I have to take my medicine now."

Before I could reach her, she put the glass to her lips and drank it down in two quick swallows. Then she set the glass back on the outer edge of the table in front of her. For a moment she stared at it blankly with her fingers caressing the rim, and then her breathing shortened and her expression started to change.

I stood up and walked out of the kitchen, down the short hallway to the steps that led down to the side door, which opened out onto the driveway. Behind me, as I was closing the door, I heard the flat thud as Mary's body hit the kitchen floor.

*

Without saying a word, I started up the Ford and pulled away from the house with the collapsed porch. Nothing in the aging neighborhood seemed to have moved or changed. We drove down the street to the first corner and slowed for a stop sign. There was no traffic moving in any direction.

"No sign of the boy?" Delilah asked finally, with a note of fear in her voice.

As we approached Main Street, I shook my head and glanced over briefly to see the melancholy in her eyes. "You were in there long enough," she said.

"Yes, just long enough."

"What did you find?"

"Nothing, the house was empty," I said. "It was the emptiest house there ever was."

"Now what do we do?"

"We'll stop at the drugstore for something cold," I said. "I need to make a telephone call."

Chapter Thirty-Two

While Delilah took a seat at the counter and ordered two egg creams, I found a telephone booth in the back and placed a call to St. Paul. My hands were shaking as I fed the nickel into the slot. The images from the house carried with me. I still saw Hector laid out on the bed and flinched as I heard the sound of Mary's body land on the kitchen floor.

Though it was Sunday, Agent Trestleman was at his desk and picked up after the second ring.

"What've you got?" he asked tersely.

I took a deep breath and focused on holding my hands still. "For one, I got far too much of nothing and it shows no hope of growing into anything I'd ever like it to be."

"Where are you?"

"I'm grinning through the fence."

"You didn't call me because you're feeling philosophical."

"No. Write down this address."

Speaking slowly, I gave him the address of the house I had just left.

"What am I going to find there?"

"The old couple from the Iowa farm, both freshly dead this morning, a few minutes ago."

"The Schulz's? Did you kill them?"

"No. The woman, Mary, poisoned her husband, Hector. Then she took the poison herself. I got there in between."

"You didn't stop her?"

"No. Didn't have a chance to. I'm not sure there would've been a reason to anyway."

"You sound comfortable about it."

"You had to be there. It happened quick and it might have been justified."

The line was quiet for a moment. "Interesting word choice: 'justified.' In this context, it has several connotations. What about the child?"

"Mary told me the child never left the farmhouse in Iowa."

"I'm listening now, what it is?"

"She said he's behind the barn there, resting; much like she told me that Hector was upstairs resting at the house."

Trestleman sighed. "Okay, I get it."

"There's no hope," I said quietly.

"We'll get a squad out there by late afternoon, or early evening."

Before responding, I paused to study my shaking hand. "Trestleman?"

"Yeah, what's that?"

"Make sure they bring shovels," I said.

Chapter Thirty-Three

We returned in the dimming light of a late summer evening to arrive at Eva's apartment in West St. Paul. It was hotter than before and stiller, if that was possible. It had rained earlier and the street was still shiny wet. At least the impatiens had finally received some water. From inside one of the apartment buildings I could hear the muffled barking of a small dog, probably the terrier I'd seen tethered outside on the lawn the day before. Something was bothering him.

I had already angled the Ford in towards a parking spot by the curb when I saw the shooters. Two of them sat in a large, pale Studebaker coupe convertible from the Commander line that was parked just ahead of us, in front of the apartment building. With the low ambient light coming from the street lamps, it was impossible to be sure what color it was, but it was probably yellow and it had large white-wall tires and a long, sleek, powerful front end. The chilling sight of double barrels flickered in the sweeping light cast by my headlamps as we pulled in behind them.

Another pair of men dressed as police officers stood together smoking under the eve of an apartment door awning on the other side of the street. Beat cops wouldn't have stood in that position for long. The glow of their cigarettes was out of place there. Maybe if they'd stayed in their cruiser I wouldn't have seen them.

"Delilah," I said, "those guys mean trouble – brace yourself, and stay down!"

We were halfway into the parking spot with no option to retreat or to go forward that would not draw attention. I gunned the throttle and rammed into the Studebaker from behind, hoping to take them by surprise.

Before either of them could get out of the coupe I was out with my .45 drawn down on them. The driver got a foot out onto the pavement. He tried to come up with a shotgun, but his own door, a "suicide door" that had reverse-side hinges, slowed him. I shot him over the top of that door, once in the chest, and he fell straight backwards against the long slope of the wheel fender. From there he slumped down onto the running board and then into the street. The shotgun clattered to the street and discharged away from me.

The man in the passenger seat was having trouble working his door open. The force of the collision might have jammed it, or in his panic he may have forgotten where it was hinged. I fired twice through the soft top of the roadster. I didn't have to look to know what a .45 slug did to a man's skull.

I moved into the middle of the street, ran about ten steps forward, and spun to my left, hunched low with my gun extended before me. The soft count in my head reminded me that I had just five shells left in the magazine. I would need to use them efficiently.

It took a few seconds for my eyes to adapt to the much darker background close up against the apartment building between the lights in the windows. There was a strained bellow that helped orient me.

The two men dressed as police officers floated into my peripheral vision as they came down off the porch where they had been standing and into the overlapping circles of lights thrown from the streetlamps. Both of them carried Thompson machine guns and they were firing prematurely, before they could aim. The street behind me skipped with bullets and ricochets. It was panicked gunfire. They'd moved too fast and they should have stayed in place or moved the other way. They ran right into my line of fire as I dropped to one knee beside the curb, sighted, and squeezed the trigger five times. When the slide catch locked, I slammed in another magazine and released the slide with my right thumb. The street echoed with the shots and the renewed frenzy of the terrier's staccato barking.

Running now myself in a low crouch, with the .45 held in both hands down in front of me, I moved down the sidewalk and veered up over the inclined tree lawn to where the two men lay. I didn't know if they were real police officers or men dressed as police officers, but it didn't matter anymore.

They were both down. One had a head wound. Still writhing in a herky-jerky fashion at his peripheral points, he was probably already unconscious and wouldn't last more than a few seconds. I ignored him and looked to the other man. He was on his back. A dark red line stained the front of his blue jacket from one shoulder down to his waist.

He was breathing and his wide eyes stared up at me, fearfully, as he struggled to hold tightly onto the tenuous line.

He was dying and he didn't want to.

It wasn't easy to watch. It never is and it never leaves you.

242

"Who sent you?" I asked quietly, standing above him.

He did not respond.

"Was it the Irishman?" I asked again, more urgently this time. "You don't owe him anything now."

"The fixer, it was the fixer."

"Who is the fixer?"

Again he did not respond. I knelt beside him and asked a different question, quietly this time: "Is there a valediction? You have only moments left." But even as I finished the words I realized he would never answer me.

He had crossed over. His white eyes now stared up at the hovering sky, sightless and blank, perceiving nothing at all anymore. I closed the lids slowly with my fingertips and moved away from the corpse, toward the street.

*

Delilah was out of the Ford, hurrying toward me, kicking up the water in the street as she moved. She wore a soft, white blouse without any buttons and a cowl at the neckline. Her skirt was black and simple, and without any pretense or attitude. In the half light and shadows, with only her blouse showing easily, she resembled a ghost moving toward me, a ghost without any legs or lower body. I shivered uncontrollably and hurried toward her, helping her close the gap between us.

"I told you to stay down," I said to her as she came up beside me and placed a hand on my hip.

"You've been hit," she declared.

I looked down to see what she was talking about and I saw the blood on my leg, soaking through the trousers beneath the right pocket. "Probably a ricochet. Come on; let's get out of here. You'll have to drive."

It was then that I noticed the pistol in her hand—a .32 snub-nose revolver that she held as if she meant it. I didn't ask where or when she had acquired the pistol.

She'd ignored my warning, but I liked her the more for it.

Chapter Thirty-Four

The bullet had torn through the skin and muscle of my outer right thigh. There was a good bit of blood and the flesh was grooved pretty badly.

We stopped behind a service station near the edge of town. The glow from a streetlamp was sufficient. After I got my ruined clothing off, Delilah took the alcohol and gauze from the first-aid kit. Working quickly in the weak light she cleansed and bandaged my leg. She did it clinically without shrinking from the sight of the wound or the pain the alcohol caused me. With a fresh pair of trousers on I climbed behind the wheel again.

"We need to eat something," I said to Delilah.

"There's a diner down the street." She pointed ahead, toward a clustering of streetlamps and neon. "I'm famished."

I was famished too. We ordered strip steaks and fries, and ate mostly without talking. When the plates were cleared Delilah ordered a piece of chocolate pie and coffee. I left her alone again and found a telephone booth in the back of the diner. After I fed my coins in and spoke to the operator, I watched Delilah quietly eating her pie.

I was hoping my request to reverse the charges on the long-distance call would be accepted by the party I was trying to reach. Somewhat to my surprise, it was.

"Mr. Duncan," the voice said with a thick Irish brogue. "It is an unexpected pleasure to hear from you."

"I'm sure it is unexpected," I replied, turning my gaze away from Delilah so that I could speak into the receiver. "Your men missed me again this evening."

"They seem to have done a lot of that lately. More is the pity." His Irish brogue was dense and pronounced.

"I imagine they were planning to fit me for a barrel suit? How is the flower business?"

"Thriving."

"Just to be clear: we do not misunderstand one another. I know where you stand."

"And I you."

"I remind you that you owe me ten thousand dollars, probably more like eleven or twelve with interest. I trust you'll be able to pay off and still have flowers enough to cover four funerals?"

"Laddie, there is no shortage of flowers in any of my hot-houses. Be assured of that. We will easily grow enough to supply all the funerals that are necessary."

"I'm glad to know that, because soon there will be more funerals. Have you yet planned the floral arrangements for your own funeral?" I asked. I said it simply, without emotion in my voice, and then hung up without waiting for a response.

Now I understood, and I knew, ineluctably, what I had to do.

I walked back to the table where Delilah sat, aware of her eyes on me as I moved. My leg was hurting badly now and each small motion aggravated it further, but I was alive. I picked up an extra fork that had been left at the table and reached across to help myself to a bite of her pie.

With a serious face, Delilah watched me and said: "You're limping. Your leg is going to need medical care."

I shook my head. "Maybe not. We'll wash it again in the morning and we'll see."

"Where will we stay?"

"There's a motor inn about fifteen miles down the road, that way."

"I don't want to stay alone tonight."

I eyed her soft face for a moment, looking for the tiny cracks. I wasn't able to spot them. "You won't have to, kid."

"And in the morning?"

"In the morning I'll take you back to Des Moines on my way through."

Delilah blinking mildly, put a cigarette to her lips, and lit it with a quick expert motion. Stubbornly, she waited for me to say something else. We sat across the table from each other without speaking.

She was two people: one was a girl-child, filled with pouting emotions and naïve hopes, still waiting to grow up and the other was unmistakably all woman, and with a toughness that I'd admired from the very start. I was thinking about how she had earlier come to my aid with a pistol in her hand, ready to use it. Not many women would have done that – not many men would have either, for that matter. Then I thought about how she hadn't flinched when she washed and bandaged my wound.

"You've got the moon in your eye, kid."

"Maybe I do. What of it?"

"Would you prefer to ride along with me for a little while?"

"Yes," she replied without hesitation and then exhaled a thin blue stream of smoke, smiling in a way that made me forget all about the pain in my leg and most everything else that had been bothering me too. "I would definitely prefer that, and I've got no place else to go."

"Nowhere?"

"Nowhere."

"Quite apart from everything else, I'm too old for you."

"I never once thought so. How old are you, anyway?"

I told her.

"That's only nine years difference. My mother was sixteen when she married my father, and he was thirty-one, almost double her age. They say Alvin Karpis' girl is only seventeen."

"Your parents were from another time," I told her. "And Karpis isn't an example you should be following, not on anything. But I might give in and let you come with me, but that's out of the responsibility I feel towards you. Don't get wrong ideas."

"Oh, phooey! You're a man, aren't you? You don't fool me any with that high talk."

"Delilah, you have to understand something." I stopped speaking suddenly as I studied her. She was young, but she wasn't quite a child anymore. I thought of the night she'd visited me in my room at the farm, naked, and how her body had looked in the moonlight. I thought of the kiss on the mouth she'd given me the next day, disregarding her own bruises. Maybe there was a chance. I wanted to believe there was.

"We'll go together then," she interrupted simply. It was a declaration, not a question. "It'll work out swell, you'll see."

She had me and she knew it.

"What about Eva? We can pass through Des Moines if you'd like to say good-bye."

Delilah looked at me between two slow drags on her cigarette. "Now, you don't seem to understand," she related. "Eva and I already said good-bye."

"When?"

"At the bus depot, when you dropped us and circled back through while she was buying her ticket. She knew it was good-bye, that we wouldn't be seeing each other for a while."

"She knew you were going off with me and she accepted it?"

"Yes, as much as she can accept something like that. She's seven years older than me and has trouble stepping out of the mother role sometimes. Maybe if she could find a man of her own, it would be different. You've seen her. Somehow she doesn't seem to make the best use of her, well her assets, and time is never kind."

"I don't hold with the old wisdom about spinsterhood. Eva's a fine woman and she'll probably find someone."

"If she's open to it."

"You can't solve that one for her. How far can love and pity take you?"

Delilah shrugged and the dark circles beneath her eyes shadowed further as she tilted her chin downward. "The rumpus between us runs hot and cold, though when the chips count she comes through for me."

"As I'm sure you do for her."

"Yes."

"She warned you that traveling with me would be a life on the run, that it would be no good life."

I didn't phrase it as a question, but Delilah treated it as one all the same. "Not exactly. She told me to take care of myself and to take care of you. She said you were a better man than she gave you credit for at first, something about you being rather good around the eyes."

"Eva said that?"

Delilah nodded and smiled at me. But her expression darkened as she stubbed out her cigarette.

"It's not all she said. She also said there would be heartache and tragedy. That our time together is likely to be measured in weeks or months, if not hours or days."

"She may be right. What happened tonight can happen again, at any moment. It's what I live with, and what you'll have to face if you're with me."

I thought about Tommy Carroll and his girl, Tommy shot down, dying in an alley in a strange town, still trying to protect his girl, and she stoically weathering the police questioning that followed.

"I'm not turning back from it."

"I didn't expect you would."

"Are you ever going to tell me what happened in that old, broken down house today?"

I shook my head. "No. I will never tell you that. I wouldn't want you to know."

Chapter Thirty-Five

We took just the one room.

When the lights were out, Delilah kissed me with fierce divinity the first time and then again slowly, with a motion that was tender and deliberate and long and her hands found my chest. Together we fell back onto the bed and then she was on top of me.

Luminous in the dark, her eyes were gems dangled from heaven. After a while she paused and whispered the kind of words that every man wants to hear in the night. Her skin pressed against mine with increased urgency and then she arched upward.

A large scarlet moon was high and illuminated the room, so that her body was framed pale and slender in the light and her face was hidden within the sheltering darkness of cascading hair around her face and shoulders. I held her face and slowly pulled her down next to me.

"Love me," she whispered.

I wanted to. The desire was there and I couldn't hide it, but there was a counter urge I hadn't fully anticipated. I guided her off me onto the bed and I lay next to her with her hand in mine as a vague sense of guilt came up to wash over me and settled in a shallow pool. I couldn't explain it.

It seemed as though some detached part of me had floated up to the ceiling and now looked down in judgment. For an instant, I was an all-seeing eye-in-the-sky, a shadow figure rooted only in that firmament and amused by my own ambivalent hesitation. Most of the men I knew had teenage girlfriends. It was common – on both sides of the law.

"I can't," I told her then. "It's too soon and I wouldn't feel right about it."

"You think I'm a child."

"You are a child," I said with only partial conviction.

"I'm a woman and I've been with men before. Murphy wasn't a monk, you know."

I nodded in the dark. "There's more to it than that."

"Is there another?"

"Not exactly that either."

"I don't understand."

"Shhhh," I hushed as soft as I could. "Let's sleep a little."

I didn't understand either, not quite anyway.

*

We lay together in the dark room after the moon had dropped low in the sky. Delilah was under the bed sheet now, and I was on top of it, still in my clothing, though my jacket and tie were tossed over a chair. The heat had lifted and we were on our sides, facing the open jalousie windows.

Lace curtains billowed against the angled glass slats, allowing in a gentle breeze that cooled the room. I had my arms around her and my cheek against the back of her neck. I held her tight. Without trying to, I liked the way the soft parts of her body felt against mine when we were not moving. My thigh was starting to ache again and I knew that in the morning I'd have trouble walking on it. But I didn't mind – I was alive and I could feel her heat emanating beside me.

In the quiet, I thought she was asleep, but after a while Delilah whispered to me, "Will you ever love me?"

"I'm here with you now," I said, evading her question. The eye-in-the-sky was watching again from above, judging.

"Will you?" she persisted quietly.

My chest pounded: a hollow, thudding sound to my ears.

I thought about Elinore. "I may not be able to anymore, sometimes you lose things."

"You can't love?"

I didn't answer. I wasn't sure if we were talking about the emotion or the physical act of love and maybe it probably didn't matter.

"There are signs that you've lost someone," Delilah said finally, coaxing me.

I nodded in the dark. Her fingertips on my cheek read the emotion in my response. "It's left me empty, cut through in a way."

"Did she die?"

"Yes."

"What was her name?"

Elinore. Her face appeared before me, silently, floating in the dark behind my closed lids for a long moment and then she faded.

"Won't you tell me?"

I said her name out loud, pronouncing it carefully.

Delilah was quiet for a while.

"It's a beautiful name," she said finally in the dark.

"Let's sleep a little now," I told her, though in my mind I'd already gone back into the past.

*

From the outside of her apartment nothing appeared amiss. The street was quiet. Nothing moved. Windows above me offered no clues to anything. I abandoned caution and went into the building.

I came up the steps slowly with one hand flexed and ready in my pocket. At the landing I turned, my eyes lifted toward the varnished oak banister that fronted the entrance to her apartment along the stairwell. Something was amiss: a stomach wrenching quarter-inch of dusk-lit air separated the door from the molding of its frame. I stop-started. Bounding the last few stairs I pushed it open and stepped into the withering light. As my eyes adjusted to the dark, I dared not inhale. Then everything came into focus. But I was too late.

She lay on the couch in a tight curl, much as she had the last time I'd been there with her. A ribbon of red silk nestled beneath her feet. She was an image from a shampoo advertisement: her full-body hair splayed forward over the pillow beneath her cheek, rode back across her whitening forehead, and swept behind her ear, down along her neck. Frail lines of black make-up had melted down her face beneath her eyes. One partially open hand tilted off the edge to dip toward the floor, as if grasping symbolically for something that was not there—an empty bottle of laudanum. It sprawled just out of reach at the edge of a gray-green Persian area rug.

Nothing could have been more still.

Without hope, I knelt beside her and held that soft errant hand, folding it close to her breast, a position more natural. My face covered hers. I wept. Warm tears did nothing to resuscitate her from the coldness that filled those eyelids.

I whispered her name quietly, aching so very deep in my soul. She died alone, and now lay there in the dark without an angel over her.

I dreamed for a moment of dropping down into that absence of light, that warm eternity, of holding myself with my own arms gripped tight as I sank into the welcomed nothingness that would simply envelope me if I were to let go and take the long, slow fall down that subterranean slide – how I wanted to. That stillness would have been so easy to accept.

The moments passed as I sat there with her.

I was recalled from this dream of eternity by a haunting specter of the Irishman, with his tuxedo in perfect order. It floated up hotly behind my eyeballs: there, on the dining table, laid out in waiting for me on carefully folded green tissue, a single yellow long-stem rose. The anger caught suddenly in the back of my throat, a hard bitter pill.

I rose up.

Shaking and with minute stars circling randomly in the periphery of my vision, I went out again, closing the door carefully and gently behind me as if not to wake a slumbering child.

Outside in the moist night air I was pounded by the darkness and the sharp, discrete pricks of the city lights as they flickered about me.

*

"Is there is any chance you can have the feeling for me?" Delilah whispered, bringing me back to the bed where we lay. It was still dark. The morning was a long way off.

The question startled me and I didn't have a ready answer.

"Perhaps with time?" she asked again. "I'll be patient."

"I already have the feeling," I said finally, and though I believed it to be true, I also considered it to be one I wouldn't be comfortable with until some distant point. "It may take a while to let it fit," I explained.

"I'll be patient," she repeated, reassuringly. She pulled my arm in tighter around her and simultaneously moved back against me. "Because I love you, utterly. I do. I won't ask you again about Elinore, about where she came from and what she meant. I won't ask about any of it because none of it matters. The past is simply what made us who we are now."

We were quiet for a while.

Eventually Delilah broke the silence again.

"There's something I need to tell you about myself. I'm not ashamed of it, but some men would care. I don't think you will, but I want you to know about it from the start so whatever happens later you can't say you didn't know."

252

"I'm listening."

"My grandmother was full blood Ojibwe—" She stopped suddenly and raised her head up from the pillow to look at me, assessing.

I rolled inward towards her. "What about it?"

"There's nothing about it, other than it makes me one quarter Ojibwe. Some men would care – it would bother them to be with an Indian woman. It's why Murphy did that thing to me. He was already jealous about you. We fought, and I threw it in his face because I knew it would hurt him. I wanted to see him twist. After that, he was very angry, enraged. He said I'd misled him and he did that thing to me because he said I was Indian blood and I deserved it."

"I didn't know."

"I didn't tell you, so how could you know? But right now, I need to know if it makes any difference to you, any part of it at all."

I stroked her shoulder, with my mouth near her ear. I whispered: "Some men make excuses to hide from their own failures and their fears. Nothing of that sort could ever make any difference to me."

My cheek was held against hers and I closed my eyes for a silent prayer that I didn't share out loud. She'd never know I made it, but I'd know and I would remember. It was quiet in the dark room. There was only the soft sound of the curtains as they billowed against the jalousies, the far off crickets, and the occasional automobile or truck on the road a quarter mile in the distance.

Finally she said, "I knew that, but I wanted to be sure. I'm one of them, you must understand. All my life I've been close to them. When I was little I lived for a few years on the Red Lake reservation. I still go up in August to help with the blueberry harvest in Littlefork, near the Canadian border. After they logged out that area the blueberry bushes took over. Many people from the tribe, entire families, go up and camp in tents together by the river. They pack everything they need onto the old automobiles and trucks that they drive. The work pays ten cents a quart and it's lovely there that time of year. When I was a child it was my favorite season. It seems so long ago now."

I kissed the back of her neck softly several times and held her tightly, relaxing slowly, drifting off to sleep as she whispered on about life in the Ojibwe blueberry picker camps in northern Minnesota during the month of August.

Chapter Thirty-Six

With the tenderness of the hour before dawn, I awoke with a certainty that I hadn't felt in some time. Delilah was cradling my head in her hands. The sheet and the bedcover were still between us, though in the night I'd unfolded a blanket at the foot of the bed and pulled it over my legs. Delilah shifted on the pillow and placed her cheek against my forehead. I could feel the moisture of her tears.

Outside in the darkness, hundreds of crickets persisted, their sounds coming together as one continuously pulsing whirr. The air was still cool from the night, but it wasn't moving now and I had a sense that by mid-morning it was going to be hot, very hot, again.

"You think Wilson is dead, don't you?" Delilah whispered near my ear.

"Yes," I said finally, in a hushed response. "I think he's been dead the whole time we've been looking for him."

The silence that followed crept on. As I wondered if maybe she'd fallen back to sleep, she spoke to me again, "Then you've been chasing nothing."

"Probably."

"How can you bear it?"

"You don't think about it too much is how, you forge on." *If you could.*

"A child isn't supposed to die."

"No, and not at the hands of an adult he trusts."

"Maybe you're wrong?"

"I hope I am."

Delilah started to weep hard. I could feel her tears at the top of my face. They were warm and ran down into my hair and along the side of my cheek. With my hands, in small unfamiliar motions, I tried to comfort her. She was tough enough, but the shock of the previous evening's violence was settling in now.

"Wilson was such a nice boy. I don't think I can bear it," she choked. Her voice was small. "Any of it. I'm talking about all of it, all of the violence. It's a catalogue of horrors. Why do men do these things?"

"Because they were born with a stain upon them. Beyond that, nobody can understand it. It's not something modern science with all its theories, formulas, and new ideas can unravel. It always comes back to the stain."

"You killed four men last night. You shot them dead, and you had to. You had no choice. They were going to kill us, and so you did the only thing you could to prevent that. Otherwise we'd be dead. I don't know how you can ever talk about 'goodness' or manage the fear."

"There was no time for fear – only the reaction. As for the goodness, it's always there, whether we talk about it or not, even when it's overshadowed by the evil."

"Answer me this: do you love the violence?"

"No."

"Some men love it, and they're drawn to it."

"I stand it because I don't have any other choice now. With your arms around me, like this, maybe I can rise above it in time."

"You have a choice; you have a choice in me."

"Sure, and where will we go? What will we do when we get there?"

"We'll go to Southern California, Brazil, or France even. We'll feel the sunshine on our skin."

It was my fault; I'd started it. "There's no great escape to be found there. The people who are looking for me, can find me there too."

"Are you telling me we won't go? It'll take them some time to find us, and by then we'll move on."

"I can't run forever with an eye over my shoulder."

"What does that mean?"

"There's a man I need to see in Chicago." *The Irishman.*

"You mean there's a man you need to *kill* in Chicago?"

"Yes."

"He might kill you."

"That's a possibility."

"If you face him, what will that gain you?"

"If I live, it ensures my survival," I uttered simply. "It also means he can never again kill someone important to me. And, I'd gain satisfaction."

"All it will get you is an eye and a tooth, and maybe you'll lose some of your own. Do you want to be an eyeless, toothless man?"

"I can't let it go now. It's gone too far for that—redemption of the debt, measure for measure, is an inviolable cause." The ancient law of *lex talionis*, an eye for an eye, was too often misunderstood as a primitive impulse. To me, it was an innate part of membership in the human species and not distinguishable from justice.

256

Delilah sighed and turned over on the bed to look up at the ceiling. She crossed her hands over her breasts and pulled one bare knee up. The sheet had slipped away. "Will we ever go away?" she asked quietly.

"Yes, though we have to stop in Chicago first. I have to do it. You don't have to like it."

"How long will it take?"

"I can't predict that – three, four days, maybe a week, maybe two."

"Why?"

I found a pack of Chesterfields and sat up to light one. "Unfinished business," I told her from the edge of the bed.

"Let's skip Chicago." The tone in her voice was pleading and urgent.

I exhaled through my nostrils and reached toward the nightstand for my watch. The sky outside was growing lighter. "I have to, Delilah. It's something I have to do."

"The men who tried to kill you last night. Were they from Chicago?"

"Probably."

"There will be others?"

"Probably."

"And so, you'll kill them all?"

"If I have to."

"It sounds hopeless, a suicide mission."

I shook my head against the pillow, slunk down now, smoking absently. Above me unfinished pine slats in the ceiling, knotted and smoke-stained, hovered impartially.

"No, it's not," I sighed.

"Once you've settled this, then what will you do?"

"I'll finish reading the book I've been working on for the past few months."

"What book is that?"

"The Old Testament."

"I guess," she said sadly, "that somebody has to bear witness to the evil."

"There's more to it than that," I answered.

I thought about Lars Hansson and the story he told me that night in the prison. I didn't mention his name. To myself, I thought about the goodness, the light that shines in the darkness. I thought about the possibility of seeing it from a worm's eye view and the inexorable likelihood that it would shame you to the very core of your soul as he had predicted it would. And in my mind, I went on, going farther than

257

Hansson had dared to: I thought about how the light could change you, if you allowed it.

I didn't give voice to any of these thoughts. Instead, I lay back down, alone again in my head, and reached out to the nightstand where I stubbed the cigarette in an ashtray. I had the feeling for Delilah. It had come upon me out of nowhere, and I hadn't been ready for it. If I could let it grow, if I could find some level of comfort with it, perhaps she was the one who could bend the light far enough to help change me away from what I had become.

It was raining gently outside, a slow, soaking pre-dawn rain. The curtains no longer billowed and it was already starting to become warm as the humidity climbed. Mosquitoes gathered at the screen on the other side of the jalousies.

Chapter Thirty-Seven

As a hot red sun crested the horizon at dawn, I stepped out into the light and there was no applause. The roadway at that hour was empty. I limped stiffly across a vacant parking area; navigating puddles left by the recent shower, to an empty telephone booth and went in to call Special Agent Trestleman.

The booth was warm and quiet – serene glass panels buffered me from the outside world. Within the artificial comfort of the tiny space I paused, letting the nearly complete lack of motion around me settle. Then I engaged an operator and gave her the number I wanted to call.

After five rings there was a gruff answer.

"Sorry to wake you."

"You didn't wake me. What time is it?"

I ignored his question. "You recognize my voice?" I asked.

"I do. We found the child's body yesterday. He was buried right where you said he would be, wrapped in bedding. His throat had been slit straight across, right to the bone. He must have been murdered in bed, while he slept. There's no evidence that he struggled. Two pillows, both soaked with dried, hard blood were folded in with his body. We also found an old baseball glove. Looked like a second baseman's mitt. It had had blood on it too. He must have brought it to bed with him. Inside the house when we overturned the mattresses we found one with a corresponding bloodstain."

I leaned back, with my head against the glass. Soft, fractured moments of time came back to me: the arc of a baseball thrown by a small hand, the scent of old leather and neatsfoot oil, the release of a caught firefly on a hot June evening.

I thought about a small child, with trembling hands and few friends his own age, approaching a grown man standing by himself to ask if he was feeling sad. I thought about a dead sparrow lying in the road after I had struck it down with an automobile – an engine of progress. I thought about another child, shot down in a bank, lying on the cold marble floor, watching me quietly as his life bled away from him.

I thought of the lines in Genesis. They had died because of me, because of actions I had taken and actions I had not taken; maybe because I had been born: *So he drove out the man; and he placed at the east of the garden of Eden cherubim, and a flaming sword which turned every way, to keep the way of the tree of life* (Genesis 3:24).

"You still there?" Trestleman asked.

I came out of it, hardened again, ready to lean into the bitter wind. "Yeah," I affirmed. My voice was different now, even to me. "I'm here. I know it was Hamilton. He had to cover his loses on International Match for the Outfit; he manipulated every one of us. Any way to prove it for a jury?"

Trestleman's voice almost cracked. "We got the knife. It was also buried with the child – whoever buried him didn't have their wits about them."

"It was the old couple, not the brightest pair you'll find. Or perhaps they were ashamed of their crime, willing to have it caught out."

"There were fingerprints all over the knife, including the blade. Forensics returned them as Hamilton's."

I took a deep breath. "He slew the child himself," I said slowly. "Over a pile of matches and some cash."

"Yes – matches and money, lots of both – and maybe also to hurt his wife. Who knows what goes on in the marital bedroom?"

"We can never know, but there was something personal there."

"You saw the two of them together. How do you read it?"

"I think it was hatred, not toward the child, but toward the mother. Killing Wilson was his way of lashing out at Mrs. Hamilton. I think she left him impotent."

"From what I saw of her, I think you've called it right. Some men, weak men, are sick that way, but we got him." There was a hard edge to his voice as he pressed on the last three words.

"Where?"

"We picked him up last night in New York City. He was boarding a steamer to Buenos Aires ... carrying a suitcase full of cash – the ransom money, almost a hundred and forty grand of it. The serial numbers matched right up, so we have him cold. He came without a whimper, hasn't spoke a word since they put the cuffs on him. He won't tell us where the missing bonds and securities are, though I'm betting they'll turn up soon enough."

"Then you've got him."

There was a pause over the line. I wasn't sure if we were still connected. I waited with the telephone booth door pushed open now, not caring about the sounds of trucks that were starting to rush by.

My heart beat faster. I adjusted the shoulder rig, pushing it up forward so I could draw the .45 quicker, ready for action – ready for anything, already thinking ahead to Chicago, to the Irishman.

After a brief flurry of static I heard Trestleman's voice again clearly: "Yes, we've got him," he told me. "I'll see it's the green room he gets."

"See that you do," I replied with the easily imagined hiss of the gas pellets singing cheerfully through my ears.

I rang off.

THE END

Acknowledgements

Very special thanks to: my agent, Sonia Land, for her encouragement, guidance, and dedication to my writing career; Leila Dewji and Anne Lupton for their editorial comments on earlier versions of this work; Charles and Sally Neblett for everything; and my publicist, Kristi L. Masuhara, for her creative and diligent efforts on my behalf.

About the Author

Christopher Bartley, a pen name, is American with a PhD in Clinical Psychology and is presently a Professor of Psychology at the University of Hawaii and Director of Clinical Research at The Menninger Clinic in Houston, Texas. The teaching responsibilities and consultancies in worthy and prestigious establishments are too numerous to list here. He still finds time to sit on a large number of editorial boards and is a reviewer of countless psychiatric, behavioural research, mental health, obesity, depression and anxiety (to name but a few) journals and academic papers. He has had his works published in letters, papers, in journals and scholarly books, often making scientific presentations, and has written for media such as *Time* and *The Huffington Post*. He directs research and conducts clinical trials on chronic combat-related posttraumatic stress disorder mostly with prisoners and combat veterans, working to improve their mental health and separate science from quackery.

He has had an interest in American history since hearing a first-hand account of the Battle of San Juan Hill from his great-grandfather as a child, and then learning later of his father's military service in Vietnam. He is also fascinated with the history of jazz, gangsters, bank robbers and baseball, all of which seems to converge in the 1920s, '30s and '40s. Writing noir crime and thriller novels set in the period just after prohibition affords him an enjoyably different aspect from his work and allows him to delve into research of one of his favourite periods.